Front
Page
Murder

Also available by Joyce St. Anthony
Writing as Joyce Tremel

The Brewing Trouble Mysteries

A Room With a Brew

Tangled Up in a Brew

To Brew or Not to Brew

Front Page Murder

A HOMEFRONT NEWS MYSTERY

Joyce St. Anthony

CROOKED LANE

NEW YORK

Published in the United States by Crooked Lane Books, an imprint of The Quick Brown Fox & Company LLC.

Crooked Lane Books and its logo are trademarks of The Quick Brown Fox & Company LLC.

Library of Congress Catalog-in-Publication data available upon request.

ISBN (hardcover): 978-1-64385-898-2
ISBN (ebook): 978-1-64385-899-9

Cover illustration by Trish Cramblett

Printed in the United States.

www.crookedlanebooks.com

Crooked Lane Books
34 West 27th St., 10th Floor
New York, NY 10001

First Edition: March 2022

10 9 8 7 6 5 4 3 2 1

To my husband Jerry.
I love you more every day.

Chapter One

Pop taught me a lot about the newspaper business. Unfortunately, he neglected to tell me the sentence I'd hear most often was *That's not how your father would do it.* It had gotten to the point where I'd have to have it engraved on my tombstone. When I mentioned this to Pop's secretary, who was now my secretary, she laughed. Peggy Reardon had been my best friend since third grade, so I didn't hold it against her.

"You should have known that's how they'd react, Irene," Peggy said. "They're not used to taking orders from a girl, let alone someone ten or more years younger." She took a seat on the metal and Naugahyde chair on the other side of my desk and straightened her black skirt. Peggy was what most men called a looker. Her legs alone put Betty Grable's to shame. She wore her platinum hair in a simpler style than the movie star, though. As a matter of fact, I wore my auburn hair in a style similar to Peggy's. A girl could do a lot with finger waves and pin curls even if she wasn't exactly movie star material.

"I hoped they'd see the light, since Pop read them the riot act before he left." My father, Pete Ingram, had joined the army at the ripe old age of forty-five. Well, not the army exactly. As a newspaperman, he'd followed and reported on the war in Europe since the beginning. He knew it was just a matter of time before the United States was drawn in. When the Japanese attacked Pearl Harbor and Roosevelt announced we were going to war, Pop had applied to the War Department to become a correspondent. A friend of his who was a big cheese there pulled some strings and got him approved, even though we were a small paper. He left a few weeks later, making me editor in chief of the *Progress Herald*.

"You just stand your ground," Peggy said. "Sooner or later they'll see that you mean business." She smiled. "You can always threaten to tell your father."

I crossed my legs and carefully straightened the seam in my stocking. I couldn't chance getting a run. Stockings hadn't been rationed—yet—but they were already hard to find. I was down to my last three pairs and had to make them last as long as possible. "I could do that, but I won't. Pop would want me to stand on my own two feet. And so do I. I'm perfectly capable of running this paper. I've been writing stories since I could pick up a pencil."

Peggy held up a flawlessly manicured hand. "You don't have to convince me. I'm on your side."

"I know you are. I shouldn't let it bother me. I'm the boss, whether they like it or not."

"Attagirl."

The telephone on Peggy's desk, right outside my office, rang, and she pushed out of her chair. "Guess I'd better get that."

I leaned back in Pop's chair. My chair. I wasn't quite used to that yet. I appreciated the fact that he'd thought I was ready to take his place, and most days I believed I was. But today wasn't one of them, and it was only nine AM. Before I could get my pity party rolling, Peggy poked her head through the doorway.

"That was Ava Dempsey," she said. "She wanted us to know that Markowicz Hardware was just robbed."

Ava Dempsey was the proprietor of Ava's Beauty Salon across the street from the hardware store. She was the town gossip and busybody and sometimes passed on information before she had all the facts straight. She was the main reason the rest of Progress had known I'd gotten engaged before my mother had. "She called us instead of the police?"

Peggy leaned on the doorframe. "She saw Chief Turner pull up in front of the store, go inside for five minutes, then rush out and speed off."

Walter Turner, chief of police and my future father-in-law, didn't rush for any reason. Ava might be onto something if she was telling the truth. And that was a big if. I got up and came around my desk. "Did she say anything else?"

"Nope." Peggy's telephone rang again, and she went to answer it.

I'd have to send someone to cover the story. I didn't have to go far to reach the newsroom. One step, to be exact. It was right outside my office. Besides Peggy's desk, there were five others in varying degrees of neatness. Every desk at the *Herald* had a typewriter, but the only one being used at the moment was Ken Stafford's. He was our sports writer and happened to be Peggy's fiancé. The only other reporter in the room was Moses Bauer, who was drumming a beat on his desk with his pencil.

"Moe," I said. "I have something for you."

He stopped tapping. "Sure thing, doll."

"Doll?" I gave him a stern look.

3

Moe considered himself a ladies' man, and he acted the part. Peggy thought he looked like Clark Gable, but I didn't see it. He looked more like Robert Taylor to me. Either way, he was certainly handsome. And unfortunately, he knew it.

"I mean boss. Sure thing, boss."

I told him about the call from Ava Dempsey.

"You do know she's the town gossip, don't you?" he said.

"That's beside the point. We have to follow up. Talk to Ava and Sam Markowicz. In the meantime, I'll give Chief Turner a call and see what I can find out."

Moe opened his desk drawer and pulled out a tablet and his fedora. "I need to talk to old man Markowicz about something anyway." He dropped the hat onto his head and gave the brim a tug. "I'll be back in two shakes of a lamb's tail."

I watched him leave. Moe was what Pop called a go-getter despite his sometimes glib attitude. He'd been with us for about a year and made no secret of the fact that he wanted to be an investigative crime reporter. Fortunately—or unfortunately, in Moe's case—there wasn't all that much serious crime in Progress, Pennsylvania, so most of his investigations didn't go anywhere. His major fault was that he sometimes disappeared for hours at a time, occasionally as long as a full day when he was following what he said was a hot tip. Last week I'd told him I needed to be kept apprised of his whereabouts. Hopefully he'd heed the warning.

Back in my office, I dialed the police station, but the chief hadn't returned. When Moe came back, I'd have him chase the chief down for a statement. In the meantime, I still had my weekly household hints column to write. Alas, my job as the home, garden, and fashion reporter hadn't ended when Pop promoted me.

I alternated my column topics each Wednesday, so I usually wrote them on Monday. The first week of the month was food and recipes, the third was usually about keeping house, and the fourth was clothing and fashions. This was the second week of May, which meant it was time to write the gardening article.

Shortly after we entered the war, the Agriculture Department had begun promoting victory gardens like the ones most Americans had in the previous war. The mayor had even set aside a plot of land in the park for a community garden. The groundbreaking for that was coming up soon. In my February column I'd encouraged readers to plan their gardens and start seeds indoors if possible. The March column was about vegetables that could be planted in colder weather, like peas and lettuce. Many farmers planted peas around Saint Patrick's Day. April had been about the best vegetables to grow in our climate.

I slipped a sheet of paper into the typewriter. With the weather warming up—a couple of scorchers were predicted for this week—it was time to begin planting in earnest. I had already interviewed Dan Petrie, who owned a gardening shop and feed store just outside of town. He had given me tips earlier on the best ways to prepare a garden. This month I would use his advice on planting seedlings and how to make sure they would grow. I also pulled some things from the information the agriculture secretary had released and included a few quotes from President Roosevelt's speeches on how important it was for the whole country to participate in the war effort. My stomach growled as I read through the finished article. I looked up at the clock—it was noon. Perfect timing.

*   *   *

The lunch counter at Woolworth's wasn't very busy. It never was on Mondays. I sat and ate my egg-salad sandwich in relative silence. I'd just taken a sip of my black coffee—unsweetened now that sugar was being rationed—when Ava Dempsey squeezed onto the stool beside me.

"Hello, Ava." I took another sip of coffee.

She didn't bother with pleasantries. "I thought you would have interviewed me by now. After all, it's not every day one witnesses a heinous crime."

"I sent Moe Bauer to talk to you this morning. You don't need to tell both of us."

"No one has been in to see me other than my clients," she said.

I turned to face her. "Moe didn't stop by?"

She pursed her lips, which were almost the same color as her impeccably styled red hair. "No, he didn't."

"Are you sure you didn't just miss him?" I asked. "Maybe you were busy or left the shop for a moment."

Ava shook her head. "The only place I went was in the back to get some towels. I would have heard the bells on the door. This is the only time I've left all day. He most certainly did not come into the beauty shop."

I sighed inwardly. Moe was supposed to interview both Sam Markowicz and Ava. I was going to have to have another talk with him. He'd better not be out chasing down one of his hot tips instead of this story—a real story. I pushed the rest of my sandwich aside and retrieved a notepad and pencil from my pocketbook. I flipped to an empty page. "Tell me what happened."

"I had just put Mrs. Feeney under the hair dryer when I heard tires screech. I ran to the door and saw Chief Turner jump out of the police car. The light on top was flashing, so I knew something bad had happened. He ran inside the hardware store, and I was just about ready to go across the street to see if there was something I could do when he ran outside, got back in his car, and raced away. That's when I called the paper." She patted her chest like she was out of air. Which she should have been, since she hadn't taken a breath through her whole narrative.

"That's all you saw? So you don't really know what happened?" I asked.

"Of course I do," Ava said. "I told Mrs. Feeney I'd be right back, and I marched right across the street. Poor Sam! He was holding a handkerchief to a very nasty cut on his forehead. I got the whole story."

And now everyone in town had probably heard it except me. And Moe. I was about to ask her what Sam Markowicz had told her when I spotted Chief Turner's car pulling up in front of the police station on the other side of the town square. In a split second I decided it would be better to get the story from the horse's mouth—or the chief's, in this case. I put fifty cents on the counter, grabbed my pocketbook and notepad, and said so long to Ava.

I felt a little bad leaving her like that. I'd just have to explain later. I dashed across the square. The Progress Police Department was in a narrow, three-story granite building that also housed the mayor's and other government offices. I made my way up the front steps and pulled open one of the heavy oak double doors. The police department and the jail—which consisted of three cells—took up all of the first floor. The mayor's office was on the second, and other town offices were relegated to the third. My stacked heels made a clacking sound as I crossed the marble floor to the front desk.

Sergeant Jimmy Feeney looked up and smiled. "If it isn't my favorite news hawk." He had been a police officer for as long as I could remember. He was well into his sixties, and for the last few years he'd spent most of his time at the front desk. He couldn't have chased a criminal even if he wanted to, but Chief Turner didn't have the heart or the desire to ask him to retire. He'd be run out of town on a rail if he even attempted such a thing. Legend had it that when Sergeant Feeney was a young patrolman, he had single-handedly chased Capone's mob out of Progress. The legend wasn't quite true—it had been a few small-time mobsters from Pittsburgh who were running hooch from Pittsburgh to Philadelphia. In any case, everyone loved Jimmy Feeney, and no one was about to correct this point.

"Good afternoon, Sergeant," I said.

"I suppose you're here about the trouble this morning."

"You supposed correctly."

"Terrible what happened."

"I understand that your wife was in Ava's then," I said. "Did she see anything?"

"She stopped by a little while ago. She only knew what Ava kept yammering on about. I told her to not believe everything that comes from that woman's mouth."

Ava certainly had a tendency to embellish things. Even though there was usually a kernel of truth in what she said, I had made the right decision in getting the scoop from the police instead of from her. "What can you tell me?"

"You'd better talk to the chief about it." Jimmy nodded his head toward the glass-windowed door behind him. "Go ahead in."

I knocked on the door before opening it.

Chief Walter Turner was hunched over his typewriter, his index fingers firmly but slowly pecking at the keys. It was odd to see him typing a report, but he was short a patrolman because of the war. The chief was my future father-in-law, and his patrolman was none other than his own son—my fiancé. The chief had been interviewing applicants to take Bill's place until the war was over but hadn't hired anyone yet. He looked relieved to be interrupted.

"Got a minute?" I asked.

He smiled, and for a brief second he looked just like his son. My heart ached. Bill had been gone only two months, and already I missed him terribly. Like many boys in town, he'd joined the army right after Pearl. He was safe for now, but it was just a matter of time before he was sent overseas. I knew he had to do his part like everyone else, but I dreaded it all the same.

"For you, I have all the time in the world," he said. "I assume you want to know what happened at the hardware store."

I took a seat in the oak straight chair on the other side of his desk. "All I know so far is that Ava said there was a robbery."

"Did she say anything else?" He leaned back in his chair and ran a hand through hair that was still the same sandy color as his son's except for the touch of gray at the temples.

I shook my head. "She was just about to tell me when I saw you pull up to the station. I thought it would be better to get the story from you."

"Smart." He paused. "I don't want to tell you what to write, but this is a delicate subject. That something like this could happen in our town pains me."

I didn't understand what he was getting at. "Why? We've had robberies before."

He was silent for a moment, then said, "How well do you know Sam Markowicz?"

"How well? I know he's owned the hardware store since he and his wife moved here a few years ago."

"Anything else?"

"He speaks with an accent. I'm ashamed to say I've never bothered to find out where he's from."

"I'll give you the short history, and if you want to know any more, you can talk to Sam." The chief folded his hands on his desk. "Sam and his wife came from Poland, but they lived in Germany for many years. Sarah Markowicz is German. And Jewish."

He wouldn't have had to tell me more. I knew why they had come to this country.

"They left Germany shortly after Hitler came to power and began persecuting Jews. They sold everything they had and moved to Sam's hometown in Poland. They tried to settle down, but they lived in fear that Hitler wouldn't be content with ruling Germany alone. They came here in 1937. They were fortunate they didn't wait longer. Another year and their entry to this country would likely have been denied."

I shuddered, thinking of what would have happened to them had they stayed in Europe. I thought of Kristallnacht in November of '38 and then the invasion of Poland in '39. They would have lost everything and possibly even their lives. Hearing all of this, I felt even worse about never having shown much interest in Sam and Sarah Markowicz. I'd have to remedy this.

I did have a question for the chief, though. "What does any of this have to do with the robbery this morning?"

"It wasn't a robbery."

"But—"

He held up a hand. "I know that's what Ava told you. She assumed that's what it was, and I understand that Sam didn't correct her."

"I'm very confused," I said. "If it wasn't a robbery, what happened?"

Chief Turner reached under his desk, retrieved a large piece of cardboard, and turned it so I could see.

I was shocked at not only the large letters, painted in red, but the content of the message:

GO BACK WHERE YOU CAME FROM JEW.

Chapter Two

Churchill Warns Nazis About Use of Poison Gas
—The Progress Herald, May 11, 1942

"That's horrible," I said. "Who would do something like this?"

"I don't know, but I mean to find out," Chief Turner said. "I won't allow anyone to be treated like this."

I didn't need to jot the words on the sign down in my notebook, but I did anyway. I thought of something Ava had told me. "Ava said Sam had a cut on his head. Did this person hurt Sam? Sam would be able to identify him, wouldn't he?"

The chief put the sign back under his desk. "Sam found the sign when he opened the store for the day. Whoever left the sign had broken in through the back door. Sam hit his head on the corner of a shelf while he was cleaning up broken glass."

"So he didn't see anyone," I said. "Does he have any idea who did this? Has anyone given him trouble lately?"

"He was pretty shook up and said he couldn't think of anyone just then. I'll talk to him again tomorrow after he's had time for it to sink in."

"I'm going to stop and see him. If I learn anything new, I'll let you know."

The chief nodded. As I got up to leave, he asked, "Heard from my son this week?"

"I got a letter yesterday." I smiled, thinking about the contents—most of which were too personal to share. "How about you?"

"Yep. He told me all about how well he did on the firing range. Guess it paid that I taught him to shoot when he was only ten years old."

I prayed that anyone who'd be shooting back at him wouldn't do so well.

"Heard from your father?" the chief asked.

"Mom got a letter last week. Pop was about to board a navy ship, but he didn't know exactly where he was headed. Somewhere in the South Pacific was all he knew."

"You tell your mother if she needs anything to let me know."

"I will."

*   *   *

I glanced up at the clock in my office for at least the tenth time in the last half hour. It was nearly time to go to press, and Moe hadn't returned yet. I was getting angrier by the minute. He had better have a good reason for not having turned in his article yet. When there was a knock on my door, I snapped, "What?"

"You don't have to be so grumpy," Donny Wallace said as he pushed open the door.

My cousin was the last person I wanted to talk to. Donny was my aunt Rita's son, and he was as much of a pill as she was. My mother and her sister got along fine—when Rita, who was the baby in the family, got her way. That was the only reason Donny worked here. He couldn't write his way out of a paper sack, so Pop had found a spot for him elsewhere to keep peace in the family. I hated to admit it, but he was good at laying out the articles and figuring out what should go where.

"I'll be grumpy if I want to be," I said.

"I'm still waiting for Moe's article."

"I know that."

Without asking, Donny sat in the chair across from me and leaned back. "This is the third time he's almost missed deadline in the last six months. If I were you, I'd give him his walking papers."

"Well, you're not me," I said. "I have no intention of firing the man. He's a good reporter."

"Uncle Pete never should have hired him. I told him he would be nothing but trouble." Donny sniffed. "And that's certainly not the only mistake your father made."

"You mean putting me in charge." It wasn't a guess by any means—he'd told me so at least a dozen times since my father made the decision. My cousin had known Pop would want the *Herald* to stay in family hands, but he'd assumed those hands would be his. Donny couldn't get over that fact that his younger cousin—a girl, no less—was now his boss, and he made sure everyone knew it.

"Of course that's what I mean. Your father isn't going to have a paper to come back to. If he even comes back. That was another foolish decision. Why in the world would a man go where he could be shot or blown up if he didn't have to? Thank heavens I'm 4-F."

I mentally counted to ten before I opened my mouth. "Men with integrity do things like that. They go where they can make a difference regardless of the personal cost."

Donny was probably disappointed he hadn't gotten more of a rise out of me. He stood. "What are you going to do about the Markowicz article? You're running out of time."

I wasn't about to let him know I had no idea. "Don't worry. I'll handle it."

After my cousin left, I glanced at the clock again. I couldn't wait any longer for Moe to come back. I'd have to see Sam and write the darn thing myself.

* * *

Sam Markowicz looked older than his fifty years, and this morning's incident had added another year or two. His pain and disbelief were palpable. I could hear it in his voice and see it in his eyes. "I do not understand why someone would do this," he said. "We came to this country to get away from such things."

"I'm sorry this happened to you," I said. "Have you had trouble with anyone before this?"

He shook his head. "Everyone has been very kind. My wife and I are happy to live here. I never imagined that someone in Progress would carry such hatred." He went on to tell me everything I'd already learned from Chief Turner.

"Have you remembered anything else since you spoke to the chief?" I asked.

"I have gone over it in my mind many times. I have not forgotten anything."

I closed my notebook. "Thank you for speaking with me. The article will be in the morning paper. I hope that if anyone knows anything about it or witnessed something, they'll come forward."

"That is my hope as well," he said. "My wife is very worried. She says she will not sleep in peace until this person is found."

"Chief Turner will do his best to catch the culprit." I left the store and hurried back to the paper. When I reached the newsroom, Peggy was waiting for me.

"Moe telephoned," she said.

I could tell by the set of her mouth that she wasn't happy. I gestured for her to follow me into my office. "What did he have to say?"

Peggy planted her hands on her hips. "He said to tell you he's sorry, but he's onto something more important than a robbery."

I knew it.

"I told him in no uncertain terms that you were very angry with him and he'd better report to you first thing in the morning," Peggy said. "I hope that was all right to say."

"It's perfect." I sat down and rolled a sheet of paper into my typewriter. "He's going to regret missing out on this story, especially when he finds out it wasn't a robbery." I filled her in as I typed the article.

"That's horrible!" she said.

"What's horrible?" Ken Stafford appeared in the doorway. "I have my story on the girls' baseball team over in Butler. I know it's not due until Thursday, but I thought I'd get it to you early."

"I appreciate it," I said.

Ken moved behind Peggy and squeezed her shoulders. "So what's horrible?"

I told him, trying to ignore the way my friends looked at each other. I was happy for them, but it reminded me of how far away Bill was. It was kind of funny—I wanted my fiancé to be here, and Ken would have given anything to be where Bill was.

Unlike my cousin Donny, Ken hated not being able to serve. He had been a star pitcher on the Progress High School baseball team. He'd been recruited by both the Yankees and the Pirates. The dream of a baseball career ended abruptly the week of graduation when he was severely injured in an automobile accident. A truck ran a stop sign and hit Ken's car broadside. The driver of the truck was killed instantly. Ken had spent months in the hospital. He walked with a limp and wore a brace on his left leg, but it was a miracle he could walk at all. It surprised me that he didn't seem at all bitter about what had happened.

"Sam doesn't have any idea who might have done it?" Ken asked.

"No," I said. "He swears no one has given him any trouble."

Peggy said, "It sounds like you don't quite believe that."

"It's not that I don't believe him, but it just seems odd to me that someone would target him all of a sudden. I would think he'd be extra sensitive to any kind of prejudice against him since he was subject to it in Germany and Poland."

Ken said, "Maybe it's someone who just moved here. We have a lot of new people in the area with the expansion at Tabor."

Tabor Ironworks was the largest employer in the area. It had been manufacturing nuts, bolts, and other metal parts since 1900. Before the start of the war, the nuts and bolts had been used in the automobile industry. When the president suspended automobile production, Tabor began a big expansion and began adding and converting equipment to make nuts, bolts, rivets, and other parts for the war industry. Most of the parts would be sent to nearby production facilities like Dravo and American Bridge in Pittsburgh and the Bantam company in Butler, where the Jeep had been invented. It always galled Pop that the army had given the contract to others because Bantam couldn't produce seventy-five a day. They now made cargo trailers for the military, which was just as important, in my opinion. Tabor Ironworks had finished their conversion a couple weeks ago, and the official dedication ceremony was scheduled for tomorrow.

"That's a good point," I said. "They've hired about three hundred people in the last couple of months." I'd have to mention it to the chief, although I was sure he'd thought of it already.

"Isn't Moe assigned to cover the dedication tomorrow?" Peggy asked.

"Yes." Considering what had happened today, I wondered if that was a good decision.

"Do you think that's a good idea?" Apparently Peggy and I were on the same page.

"I don't know," I admitted. "I don't want to just pull it from him, and Rex and Frank are working on other stories. I'll decide after I talk to him in the morning."

After my friends left, I finished the article and made sure Donny had everything set for printing the morning paper. He took it personally when I did this, even though it was part of my job as editor in chief. Donny had never complained when my father did it—and Pop sometimes triple-checked the layout. Though it did give me a certain satisfaction to hear Donny whine.

* * *

I walked the six blocks home thinking about Sam Markowicz and Ken's theory that one of the new employees at Tabor Ironworks had left that message. It was certainly possible and, to my way of thinking, probable. I couldn't think of a single longtime resident who would do such a thing.

When I turned onto our street, I spotted my fourteen-year-old sister, Lily, sitting on the porch steps. Our Victorian-style house wasn't the largest on the tree-lined street, but I had always thought it was the nicest. Last summer Pop had painted it pale yellow with green shutters, and it looked warm and inviting. The porch stretched across the entire front of the house, and the daffodils growing along it were almost the same color as the clapboards.

Lily saw me and waved. She hopped up and headed my way. "We have a new boarder," she said, locking arms with me.

"Already? That was quick." My mother had advertised less than a week ago. Pop was now drawing an army salary, which was short of what he had earned at the paper. I contributed most of what I made, but it still wasn't quite enough. Mom and I had discussed it and decided together that it would be prudent to rent one of the bedrooms, which meant that I now shared a room with my younger sister.

"Wait until you see her," Lily said. "She's beautiful. She looks like a movie star."

I couldn't help smiling. Many of the new hires at Tabor were women, since most young men were now on their way to fight in the war. Lily thought it was so glamorous for women to be working in a factory. She didn't realize it was much harder work than what they showed in the latest newsreel at the movie house.

"You'll get to meet her at dinner," she continued. "She's on the night shift tonight, so she doesn't have to be at work until eleven. Can you believe that? The night shift! She's at work while we're all sleeping!"

"That means you'll have to be quiet during the day when she's asleep," I said. "No phonograph or radio after school."

Lily shrugged, making her dark-brown hair bounce on her shoulders. "I don't mind. We can all listen to it in the evening. Besides, we all have to make sacrifices for the war effort."

It would definitely be a sacrifice for my sister to not play the few Tommy Dorsey records she owned—especially the ones with Frank Sinatra singing. As much as I liked "I'll Never Smile Again," hearing it ten times a day was more than enough.

When we went inside, Lily ran upstairs to wash up for dinner while I made my way to the kitchen. My mother was stirring something in a pot on the gas stove. Despite the fact that she'd probably been in the kitchen most of the day, she still looked fresh. Her dress was a pale lilac color and didn't have a wrinkle in it anywhere. Her ruffled apron matched the dress. I gave her a peck on the cheek. She smelled like White Shoulders, her favorite perfume. She never went a day without wearing it. "Need some help?" I asked.

Mom put the spoon down. "This stew is about ready." She opened the icebox, took out the butter dish, and handed it to me. "You can put this on the table. And the bread over there." She pointed to a freshly baked loaf that she had already sliced. "How was your day?" she asked.

"Long, but interesting," I replied. "I'll tell you about it over dinner."

"Did Lily tell you about our new boarder?" Mom spooned beef stew into a serving bowl.

I smiled. "Lily thinks she's oh-so-glamorous."

Mom returned my smile. "She's very nice, but she doesn't seem like the factory type."

"Factory type?"

"Oh, you know," Mom said. "Sort of rough. She's anything but. You'll see what I mean."

"Not everyone who works in a factory is the rough-and-tumble sort." We carried the food into the dining room and placed it on the table. We'd had similar conversations before. According to my mother, women had no business doing what she called "men's work," although she had conceded that it was necessary with the war on. She was still getting used to the fact that I was now running the *Herald*. She'd been fine with me writing women's columns, but running the paper was another story.

Mom rang the dinner bell that she kept on top of the mahogany buffet. She didn't believe in hollering *Dinner's ready!* I heard Lily talking to someone, followed by quiet laughter. My sister entered the dining room, followed by our new boarder.

"Irene, I'd like you to meet Katherine Morningside," Mom said.

I finally realized what Lily and my mother had meant. They'd both been right. Our boarder definitely didn't look like the rough-and-tumble sort Mom had expected. And I could see why Lily was fascinated with her.

Not long ago, Peggy, Lily, and I had gone to the Strand to see the movie *Belle Starr*, featuring Randolph Scott and Gene Tierney. Other than the fact that Katherine Morningside had the blackest hair I'd ever seen and bright blue eyes, she was the spitting image of Gene Tierney.

I couldn't wait to hear her story.

Chapter Three

British Hospital Ship Bombed and Sunk by Luftwaffe
—*The Progress Herald*, May 11, 1942

Katherine Morningside held out her hand to shake mine. "I'm pleased to meet you. Your sister has told me so much about you already." Her handshake was firm. She wasn't as delicate as she appeared. Although she wore a simple skirt and blouse not all that different from the ones I had on, I looked downright drab in comparison. "I hope you like it here," I said as we sat at the table.

Katherine unfolded her napkin and placed it on her lap. "Thank you all for sharing your home with me. I don't know what I would have done otherwise. I started at the plant a few weeks ago, and I've been staying in Butler. I felt like I wasn't doing my part by driving thirty minutes to and from work. I had to find something closer, and here I am."

My mother ladled stew into a bowl and passed it to Katherine. "I would have been appalled if you had had to stay in one of those awful rooming houses by the factory."

The rooming houses were more like dormitories and weren't as bad as my mother made them out to be. Frank Mitchell had done a story on them a few weeks earlier. Tabor Ironworks had put them up, expecting an influx of workers. Granted, they weren't the Ritz, but they were warm and dry and cheap. There were separate buildings for men and women. The problem was that they were already filled to capacity and Tabor had no plans to build more. Any new employees who hadn't already made arrangements to stay there were out of luck. They either had to find a private house to room in, like Katherine had, or travel to Pittsburgh or Butler.

"Now that I'm here, I can't imagine staying anywhere else," Katherine said.

I slathered butter on a slice of bread. "What made you decide to come to Progress and work at Tabor?"

"Money," she said. "Pure and simple."

"Do they pay a lot?" Lily asked.

Mom's face grew red. "Lily, dear, we don't ask questions about money. It's impolite."

"That's all right. I don't mind," Katherine said. She smiled at Lily. "They pay very well. More than I would make most anywhere else. I'll be able to save up quickly."

I almost asked what she was saving for but figured Mom wouldn't like it. Not that Mom not liking something had ever stopped me, but I didn't want to frighten off our guest on her first day by being too nosy.

Katherine turned to me. "Your mother told me you write a household column for the newspaper. That must be so interesting."

What was telling was that Mom hadn't told her I did a lot more than that. "It is. Most days, anyway, especially now that I'm editor in chief."

"Oh! How fabulous!" Katherine said. "I want to hear all about it."

I glanced sideways at my mother. Her lips were pursed. I squelched the urge to sigh. "Pop owns the paper. Before he left for the war, he put me in charge."

"How did that go over?" Katherine asked.

I shrugged. "About as well as I expected."

She nodded like she knew very well what that meant. I imagined it wasn't all that different at the plant, which gave me an idea for a story. I'd ask her about it later.

Katherine sipped her water. "What's the news of the day?"

I gave them the short version of what had happened at Markowicz Hardware.

"Poor Mr. Markowicz," Lily said. "How can people be so mean?"

Mom said, "We should do something nice for Sam and Sarah. I can make a casserole and take it to them."

Food was her answer to everything. A casserole might make them feel better temporarily, but finding the culprit was a better solution.

"That's a great idea," Katherine said. "I'd like to help, if I may."

Mom beamed. "That would be so kind of you."

We spent the rest of dinner discussing what kind of casserole to make. Lily suggested sending a cake instead, but Mom reminded her about the sugar rationing that had just begun. A half pound—a little over a cup—per person every week sounded like a lot until you figured how many things one put sugar in or on. Pop would have used his portion just in his coffee. We finally decided a tuna casserole would fit the bill.

While Mom and Lily cleared the table and washed dishes, Katherine and I crossed the hall to the living room. She took a seat on the floral sofa. I sat on the opposite side of the room beside the radio and turned it on, keeping the volume low. I didn't really need to listen to the news. The paper got any news firsthand on the wire, so nine times out of ten I already knew what would be broadcast in the evening. There hadn't been much good news on the war front lately anyway, especially with the fall of Corregidor last week. Fortunately, there were enough music and other entertainment programs on the air. *Cavalcade of America* was on tonight at seven, and it usually aired a good story. We had some time to kill before it started, so I figured I'd get to know our boarder a little better. I asked her where she hailed from.

"Promise you won't tell?" Katherine asked with a smile.

"My lips are sealed."

"I come from a tiny town in the mountains of West Virginia. I'm the first one in my family to escape. The first girl, anyway. Two of my brothers are off fighting in the Pacific."

"That's where Pop was headed," I said. "At least I think that's where he thought he was going. He didn't say much in the last letter Mom got."

"Your mother told me your father is a correspondent. That sounds so interesting."

I nodded. I didn't want to talk about Pop. I wanted to know more about her. "What about the rest of your family?"

She reached into the pocket of her skirt and lifted out a pack of Chesterfields. She tilted it toward me.

"No thanks," I said. I'd tried smoking once and didn't much like it. Pop smoked like a chimney. When he got up in the mornings, he always sounded like he was going to hack up a lung. I could do without that.

"Do you mind if I do?" Katherine asked.

"Go right ahead."

After she lit her cigarette, she said, "My father died in a coal mining accident when I was twelve."

"I'm sorry to hear that," I said.

"My oldest brother still works in the mine, and my mother takes in laundry and ironing. I'm her only daughter. I love my family, but I couldn't stay there and end up with the same life as my mother. We write to each other, but I haven't been back in ten years."

"What have you been doing since then?"

Mom and Lily entered the room before she could answer.

Lily turned the volume up on the radio. "I wish Frank was on tonight."

"Frank?" Katherine said.

"Frank Sinatra." Lily let out an exaggerated sigh. "His voice gives me the shivers. And he's so handsome." She flopped down onto the floor.

Katherine smiled. "He is that."

Mom shushed us. "The show is about to start."

There was no more talk about Sinatra or anything else while we listened to tonight's episode on *Cavalcade*. "A Tooth for Paul Revere," about a farmer with a toothache who traveled to Boston to see Paul Revere and started the Revolutionary War by accident, was quite entertaining. It was good to hear about a distant war instead of the current one for a while.

*   *   *

"Has anyone heard from Moe?" I asked. We were ten minutes into our morning staff meeting in the newsroom, and he was nowhere to be found. Frank Mitchell had already gone out to interview the Progress High School principal about graduation plans, so it was just Rex Griffin, Ken, Peggy, Donny, and me.

"He hasn't called in," Peggy said.

Par for the course. "Does anyone know what story he was chasing?"

"Some imaginary one, I'm sure," Rex said. "You know what the problem is, don't you?"

I knew what he was going to say: the same thing he had been saying since Pop left. Rex had worked at the paper for twenty years. He still saw me as the toddler he used to ride around on his shoulders when Mom and I would visit. He didn't see me as a woman who had grown up in this business. I knew as much about it as he did. I'd learned more than just reporting from Pop. He'd taught me what it took to publish a successful newspaper. He'd taken the *Herald* from a weekly town newsletter to a daily paper. Almost daily, that is. We combined Saturday's and Sunday's news into one weekend edition. Our circulation was growing. We had subscribers from not only Progress but all the surrounding towns in our county. Pop had a knack for anticipating what people wanted to read, and I had inherited that ability from him.

"Moe pushes you around because you're just a girl. I know Pete hired him and he's a good reporter, but your dad wouldn't put up with his not showing up for work and not even letting you know what he's onto. Excuse my French, but you don't have the balls to do anything about it. Pete should never have put you in charge. It's unnatural."

"I've been telling her that every day," Donny said. "Moe should be canned. I would have done it weeks ago."

"Oh, put a sock in it. Both of you," Peggy said. "Irene knows what she's doing."

Rex put his feet up on his desk and leaned back in his chair. "She knows how to write, I'll give her that. But she ain't no boss."

"You got that right," Donny said. "The boss part, anyway."

"How about you quit talking about me like I'm not here." I reached over and shoved Rex's feet off the desk. "And keep your feet on the floor where they belong."

Rex looked surprised.

Donny backed up toward the hallway that led to his office. "I just remembered something I have to do." From the numerous times I'd popped him one as a kid, he knew when I'd been pushed too far.

I stood from where I'd been leaning on Ken's desk. "Like it or not, Rex, I am the boss until Pop comes home. I'm not a kid anymore. Get used to it, and if you can't, you know where the door is."

I heard Ken snort.

"I still think it's unnatural," Rex said.

"There's nothing wrong with having a woman in charge," Ken said.

Rex leaned back in his chair again but didn't put his feet back up on the desk. "I don't like it. I can't wait until this war is over and things get back to normal."

I couldn't help but wonder whether that would ever happen.

* * *

I still hadn't heard from Moe by ten o'clock. I'd give him until noon, then I'd cover the ceremony at Tabor Ironworks myself. And like it or not, I'd have to decide what to do about him. I didn't want to fire him, but it might have to come to that. After Rex and Ken left on their assignments, I walked over to Markowicz Hardware to see if Sam remembered anything else about what had happened yesterday.

Sam was dusting a display of wrenches and looked up when the bell on the door jangled as I entered.

"Good morning, Miss Ingram," he said.

"Please, call me Irene."

"Irene. A beautiful name." Sam placed his feather duster on the counter. "What can I do for you?"

"I'm just stopping to see how you're doing after what happened yesterday."

"I am a little bit better today." He reached up and touched the bandage on his head. "I still do not understand it."

"Have you remembered anything else? Someone who might have come in and given you trouble? Someone who made a comment in passing?"

Sam shook his head. "Chief Turner asked me the same questions earlier. Some customers have been rude, but no one has given me that kind of trouble."

It wasn't much to go on, but I'd take it. "What customers? Can you give me their names?"

"I cannot," Sam said. "I had never seen them before."

Drat. "If you do happen to see them again, would you telephone the paper?"

"I doubt that I would recognize them. I would much prefer to forget this ever happened, but I will call."

I thanked him and headed over to the police station, hoping that Chief Turner had better news.

Sergeant Feeney was behind the main desk as usual. He gave me a big smile. "Here for the blotter from last week? You ducked out yesterday without it. Not that there was much that was newsworthy."

I'd forgotten all about it with what had happened to Sam. I usually checked the blotter on Monday and wrote it up for Wednesday's paper. "What did I miss? I'll write it up this afternoon."

"Here you go." Jimmy slid a sheet of paper across the desk. "Besides the Markowicz incident, Mrs. Anderson's goat got loose, and two of her chickens are missing. Someone got beat up in a parking lot at Tabor. Mr. Russell got a flat tire out on Route 8, and the chief changed it for him. Three people got tickets for speeding. That's about it."

I jotted the information down in my notebook. It would take me all of five minutes to type it up for the paper. "Is the chief in?" I asked.

Jimmy shook his head.

"I wanted to see if there was any more news about what happened at Sam's."

"There's nothing as far I know. If you're going out to Tabor this afternoon, the chief will probably be there."

"I'll talk to him then," I said. I headed back to the paper. I had plenty of work to do, and if Moe hadn't checked in yet, it was more likely than not I'd see the chief that afternoon.

* * *

By eleven thirty I had finished the police blotter article, plus a piece about the upcoming senior high school prom with the list of those in contention for prom king and queen. I'd been reminded by Rex no fewer than three times that Moe still hadn't reported in. I'd been elated when Peggy had let me know there was an automobile accident out on the state road—not that there was an accident, of course, but that I could send Rex out to cover it.

I dialed Moe's home at noon, and there was no answer. I'd cover the ceremony at Tabor Ironworks myself and deal with Moe whenever he decided to grace us with his presence. Besides, I still wanted to talk to the chief.

After a quick lunch at home, I took Pop's Pontiac out of the garage behind our house and headed out on the five-mile drive to the Tabor factory. Pop had bought the car at the end of 1940, and it was seldom used now that he was away. Mom didn't drive, and most things I did were within walking distance. I drove only when necessary. If I blew a tire, there'd be no way to buy a new one. There was already a gasoline shortage, and rationing was set to begin this week.

Tabor Ironworks had expanded so much recently that in addition to their two paved parking lots, they'd had to add a makeshift one in a field a quarter of a mile away. They were all full. I drove back to the factory and parked behind Chief Turner's squad car in front of the section that housed the offices, even though the spot was marked NO PARKING. I retrieved a cardboard sign that read PRESS out of the glove box and placed it on the dashboard. I figured I was safe either way. Surely the chief wouldn't ticket his future daughter-in-law.

I reapplied my lipstick, powdered my nose, and headed inside. I found my way through the office area into the newest section of the factory, weaving through the crowd until I reached the front where the ceremony would be held. Someone had built a wooden platform with a podium, and I spotted our photographer, Matt Redmond, already snapping shots. I waved to him.

He gave me a big grin and walked toward me. Matt had been a couple of years ahead of me in school. Like Ken, he wished he could be one of our fighting boys. Unfortunately for him, he was almost blind without his Coke-bottle-thick eyeglasses. He'd been teased relentlessly as a kid, and I'd always felt a little protective of him despite the fact that he was older and could handle himself. He'd decked more than one bully, and eventually they'd left him alone. He had been the photographer for our school newspaper, and Pop had hired him right after graduation. His photos were as good as and often better than some I'd seen in much bigger newspapers.

"Hiya, Irene." Matt snapped a photo, almost blinding me with the flash.

"Sheesh, Matt. Why'd you do that?" I blinked several times. I'd be seeing spots for the next five minutes.

"I wanted a picture of the cutest girl in Progress."

I rolled my eyes. "Your eyesight is worse than I thought."

He laughed. "You here on official business? I thought Moe was covering this."

"Yeah, so did I," I said. "I haven't heard a peep from him since yesterday. I'm going to wring his neck when he shows up again."

Matt took a handkerchief out of his pocket and removed the used flashbulb from his camera. "You and me both." He popped a new bulb in. "He borrowed one of my cameras and was supposed to meet me for a drink last night and bring it back. He never showed."

"Why did he borrow a camera?"

"No idea."

"And you let him have it without knowing why?"

Matt shrugged. "I figured he was either onto one of what he calls his 'hot tips' or taking compromising pictures of his latest conquest."

That was Moe in a nutshell. I sure wouldn't have lent him an expensive piece of equipment, though.

Mayor Ralph Young, who was anything but—he was coming up on his eighth term in office—hobbled to the podium. Pop had once written an article about the mayor's time serving with Teddy Roosevelt's Rough Riders. The fact that he'd ridden with Teddy was likely the reason he'd almost always run unopposed. Mayor Young was followed by Wilfred Tabor, head of Tabor Ironworks, and another man I didn't know.

I pulled on Matt's sleeve. "Who's that behind Tabor?"

"Dunno," he said. "Looks a little like Gary Cooper, if Cooper was half a foot shorter."

The mayor began speaking, so we stopped talking. I jotted down anything pertinent in my notebook while Matt took pictures. Mayor Young's speech was rather ordinary, focusing on how important Tabor Ironworks was to the town and to the war effort. When the mayor finished, he introduced Wilfred Tabor.

Tabor was in his midfifties but looked older. He pulled a handkerchief from his suit coat pocket, removed his wire-rimmed glasses, and wiped his brow and bald head. After he put his glasses back on, he cleared his throat.

"Welcome, ladies and gentlemen, to this historic event."

Although I was in the front row, I had to strain to hear his voice. The man who resembled Gary Cooper went up to him and whispered in his ear.

Tabor repeated his welcome, louder this time. "Tabor Ironworks has been in my family for many, many years, and I have to say that what we are embarking on is the most important thing we've ever done. It's an honor to be making nuts and bolts for the war effort. I hope and pray that our work will make a difference"—his voice cracked—"in the outcome of the war."

The crowd burst into applause.

Tabor moved from the podium, and the Gary Cooper man took his place. "Thank you, Wilfred. Now how about we get this show on the road." He waved his hand in the air, and one of the employees, a woman dressed in dungarees, trotted up and handed him something. He held it up in the air. "Here it is, ladies and gentlemen. The first bolt off the line. Here's to winning the war!"

Chapter Four

Navy Trawler Sunk by U-Boat off Ocracoke Island
—*The Progress Herald*, May 12, 1942

First bolt off the line was a bit of an exaggeration. Tabor had finished the actual conversion weeks ago, so this was more of a ceremonial bolt. I wondered if they'd have it bronzed or dipped in gold or something. Instead of the Golden Spike, it'd be the Golden Bolt.

Mayor Young, Wilfred Tabor, and Gary Cooper Man posed for a few photographs, then I waylaid them as they left the makeshift stage. I didn't need statements from them, but I wanted to know who the newcomer was and how he fit into the scheme of things. The mayor repeated what he had said at the beginning of the ceremony, then excused himself.

"Thank you for coming, Miss Ingram," Tabor said. "This is an exciting event for our company."

"It certainly is," I said. "Is there anything else I need to know for my article?"

While we spoke, Tabor's sidekick was giving me the once-over. I refrained from checking to make sure I was fully dressed.

"Yes. Miss Ingram, I'd like you to meet Arnold Moss, our new vice president of production. Arnold, this is Irene Ingram, the editor in chief of the *Progress Herald*."

"Call me Arnie," he said, shaking my hand and holding it a few seconds too long.

Tabor waved to someone across the room. "Excuse me. I have to take care of this." He walked away.

"Aren't you a little young to be an editor?" Moss asked.

I looked him straight in the eye. "Aren't you a little old to be so rude?"

He laughed. "Touché."

"In case you're wondering," I said. "I've been writing since I could hold a pencil, and I've been writing articles for the paper almost that long."

Moss held up his hands. "You don't have to convince me. I've heard good things about the *Herald*."

"Do you mind answering a few questions, then, Mr. Moss?"

"Not at all. And please, call me Arnie. All my friends do."

"We're not friends."

"Yet," Moss said. "We could fix that."

I ignored his comment. "When did Mr. Tabor make you vice president of production?"

Moss brushed an invisible speck from the lapel of his suit jacket. I hadn't noticed until now, but it looked expensive. Tabor's suits always looked like hand-me-downs. I wondered what it said about Moss that he dressed more nicely than his boss.

"About a month or two ago," Moss said. "A friend of a friend put me in touch when he heard that the company had expanded. I had the right experience, and Wilfred hired me."

"Where are you from?"

"I grew up in Ohio."

"How about after that?" I asked. "What kind of work did you do?"

"I've lived all over. Most recently in New York State." He reached into his trouser pocket and pulled out a gold watch. "I have a meeting in a few minutes. Let's continue this over a drink later."

"I'm afraid not," I said. "I have to get this in before we go to press." I held out my hand. "Thank you for taking the time to speak with me, Mr. Moss." I shook his hand firmly.

As I turned away, I saw Chief Turner going through the door leading to the exit. I hurried and caught up with him outside.

"That was quite a to-do," he said.

I agreed. "I stopped at the station earlier, but you were out. Do you have any more information about what happened at Sam's? Any suspects?"

He smiled. "Somehow I knew you were going to ask me that. No suspects and nothing new."

"Drat. Have there been any similar incidents? It has to be one of the newcomers to town, doesn't it?"

"Don't go reading too much into it. No one else has reported any trouble. I'm hoping there won't be any more."

"But—"

He patted me on the arm. "I know you'd like to get a nice, juicy story out of this. I talked to Sam this morning, and he wants to forget about the whole thing. Even if I find the culprit, Sam may not want to press charges."

Sam might want to forget it happened, but it *had* happened. Sure, it would make a good story, but that was secondary. I wanted to find the person responsible because it was the right thing to do. Another thing I'd learned from Pop.

* * *

The rest of the afternoon passed quickly, and I finished my Tabor article in plenty of time for Donny to match up my words with Matt's pictures for tomorrow's morning paper. I think my cousin was disappointed. I'm sure he was hoping I'd fail. I headed home instead of listening to his whining.

I expected Lily to meet me on our porch like she usually did, but when I neared the house, I heard music drifting out the living room window. Frank Sinatra, of course. Lily ran to the front door as soon as I opened it.

"Katherine has the best records!" Lily said. "And her stories! Wait till you hear!"

Katherine laughed as she entered the hallway. "Lily, give your sister a chance to catch her breath."

"But it's so exciting!" Lily said.

I smiled at her enthusiasm. Had I been like that at fourteen? It wasn't all that long ago, but it seemed like forever. "Let me check on Mom, then you can tell me all about it."

My mother was standing at the stove as usual. She was humming along to the song playing in the living room, which was not usual.

"You're in a cheerful mood." I kissed her on the cheek.

"I got another letter from your father," she said. "He still can't say where he is, but he's not near the fighting, thank goodness. I hope it stays that way."

"Me too," I said. "Lily is in seventh heaven right now."

Mom opened the oven door and took out a roast chicken. "I'm not sure our new boarder is a good influence on her. After school today, Lily asked if the war would go on long enough that she could go to work in the factory. I told her that it would be over long before then. The men coming home from the war will need those jobs."

"Some women might not want to give them up."

"They'll have to," Mom said.

I could have argued with her, but it wouldn't change her mind. "Did Pop say anything else?"

"He said the weather is very hot and humid. Nothing important. He did ask about how you were faring. You should send him a note."

"I will."

My sister had already set the table, so I helped Mom take dinner into the dining room, then told Lily and Katherine dinner was ready.

Lily was still in high gear even after we were seated and had said grace. "I just can't believe it. You are so lucky, Katherine!"

"Lucky about what?" I asked.

"She knows Frank Sinatra! Oh, I would just faint dead away."

"Lily," Mom said. "Miss Morningside does not know Mr. Sinatra."

For once, I agreed with my mother.

"Tell them, Katherine," Lily said.

Katherine dabbed her mouth with her napkin. "I had dinner with Frank a couple of times in New York."

"Sure you did," I said. The chances of a small-town girl from West Virginia dining with Sinatra were slim to none. Even dining with a lesser-known star was unlikely.

Katherine smiled. "I know it's hard to believe."

More like impossible to believe. I was about to ask her to explain when the telephone rang. Before the war, we'd ignored the ringing during dinner. Bad news almost always arrived by telegram, but we'd hate to miss a call from Pop or Bill if they had a chance to call. I jumped up and rushed to the phone in the hall.

"Is this the number where I can reach Katherine Morningside?"

I didn't recognize the man's voice. "Yes."

"Could I speak to her please?"

Disappointed it wasn't Bill or Pop but a little more than intrigued, I set down the receiver and told Katherine it was for her.

"Hello?"

I stood in the dining room doorway trying to listen in, wishing we had put in an extension phone. It wasn't much of a conversation anyway. Katherine listened to the caller and finally said, "I understand. I'll be right there."

I sat back down as she hung up the phone.

A minute later she returned to the dining room carrying her pocketbook. "I'm terribly sorry, Mrs. Ingram, but I have to leave for a bit," Katherine said.

"I'll keep your plate warm for you," Mom said.

Katherine shook her head. "That's not necessary. I'm not sure if I'll be back before my shift tonight. Thank you, though. Dinner was delicious."

When the front door closed, Mom looked at me. "I told you she's a bad influence."

Lily sighed. "I think she's wonderful."

I wondered which one of them was right.

* * *

My pencil tapped out a muted drumbeat on my desk blotter. I hadn't slept well, and despite drinking two cups of coffee, I had trouble keeping my eyes open. After Lily had gone to bed, my mother and I had listened to the radio and talked about where Katherine might have gone. My theory was she had a secret boyfriend, while Mom's thoughts ran more toward something criminal. Katherine hadn't returned by eleven o'clock, so our curiosity was put on hold. I tossed and turned most of the night and finally got up at six and headed in to the *Herald*. I sketched out a few ideas for upcoming articles. The first one I'd tackle would be about women working in jobs that men had traditionally held. I planned to interview a few women working at Tabor. I'd start with Katherine after dinner, unless she had other plans.

Peggy came in at eight and poked her head in my office. She took one look at the papers scattered all over my desk and said, "Looks like you got an early start. What's going on? Has something happened?"

"Nothing happened. I just woke up early and figured I'd get some work done."

She took the seat on the other side of my desk. "Ken and I have been talking."

I leaned back in my chair. "What a novel thing to do."

She ignored my sarcasm. "We think you need a night out. We want you to come to the Starlight with us tomorrow night. We'll have some drinks and listen to the music. It will do you good."

"Thanks, but no thanks. I'm not going to be the fifth wheel. Or the third wheel in this case."

"You're not. If we didn't want you to come, we wouldn't ask you. I'm not taking no for an answer."

Peggy had always been persistent.

"I'll think about it," I said.

"Good. That's settled then." Peggy stood.

"When Moe shows up, will you let me know right away?"

"Sure thing."

"I hate to admit it, but Donny may be right about him. If he doesn't have one heck of a reason for being gone, I'm going to let him go."

"Just don't let Donny know you think he's right. You'll never hear the end of it."

In the next two hours I finished my notes on three articles and wrote a follow-up to a piece we'd published a week ago on sugar rationing and what would likely be rationed in the future. I also had Peggy call and set up an appointment with Mayor Young for next week to discuss his plans for setting up a scrap-metal drive and collection site and talk about the groundbreaking ceremony for the town victory garden.

By eleven thirty, Moe still hadn't shown up. He'd never gone this long chasing a story without at least telephoning. When Matt passed my office on the way to the darkroom, I waved him in.

"Have you heard anything from Moe?"

"Nope," he said. "Not a peep. And he still has my camera. That's the last time I'm lending anything to him."

"I can't decide whether to be angry or worried."

"Don't waste your time worrying. My guess is he met up with some skirt and he's off having a high old time."

"If that's true, he's in a heap of trouble."

After Matt left my office, I decided I needed a break. Besides, it was lunchtime and I was starving. The Wednesday special at the Woolworth's lunch counter was meat loaf, which I'd had before and regretted. Dempsey's Diner had grilled cheese and tomato soup today—a much better option.

Dempsey's Diner was located at the east end of town, a nice quarter-mile walk this time of year. The diner had been a fixture in Progress ever since Ava Dempsey's father, Ned, opened it in 1915. Even when business was slow through the Depression, it managed to survive, most likely because of Ned's side business selling bootleg liquor.

The diner was almost always busy for lunch, and today was no exception. All the booths were filled and the only open spot was a stool at the counter next to Ava Dempsey. I considered walking out before she saw me but changed my mind. Maybe she had found out more of what happened at Sam's.

"Hi, Ava," I said as I slid onto the red-and-chrome stool.

"I'm a little miffed at you, Irene, the way you ran off the other day."

"Sorry about that. I had to get Chief Turner's statement while I had the chance."

Ava sniffed. "It was rude. I was in the middle of a sentence, for heaven's sake."

"I won't do it again," I said. "I promise."

Ned Dempsey came through a swinging door carrying a platter of today's special and placed it on the counter in front of Ava. "Well if it isn't little Irene Ingram."

"Hello, Mr. Dempsey."

"I haven't seen you in weeks," he said. "I guess you missed my grilled cheese."

I smiled. "No one makes a better one."

"I'll get cracking on yours." He headed back through the swinging door.

"I don't know how your dad does it," I said. "How old is he now? Seventy?"

"Seventy-two. I keep telling him he should sell this place, but he wouldn't know what to do without it."

Ned returned with my sandwich and soup, then went to check on the other diners.

Although Ava began eating before I did, we finished at the same time. While she lit a cigarette, I asked her if she'd heard any more about what had happened at Markowicz Hardware.

She took a deep drag. "So now you want to hear about it. A little late, don't you think?"

"I told you why I left." I put a dollar down on the counter and stood. "If you don't want to talk, that's fine with me."

Ava grabbed my arm. "Sit back down."

I did.

"I've heard some things from a couple of women who work at Tabor."

"Like what?" I asked.

"There was a fight or something last week in the parking lot. A janitor ended up with a black eye and a bloody nose."

"I saw that in the police blotter. What's that have to do with Sam?"

"The janitor is Jewish. The janitor told everyone it was a big misunderstanding, but one of the girls was near the lot and heard what happened. The other man called the janitor a dirty Jew. The janitor told him to leave him alone, and the man hit him." She crushed out her cigarette in the ashtray. "That doesn't sound like a misunderstanding to me."

* * *

Ava didn't know any more than what she'd told me. I wasn't sure it was connected to the incident with Sam, but it would be worth getting the janitor's story to check it out. When I got back to work, Rex was at his desk, so I told him to follow up. For once, he didn't argue with me.

There was still no word from Moe. I doubted that he was holed up at home, but there was only one way to find out. I looked up Moe's address, told Peggy where I was going, grabbed my pocket-book, and left.

Moe lived in a neighborhood of small houses that had seen better days. They weren't exactly seedy, but most needed some work. Moe's house was one of the better-kept ones. The front yard was mowed, and the porch had recently been painted. I hadn't pegged Moe as the handyman type, so it surprised me.

The main door behind the screened one was open, so I figured Moe must be home. I pushed the button for the doorbell and heard it buzz inside.

"Moe?" I called when he didn't come to the door.

Maybe he was in the kitchen and hadn't heard. I called again, opened the screen door, and went inside. The living room was a mess. Papers were strewn everywhere. Despite the tidy outside appearance, he was not a good housekeeper. I walked down the hallway to where I figured the kitchen was. Dirty dishes filled the sink, and an odor I couldn't quite place hit me. There was an open door with a staircase leading down to the cellar. The odor got stronger as I neared it. "Moe? Are you down there?"

There was no response. I found a light switch at the top of the stairs and turned it on. I stumbled back a step when I saw what—or rather who—was at the bottom of the steps. There was a good reason Moe hadn't been to work.

Chapter Five

U-Boat Sinks 4 British Ships in Same Night
—The Progress Herald, May 13, 1942

I ran outside as fast as my legs would carry me. I sank down on the porch step and took some deep breaths, trying not to throw up. My stomach settled somewhat, and I pushed myself up on shaky legs. The last thing I wanted to do was go back into the house, but I needed to call the police.

I dialed the number to the police department, and Jimmy picked up on the second ring.

"Is the chief there? I need to speak to him."

Jimmy must have heard something in my voice. "What's wrong, Irene? Are you all right?"

"Yes. No. Maybe." That didn't make much sense. I took a breath. "I'm fine. I'm at Moe Bauer's house. He's . . . he's dead."

"What happened?"

"I don't know." My voice cracked. "He's at the bottom of his cellar steps."

"I'll get the chief on the radio," Jimmy said. "He'll be there as soon as he can."

I went outside and paced back and forth across the porch. I felt terribly guilty. All I'd done the last couple of days was complain about Moe. I had a horrible thought—what if he'd been lying there alive and I could have saved him if I'd checked on him sooner? It was all my fault. I sat down and burst into tears.

I heard the siren before I saw the squad car. I quickly wiped away my tears. Seconds later, Chief Turner screeched to a stop in front of the house. He hopped out of the car and rushed to the porch. I'd never seen him move so fast.

"Are you all right?" He put an arm around me.

"I've been better."

"What happened?"

"I hadn't heard from Moe, and he hasn't been to work since Monday. I came to check on him."

"I'm going in to take a look," he said. "You wait here."

He didn't have to tell me that. There was no way I wanted to see Moe again. Not like that. The chief returned a few minutes later and went to his car. I couldn't hear what he said over the radio, but I imagine he was talking to Jimmy. He returned to the porch.

"Jimmy already notified Doc Atkins. He should be here any minute. I'm going back inside. Can you send him in when he gets here? And go home after that. You don't need to stay any longer."

I nodded. Doc Atkins was a local dentist and part-time coroner. I was never quite sure how those two occupations mixed. I only knew that I never wanted him to touch my mouth—or anything else, for that matter. I had no idea what his first name was—everyone just called him Doc. When he arrived, he was still wearing his white smock. I hoped he hadn't left a patient with a tooth half-filled.

"Where's the corpse?" he asked, without even saying hello. He tossed the cigarette he'd been smoking onto the sidewalk and crushed it out with his shoe.

"Moe Bauer. His name is Moe Bauer."

He stared at me. "I don't believe I know you."

Thank God for that. "Irene Ingram. Editor of the *Progress Herald*."

"You're a little young for that."

I ignored him. "Moe is one of my reporters."

"Sorry for your loss."

It didn't sound like he meant it. I was tired of this nonconversation. "The chief is inside. He said to send you in."

*   *   *

I'd hoofed it halfway home when I decided I couldn't face my mother just yet. I turned around and went back to the paper. Besides, I still had work to do. Pop wouldn't have gone home. He'd be writing up what had happened, and that's what I was going to do.

Peggy was at her desk and glanced up when she heard the door. "What happened? Was Moe at home?"

"In a manner of speaking."

She got a good look at my face. "You've been crying! What did that jerk do to you?"

"Come into my office." The newsroom was empty, but if Donny was lurking around, I didn't want him to hear me. I'd have to tell him and everyone else later, but I wasn't ready yet.

I sat at my desk, opened the bottom drawer, and pulled out the bottle of Scotch that Pop kept there for certain occasions. I'd never had Scotch before, but I sure needed something now. How bad could it be? It was supposed to be the good stuff.

"Uh-oh," Peggy said. "It must have been bad. Did you fire him? Did he threaten you?"

"You want some of this?" I asked, taking two glasses from the drawer.

She shook her head.

I poured a half inch of Scotch into a glass. "Moe's dead."

"What?"

"Moe is dead," I said. "I found him at the bottom of his cellar steps."

"I changed my mind. I'll take one of those after all."

I poured some into the other glass and passed it to her. I knocked back what was in my glass just like in the movies. What they don't tell you in the movies is that it burns like crazy going down. My throat was on fire. I gasped for air and pounded my hand on the desk.

Peggy had the good sense to sip hers.

When I could speak again, I poured another half inch into my glass and sipped it while I filled her in. It didn't taste any better the second time around, but I was certainly feeling better by the time I finished. "That's all I know. When I left, Doc Atkins and Chief Turner were still there."

By this time the rest of the staff had returned and were writing their bits for tomorrow's paper.

"Do you want me to tell everyone?" Peggy asked.

I shook my head. "Thanks, but it has to come from me."

I hated giving bad news, and this was the worst. I needed to be as strong as Pop would be. I couldn't show any hesitation or weakness.

I considered another drink, but when I stood and the room spun, I figured it wasn't a good idea. I got my bearings, and Peggy and I walked into the newsroom. I cleared my throat. "Can I have everyone's attention, please?"

Frank, Rex, and Ken stopped typing, and Donny looked up from the table where he was going through a stack of Matt's photos.

"I have some bad news." I didn't give anyone a chance to respond. "Moe is dead."

"Oh my God," Frank said.

Donny snorted. "I thought you said bad news."

That shocked even Rex. "You're out of line, Don."

Ken put his arm around Peggy.

I went on. I'd deal with my cousin later. "As you know, we haven't seen him for a couple of days. He hadn't even checked in, so I went to his house." I took a breath so my voice wouldn't crack. "I found him at the bottom of his cellar steps."

Ken said, "That must have been awful."

"It was. I'll write something up to get into the morning paper."

The newsroom door opened, and Chief Turner came in. The other reporters began asking him questions, and he put up his hand. "Later. I need to talk to Irene."

I motioned for him to come to my office and closed the door behind him. He sat down wearily.

"Would you like some coffee?" I asked. "There's probably some left in the percolator, if it hasn't solidified by now."

"No thank you. I figured you'd be here instead of at home." He spotted the bottle of Scotch I'd left sitting on my desk. "Is that yours?"

"Pop's. For medicinal purposes." I don't think he believed me, but he didn't say anything.

"I'll get right to the point," he said. "It appears Moe tripped and fell down the steps. Doc said his neck was broken, so he died instantly."

I was relieved that he hadn't lain there hurt. "I'm glad he didn't suffer."

Chief Turner gave me a little smile. "That's one reason I stopped. I know you. I didn't want you thinking there was something you could have done."

"Thanks for telling me."

"Do you know if Moe has any family?" he asked. "I'll have to notify someone."

"I don't know. He never mentioned anyone. I can ask Frank and Rex, and I'll check his desk. He might have an address book in there."

The chair creaked as the chief rose. "Let me know when you can." He walked to the door, then turned. "Pete would be proud of the way you handled yourself today. Heck, just about every day."

Tears formed in my eyes. "I hope so."

He smiled and pointed to the Scotch. "Just go easy on that medicine."

*　　*　　*

It was a pleasant, warm evening. It had reached the eighties today and was beginning to cool a bit. Katherine and I parked ourselves on the front porch while Mom and Lily did the dishes. I was more than glad dinner was over. My mother did her best to . . . well . . . *mother* me, but it grated on my nerves. I knew she was only trying to make me feel better, but I wasn't six years old anymore.

We sat in silence for a few minutes while Katherine smoked her cigarette. She crushed it out in the ashtray on the metal table beside her chair. "Rough day for you."

"Yep." I didn't want to talk about it anymore. "I hope Lily isn't driving you crazy."

Katherine smiled. "Not at all. I haven't been around many young girls. She's delightful."

"I imagine it's a big difference from what you're used to, having all brothers."

"A sister would have been nice, but I do love my brothers."

"Two of them are Marines, right?"

Katherine nodded. "In the Pacific."

"Have you heard from them?"

"My mother has. They're safe at the moment, but . . ."

She didn't need to finish her thought. The battles in the Pacific hadn't gone well for us so far. When we'd first entered the war, some people had thought it would be over in a month. Pop had gotten a lot of criticism when he wrote in his editorials that the Japanese weren't going to be easy to beat. Neither were the Nazis. We might have good old American ingenuity, but our production for airplanes, tanks, and just about everything else was only just beginning.

"Mom got a letter from Pop, but he didn't say much other than it's hot." I realized I'd have to write and tell him about Moe. I'd do that later tonight. "How do you like working at Tabor so far?"

"It's all right, I guess. I don't plan on staying there forever."

"I don't blame you. I don't think I could work in a factory."

Katherine lit another cigarette. "I wouldn't either if I had a choice."

"Of course you have a choice," I said. "There are plenty of other jobs. It's also not forever. What would you like to do?"

"Sing."

I didn't expect that answer. "Sing? Like Dinah Shore or the Andrews Sisters?"

"Not the Andrews Sisters," she said. "There's only one of me."

"Good point. What's the scoop? What's an aspiring singer doing working in a factory?"

"It's a long story," Katherine said.

"I'm not going anywhere."

Katherine shifted in her chair. "I'll skip the boring parts and cut right to the chase. I have some nodules on my vocal cords, and I'm saving up to have surgery."

I got the little tingle in my neck that I always got when I knew something would be a great story. I could see the headline: *Beautiful Singer Works in Factory to Earn Money for Surgery*. She wouldn't have to work there long. The donations would pour in. I was just about to pitch the story to her when I heard Mom and Lily on their way outside.

Katherine touched my arm. "Please don't say anything about this. I couldn't bear for anyone to pity me. Let's keep it our secret."

So much for my great idea.

*   *   *

It was another sleepless night. Every time I dozed off, I saw Moe lying at the bottom of his steps. I got up early, trying not to wake Lily, and took a hot bath, thinking it would make me feel better. It didn't, but at least I'd smell nice. I put an extra dab of rouge on my cheeks, hoping it would disguise the circles under my eyes. It made me look like a clown. I wiped it off.

Lily woke up while I was dressing.

"I didn't mean to wake you," I said.

"You didn't. It's time for me to rise and shine anyway." She sat on the edge of her bed. "What did you and Katherine talk about last night?"

"Nothing much." I finished buttoning my blouse and reached for my skirt. "We talked about her family a little."

Lily picked up her brush from the bedside table. "I thought maybe she'd tell you about New York." She began brushing her hair.

"New York? What about New York?"

"That's where she was before she came here. That's where she had dinner with Frank."

"You shouldn't believe everything you hear." I didn't like Katherine filling my sister's head with these stories.

"But it's true," Lily said. "Katherine said when she sees Frank again, she'll have him send me a picture."

I sat beside Lily on her bed. "Katherine seems very nice, but we really don't know her. We don't know anything about her. It's best to take what she says with a grain of salt."

Lily put her brush down and stood. "You sound just like Mom. Katherine is too nice and too pretty to lie. You'll see." She stomped off to the bathroom.

My sister was going to have a hard lesson to learn.

I finished dressing, gathered up the letters I'd written last night to Pop and Bill, and left them on the table by the front door to be mailed. I'd been all business in my letter to Pop, telling him about Moe and that everything else was swell at the paper. My letter to Bill was more personal. I missed him so much. I tried to keep a chipper tone in the note and made no mention of Moe. I told him about the ceremony at Tabor, a little about our new boarder, and how everyone in Progress was rooting for him and the other brave boys serving our country. It wasn't much, but it would have to do for now.

* * *

Once again, I was the first one at the paper. I went to our small kitchen and put the percolator on for some much-needed coffee. Back in my office, I fine-tuned the notes I'd written for my article about women in the workforce. I'd still need to interview some women at the factory, and I'd forgotten to mention it to Katherine last night. I'd talk to her tonight. I'd also need to get comments from townsfolk who didn't like the idea of women working, especially in jobs that men usually held. I'd have no trouble finding some of those. Heck, I worked with a couple.

I poured a second cup of coffee and went to tackle cleaning out Moe's desk. I hadn't been able to bring myself to do it yesterday, but the chief needed to know if Moe had any next of kin. Moe's desktop was devoid of papers, unlike the other reporters'. Rex's and Frank's desks looked like a tornado had dumped a ream of paper on top. Ken's desk had neatly stacked papers held down by a paperweight. I sat down in Moe's chair, thinking about the last time I'd seen him. Only three days ago, when I'd told him to talk to Ava and Sam. What had he done instead? I'd never know now.

I opened the top drawer on the left. It held an assortment of pencils and tablets, matches, and an unopened pack of Lucky Strikes. I flipped through the notepads, searching for anything he'd written down, but the pages were blank. I moved on to the drawer below it and found it empty. The top drawer on the right side was also empty. I opened the bottom right drawer and was surprised to find three hardback books. Moe had struck me as more of a magazine/quick-read kind of guy. I lifted the stack and placed it on top of the desk.

The first book was *Berlin Diary: The Journal of a Foreign Correspondent, 1934–1941*. I remembered Pop reading this one when it had come out last year. The next book was an Agatha Christie. I hadn't known Moe was a Christie fan. This one was *N or M?*, the latest Tommy and Tuppence book. I loved that duo. If no one claimed Moe's things, maybe I'd keep it. The last book in the stack made me smile. This was more Moe's speed, or what I imagined he'd be likely to read—*The G-String Murders*, by the infamous stripper Gypsy Rose Lee. I definitely wouldn't take that one home.

I'd have to call Chief Turner and tell him I couldn't find the name of a next of kin. I pushed myself out of the chair and in the process knocked *Berlin Diary* off the desk. I leaned over and picked it up. When I placed it back on the desk, the corner of a white envelope protruded from the middle of the book. I sat back down and slipped it out. My name was on the front.

I heard the door open and someone coming in, so I quickly put the books back in the drawer, took the envelope back to my office, and closed the door. What in the world was my name doing on an envelope secreted away in one of Moe's books? Maybe it was a resignation letter. There was only one way to find out.

I picked up my letter opener and sliced through the top of the envelope. Enclosed was a single sheet of paper folded in thirds. I spread the paper out on my desk.

Hey, Doll. You gave me that look, didn't you? Let me start over. Hey, Boss. That better? If you're reading this, it's probably not a good sign. Either you canned me or I'm no longer around. If it's the first one, I'll get over it. I know you don't like it when I'm chasing a story and don't report in. This time there's no choice. It's too big. I'm sorry I'm such a pain in the keister. Anyway, I want you to know that if something happens to me (as in I end up dead), it's not an accident. No how. No way.

It's been nice knowing you, kid.

Moe

Chapter Six

Fierce Fighting Between Reds and Nazis in Kerch Peninsula

—*The Progress Herald*, May 14, 1942

I read the note three times before it fully sank in. Surely if Moe had been murdered, Chief Turner and Doc Atkins would have determined his death wasn't an accident.

There was a quick knock on my door, and Peggy peeked in. "You're early again," she said. "That's two days in a row I didn't have to put the coffee on."

"I hope you won't have to get used to it."

"After yesterday, I don't know how you slept at all." She came in and sat down. "I tossed and turned all night, and I usually sleep like a rock."

She didn't look any worse for the wear. My best friend always looked like she had stepped from the pages of a movie magazine. Right now, the bags under my eyes were big enough to qualify as luggage.

"I didn't sleep. Every time I closed my eyes last night, I saw Moe lying at the bottom of his steps," I said.

Peggy pointed to the paper on my desk. "Is that Moe's handwriting?"

I nodded, slid the note to her, and got up and closed my door. I didn't want anyone else to know just yet.

"Holy cow," Peggy said. "Does this mean what I think it does?"

"That Moe was murdered?"

"It can't possibly be true. Moe's imagination got the better of him. We haven't had a murder here in at least ten years. There aren't any killers in Progress."

"We didn't think anyone would tell Sam Markowicz that Jews weren't wanted here, either," I said.

"But murder . . ."

"I know." We sat in silence for a moment.

Peggy picked up the note again. "Where did you find this?"

I told her.

"I just can't believe it," Peggy said. "Why would someone kill Moe? He was a bit of a ladies' man. A woman scorned? Maybe a disgruntled husband or beau?"

I shook my head. "Not from the way this is worded. Someone must have gotten wind of what he was working on. I wish I knew what it was." I folded the note and put it in my pocketbook. "I'll take it over to the police station when Chief Turner comes in."

"Good idea." She got up and went to the door. "Let me know if you need anything. "We're still on for tonight, by the way."

I'd completely forgotten about it. The last thing I felt like doing was spending an evening dancing. Or anything else, for that matter.

Peggy must have read my mind. "I'm not letting you back out. You need a break."

"Fine." I'd have to find some way to get out of it. Maybe I'd get lucky and a meteor would strike. I changed back to the subject at hand. "Keep mum about the note until I talk to the chief."

"My lips are sealed."

When Peggy opened the door, Donny was standing there. He took a step back to let her leave.

"Do you want something, Donny?" I asked.

His normally pale face was red. "I—I just came to see how you were feeling after yesterday."

I didn't believe that for a second. "What do you really want?"

Without asking, he sat down. "I want to know if you're going to hire another reporter. You really don't have to, you know. I can do Moe's job and do it better."

"It's too soon to decide if I'll hire anyone." I hadn't even considered it. One thing I knew was that if I did, it wouldn't be my cousin.

"Unlike Moe, I'll keep you informed of my whereabouts. I have lots of ideas for stories. Give me a chance."

"Like I said, it's too soon to make a decision like that. We'll talk about it later."

"I should have known you'd say that," he said. "You're jealous. You know I'd be better than you."

I leaned forward and folded my hands on my desk, mainly to keep myself from using them on Donny. "I'm not sure we need another reporter yet. Besides, what would we do about layout? That's where Pop wants you, and that's where you're needed the most."

"Horse hockey," he said. "Any idiot can lay out those articles. I want to do more. Make a name for myself. I can't believe you won't give me a shot."

I didn't answer, and he blustered on.

"You gave Moe all the chances in the world, and where did that get you? It sure didn't get him anywhere, other than in the morgue. I wouldn't be stupid enough to want to write something that would get me killed."

My blood pressure shot up a few points. "You were listening in on my conversation with Peggy."

"Not on purpose. I couldn't help it."

Couldn't help it, my patootie. "How much did you hear?"

Donny straightened his collar, a sure sign he was nervous. "You think Moe was murdered."

"What else?"

"That you're taking some kind of note to show Chief Turner." He paused. "Can I see it?"

I couldn't believe he had the nerve to ask that. "Absolutely not. And I don't want a word of this to anyone else until I talk to the chief. If I find out you've told anyone, you will be out of a job." It was an empty threat, because I'd never hear the end of it from my aunt Rita. Or my mother, for that matter. As far as her younger sister was concerned, Mom was as big an appeaser as Neville Chamberlain had been.

"Where did you find the note?" Donny asked. "Did he mail it to you? Or was it at his house?"

"I told you I'm not discussing this with anyone until I talk to Chief Turner." I went over to my door. "We both have work to do." When he didn't get up, I added, "That wasn't a suggestion."

On his way out the door, he said, "I'm serious about the reporter position. I'd do a great job."

I closed the door behind him without answering. Hell would have to freeze over first.

* * *

I passed Moe's note across Chief Turner's desk. "I found this in a book when I cleaned out Moe's desk."

He read the note, then put it down on top of a folder on his desk.

"What do you think?" I asked.

The chair squeaked as he leaned back. "It's an interesting note."

"That's it? Interesting?" I tried to keep my voice even, but it didn't work. "Moe was murdered!"

"There's no evidence of that. He fell down the stairs and broke his neck."

"But the note . . ."

"Irene," he said, "there was no sign of foul play."

"Moe said if he ended up dead, it wasn't an accident. Someone could have pushed him down the steps."

"Don't you think there'd be some sign of that? A struggle? Anything?"

"He could have been caught off guard," I said. "Or maybe it was someone he knew."

The chief let out a sigh. "Do you know what he was working on?"

I felt my face turning red. "No. He never told me." I should have known what he'd been working on. I should have forced him to tell me. I was his boss, for heaven's sake. Pop would have known every detail.

"Don't you think if it was something that would get him killed, Bauer would have filled you in? Or even better, notified me if he was that concerned?"

"Probably. Maybe. I honestly don't know. He was always chasing some story or another, and it often came to nothing. He thought his next tip was always going to lead to something big."

"See? This was the same thing. He might have been going after a story, but nothing leads me to think anyone killed him." The chief leaned across the desk and patted my hand. "I don't want you to worry your pretty head about this. Bauer's death was nothing more than a tragic accident."

* * *

"Don't worry your pretty head? Can you believe that?" I said to Peggy as we sat in my office when I returned from the police station. "He insists Moe fell down the steps. Chief Turner might be my future father-in-law, but he's wrong about this. Why would Moe write that note and put it where I'd find it? Moe knew that I'd be the one cleaning out his desk if something happened to him."

"What if the chief is right?" Peggy said. I opened my mouth to answer, and she held up her hand. "Hear me out. If Chief Turner didn't find any evidence that someone broke into the house and pushed Moe down the steps, he could be right. I certainly like that better than a murderer running around Progress."

"I don't want one in our midst either. But if Moe was murdered, whoever did it needs to be brought to justice. Since the chief doesn't believe me, the only way to find out who offed him is to figure out what he was looking into."

"I don't like the idea," Peggy said.

"Of what?"

"Of you looking into it. It might be dangerous."

"Since when did you become such a chicken?"

Peggy shrugged. "Maybe since this war started and I realized none of us are immortal. Look how many boys have died already, including some we know. And now Moe. I sure don't want my best friend added to the list."

"Look, I'm not going to do anything stupid. I just want to figure out what Moe was working on. If it leads to whoever killed him, I'll let Chief Turner handle it."

"Promise?"

"Cross my heart." I made an X across my chest.

Peggy grinned. "So, where do we start?"

*　　*　　*

That afternoon I wrote an article on that day's congressional approval of the Women's Army Auxiliary Corp, which was to be signed into law by Roosevelt tomorrow. I'd follow up with another article on Oveta Culp Hobby, who would be sworn in as the first director of the WAACs on the sixteenth.

I proofed Frank's article on the latest German U-boat attacks off the coast, which were happening all too frequently. U-boats had attacked over two hundred vessels since the middle of January. Yesterday, an American cargo ship had been targeted between Pensacola, Florida, and Venezuela, and two tankers south of New Orleans. Loss of life wasn't confined to those serving in the armed forces.

I'd just finished when Rex knocked on my door. "Got a minute?" he asked.

"Come in and take a load off," I said.

"I followed up on the incident at Tabor. Nothing newsworthy to speak of. The janitor said it was all a misunderstanding. He insists he gets along fine with everyone."

"Do you believe him?" I asked.

Rex shook his head. "Not for a minute, but he's not talking. Probably doesn't want to lose his job. I'll keep an ear open, though, in case anything else happens."

"Thanks for checking," I said.

He went to the door, then turned. "Did you ever find out if Moe had any family?"

"No, I haven't. Not so far, anyway."

"Let me know if you do," he said. "I'm going to take up a collection or something."

That surprised me. He hadn't liked Moe all that much. It also surprised me that his attitude toward me had improved. I wasn't sure if it was because I'd made it clear I was his boss, whether he liked it or not, or due to the shock of Moe's death. Whichever it was, I'd take it.

After he left, I leaned back in my chair. I should have thought of doing something for Moe and any family he might have. If no next of kin turned up, I'd plan a memorial service. I had no idea if Moe had been a religious man, but I could get Father O'Connor to say a few prayers either way. It was the least I could do.

*   *   *

I walked past the Thrift Drug on my way home before I remembered I'd put an empty toothpaste tube in my pocketbook that morning. As of the first of April, we couldn't buy a new toothpaste unless we turned in the old one to be recycled. Every little bit of metal helped the war effort. The A&P had a bin in front of the store for tin cans, and Progress would be holding a countywide scrap drive soon. I backtracked and went inside. I turned in my empty toothpaste and purchased a new one—resisting the urge to look at the makeup displays, since only a week ago I'd bought a Dorothy Gray lipstick called Headline Red. I had plenty of lipsticks, but it was my new favorite, and not just because of the name.

I left the store, and as I tucked my package into my pocketbook, I saw a man with a large bruise on his cheek and a black eye enter Markowicz Hardware. He wore dark-blue work pants and a dark-blue shirt with the sleeves rolled up to his elbow. I'd never seen him before—which wasn't unusual, with all the newcomers in town—but I didn't like the fact that he looked like he'd been in a fight. It could mean trouble for Sam if this was the person who had left the threatening message. I jaywalked across the street.

Sam was behind the counter, adding up plumbing supplies for Dennis Roscoe, a local plumber. The only other person in the store was the bruised man, who was studying a display of screwdrivers. I went to the next aisle, where I could keep an eye on him, and pretended to be interested in paintbrushes. The man picked up a screwdriver and put it back. He did this three times, glancing at Sam each time.

If he was planning to attack Sam with one of the screwdrivers, I needed a weapon. I looked around. There was a wall display of hammers on the other side of the store. Bruised Man might see me, but I had to take the chance. I wasn't going to let him hurt Sam. I tiptoed around the end of the aisle and over to the hammers.

Sam and the plumber finished their transaction, and I ducked as Mr. Roscoe turned and headed toward the door. When he'd gone, I straightened up. Bruised Man was walking toward the counter. I couldn't see if he was carrying a screwdriver or not. I grabbed a hammer just in case. As I walked toward the counter, I saw Sam smile at the man.

"What can I do for you today, Benjamin?" Sam said.

Chapter Seven

American Cargo Ship Sunk in Atlantic off Coast of Florida
—*The Progress Herald*, May 14, 1942

Benjamin? Sam knew this man? As I put the hammer down, Sam spotted me.

"Irene," he said. "There's someone I'd like you to meet."

The man turned and gave me a smile. He winced and touched his cheek. I felt foolish for thinking this man was going to hurt Sam.

"Benjamin Cline, this is Irene Ingram," Sam said. "She's in charge of the *Progress Herald*."

I waited for the usual comment about me being too young for that, but it didn't come.

Benjamin reached out his hand. "I am pleased to meet you. You can call me Ben." His soft voice carried a slight accent.

"We go to the same synagogue," Sam said.

The bruises. The work clothes. I suddenly put two and two together. "You work at Tabor, don't you?"

"Yes, I do," he said.

"You talked to one of my reporters."

"I did."

No wonder Rex couldn't get a story. The man didn't say more than a few words at a time. "What happened that you ended up with those bruises? Can you tell me about it?"

"It was nothing. Just a misunderstanding."

"Benjamin, tell her," Sam said.

Ben shook his head.

Sam looked at me. "I said I wanted to forget what happened to me. But this is different." He turned to Benjamin. "If you don't tell Irene, I will."

Ben's face turned white under his bruises. "If you do, I am a dead man." He said something to Sam in what might have been Polish.

Sam frowned. They continued back and forth, and finally Sam turned to me. "I am sorry, Irene. This matter has ended."

"Ended?" I said. "What were you saying just now?"

"I will say no more," Sam said. "It is for the best."

"I don't believe that," I said. "If someone is giving both of you trouble, you should at least go to the police."

"Bah, police." Ben practically spat the words. "Police are not to be trusted."

"Chief Turner can certainly be trusted," I said. "He's a good man."

"He is," Sam said. "But this situation is different."

"How? If you tell me what's going on, I can help."

"By printing it in your paper?" Ben said. "That will make it worse." He strode to the exit. "I'll speak to you later, Sam."

I turned to Sam. "Won't you please tell me what's going on?"

Sam touched my arm. "I cannot, Irene. I gave my word to Benjamin."

I left the store confused, frustrated, and determined to get to the bottom of whatever it was they were keeping to themselves.

* * *

When Katherine said she didn't have a shift that night, I asked her to come with us to the Starlight. Ken honked his car horn, and Katherine and I hurried out of the house and hopped into the back seat. I made the introductions as we sped off.

"I'm so glad Irene invited you," Peggy said.

"I appreciate it," Katherine said. "I don't get out much these days. It will be a nice change."

Twenty minutes later we pulled into the parking lot. The Starlight was a nightclub located between Progress and Pittsburgh. The name of the place was much fancier than the reality. The building was rather nondescript—a one-story wood-frame structure that at one time had been a roadside tavern. The owners had put a new coat of plaster on the walls, applied a fresh coat of paint, and added a stage and new tables and chairs. They'd kept the smooth wooden floor, which was great for dancing. The Starlight had become well known for hosting live music on Thursday, Friday, and Saturday nights. On occasion it hosted popular big bands. The band tonight, the Cal Rivers Orchestra, was from Pittsburgh, and Katherine said they were quite good. I'd take her word for it.

The Starlight was crowded, but not so much that we couldn't find a table. That was one reason we preferred Thursday nights. The weekends were standing room only, and I didn't much like being packed in like a sardine. At least tonight there would be room to dance. We settled down at our table with time to spare—the band was only tuning up.

I hadn't wanted to come, but now that I was here, I planned to enjoy myself. We ordered drinks, and I'd just taken a gulp of my rum and Coke when I spotted Matt Redmond coming our way. When he reached our table, he let out a big whistle.

"Ken, you sly dog, you," he said. "How did you manage to surround yourself with three beautiful women? I am jealous."

Ken laughed. "Just lucky, I guess."

"Why don't you join us," I said. "Unless you have a hot date or something."

He pulled out the empty chair across from Katherine. "Alas, no date for me tonight."

I introduced him to Katherine. "Matt's our staff photographer and a good friend."

"Anyone ever tell you that you look like Gene Tierney?" Matt said.

Katherine smiled. "Only about three times a week."

He leaned across the table. "I would love to photograph you."

"I bet you would," Katherine said. "And probably every other woman in this room."

Matt put his hands over his chest. "You wound me." He grinned. "And it's only half the women. Maybe three-quarters. I'd really need a closer look." He turned to me. "Speaking of photos, did you happen to find my camera? I'd really like to get it back."

I'd almost forgotten that Moe had borrowed Matt's camera. "It wasn't in Moe's desk, but I can look in his house." I wasn't thrilled with the idea of making another visit there, but I had a feeling it was the only way I was going to find out what story he'd been chasing. Peggy and I had talked about it earlier. If the chief or anyone wanted to know why I was rooting through Moe's things, I could always say I was looking to see if he had a next of kin.

"That'd be swell."

Conversation ended when the band broke into Glenn Miller's "In the Mood." Matt jumped up and grabbed my hand. "Come on, doll, you're dancing with me."

I wouldn't have had a chance to object even if I wanted to. By the time the song finished, I was out of breath. He and Peggy hit the floor for the next number. Peggy and Ken danced a few slow songs after that, and Katherine had no shortage of dance partners. I didn't either, for that matter. When the band took a break, we did too. After a quick trip to the ladies' room to freshen up, Peggy, Katherine, and I joined Ken and Matt back at our table.

While I sipped my third rum and Coke, I thought about the encounter at Markowicz Hardware that afternoon. No matter how hard I tried, I couldn't understand Sam and Benjamin's reluctance to talk to me. I didn't realize Peggy had said something to me until she poked me on the arm.

"You're miles away," she said. "Thinking about Bill?"

I shook my head. "I was thinking about something that happened on the way home this afternoon." I told them about meeting Ben Cline and how he'd insisted the incident at Tabor was all a misunderstanding. "I think it was more than that. Sam wanted him to talk to me, but he refused. He told Sam if he did, he was a dead man."

"That sounds like something out of a detective novel," Peggy said.

"Then they discussed something in Polish—at least I think it was Polish—then Sam told me the matter was ended. I can't figure it out."

Katherine spoke up. "Did you say he's a janitor at the factory?"

"Yes," I said. "Do you know him?"

"Not personally. I've seen him a few times, that's all."

"Do you know who he's had trouble with?" I asked. "Maybe I can get that person to talk."

Katherine shook her head. "I don't, but I can ask around."

The music started up again—a slow song this time. Matt and Katherine headed to the dance floor along with Peggy and Ken. As I watched them, I wished Bill were here. I felt guilty that I hadn't given him a thought all evening until Peggy mentioned him. Bill should be first and foremost on my mind. I'd write him another letter this weekend.

"Would you like to dance?"

I looked up to see Arnold Moss. "No thanks," I said.

He sat in the chair beside me without being invited. "You don't know what you're missing."

I rolled my eyes. All I'd be missing would be keeping his paws from getting a little too friendly. "I'm all danced out."

"Suit yourself," he said. "It's my first time here. It's quaint. Not exactly the Copacabana."

"I wouldn't know."

Moss took a pack of Camels from his dinner jacket and tilted it toward me.

"I don't smoke."

He lit his cigarette with a gold lighter. "So, how's the news business? I hear you lost one of your reporters."

"Yes, I did."

"That's too bad."

"Moe was a good guy and a good reporter."

"I can't imagine how you find anything newsworthy to print in this town."

"You'd be surprised," I said. "Maybe you should read the *Herald* once in a while."

Moss laughed. "I do. Some of it, anyway. And I'll be sure to read the articles you write, now that we've met. I enjoyed your write-up about the ceremony the other day. I usually skip the Tabor articles, since I know just about everything that goes on there."

Everything? I had a thought. "What can you tell me about the guy who was beaten up in the parking lot recently?"

"Not much. I heard it was a verbal squabble that got physical. Fights of some sort are an almost daily occurrence," he said. "Not very newsworthy."

"I understand it wasn't exactly a fight. A Jewish man was beaten up."

"Like I said, it was nothing newsworthy. I spoke to the man," he said. "He said it was a big misunderstanding and assured me he was all right and didn't want to do anything about it."

The song ended, and the others headed toward the table. Moss stood as the band began playing "Sing, Sing, Sing." "It's been an enjoyable conversation, Irene," he said. "Perhaps we can continue it over dinner some night." He nodded to Matt, who was the first to reach the table, and walked away.

"Wasn't that Arnold Moss?" Katherine asked seconds later.

"Yep."

"This isn't exactly his kind of place," Matt said. "What was he doing here?"

I shrugged. "Slumming, I guess."

* * *

The rest of the evening was uneventful. On the way home, I talked to Katherine about the idea for my article on women in the workforce. She promised to ask a few of her coworkers if they'd like to be featured. I wasn't sure if it had been the dancing or the three rum and Cokes, but I slept well and woke up refreshed and ready to go.

I didn't have a lot on my plate for the day. I had the article to write about Oveta Culp Hobby, the director of the WAACs, and some background information on the upcoming scrap drive. It left plenty of time for me to go to Moe's house after lunch and snoop around. It took me longer than I planned to get a hold of someone at the War Department who would give me what I needed for the WAAC piece, but I finally managed to get enough for my article. By the time I finished, it was lunchtime.

Since it was Friday, I opted for Woolworth's. They had a pretty good tuna salad on toast. When I took a seat at the lunch counter, Mr. Lemon, sitting at the end, was biting into a big, juicy hamburger. I almost risked ordering one and going to hell by eating meat on a Friday. At the very least I'd have to confess it to Father O'Connor. My inner angel prevailed, however, and I got the tuna.

As I left the counter after lunch, I saw Sarah Markowicz in the sock and hosiery aisle. Perhaps she'd be able to tell me what was going on with her husband. Sarah was an attractive woman. She was a little on the plump side but carried it well. Her black hair, which she wore in a braid wrapped around her head, had two white streaks at the temples. She smiled when she saw me approaching.

"Irene, it is good to see you," she said. "Thank your mother for the casserole. It was delicious. I will return the dish to her tomorrow."

"There's no hurry," I said. "How are you doing?"

"I am a nervous wreck. I don't understand what is happening."

"You mean with Sam?"

"Yes. It is frightening that there would be hatred like that here."

"Has Sam said any more about it besides what he told Chief Turner and me?"

Sarah shook her head. "He will not talk about it. I have asked him, but he tells me not to worry. How can I not worry?"

"I met a man named Benjamin at the hardware store yesterday. Sam said he went to your synagogue."

"I'm sorry. I do not know him."

I found that odd. Sam and Ben seemed to be well acquainted. But she didn't appear to be lying. "Are you sure? He's about five foot ten, medium build, dark hair."

Sarah smiled. "That description fits half of the synagogue. I may know him to see and just do not know his name. Why do you want to know?"

If Sam was keeping something from her, I didn't want to be the one to spill the beans. "No reason. I just thought I'd mention that I'd met him." I looked at my watch. "I'd better be getting back to work."

Sarah thanked me again for the casserole, and we parted ways. I walked back to the paper, no further along in figuring out what was going on.

* * *

Everything was running smoothly at the *Herald*, an accomplishment for a Friday afternoon. Although the Saturday and Sunday editions of the paper were combined into one weekend edition delivered on Sunday morning, there were usually last-minute changes and late submissions. It looked like I'd have to spend only a few hours over the weekend finalizing it all. Even the telephone was quiet for a change. I asked Peggy if she wanted to go to Moe's house with me. She hesitated until Ken said he wasn't going anywhere and would answer the phone if it rang.

"Are you sure this is a good idea?" Peggy asked as we hoofed it to Moe's house. It had been raining on and off all day, and we walked quickly in case it started up again.

"Maybe, maybe not. But it's the only way I'm going to find out what got him killed."

"There might not be anything there."

"There has to be." We turned onto Moe's street. "There weren't any notes in or on his desk, so they have to be in his house."

"Shouldn't you let Chief Turner know you're doing this?"

I rolled my eyes. "Don't be such a worrywart."

"So you didn't tell him."

"I'll tell him when we find something of significance. Remember, he thinks Moe's death was an accident. He'd tell me again not to worry my pretty head."

When we reached Moe's front door, I turned the knob and pushed, but it didn't budge. Locked. Just my luck.

Peggy turned to leave. "I guess we'll have to ask the chief to let us in."

I grabbed her arm. "Wait. Let me check the windows."

"You can't be serious," she said. "Wouldn't that be breaking and entering?"

"Only if we get caught, and I have no intention of that happening." I didn't wait for her to try to talk me out of it. Peggy followed me while I checked the windows on the front and sides of the house.

"They're all locked," she said. "Let's call the chief."

"We haven't checked the back yet. Or the second floor."

"And just how do you propose reaching a second-floor window? You can't go shimmying up a drainpipe, and I don't see a ladder anywhere. Plus you're not exactly dressed for it."

She was right about that. I'd have to go home and change into slacks. And my mother would surely ask what I was up to. "I'll figure it out if the time comes." I opened the gate in the chain-link fence surrounding the backyard.

There were two windows at the back of the house on each side of a door. As luck would have it, I wouldn't have to shimmy up anything. The back door was wide open.

Chapter Eight

Roosevelt Announces Army to Take Over Air Lines

—The Progress Herald, May 15, 1942

I was heading straight for the door when Peggy ran in front of me and blocked my way.

"You can't go in there," she said. "What if someone's inside?"

"Anyone with half a brain would have left when we started trying all the windows. We weren't exactly quiet about it. Whoever broke in is long gone."

Peggy chewed her lip. "Maybe we'd better call the police."

"After we have a look around."

"I don't like this. At all."

"You can wait out here if you want, but I'm going in."

It took her only a second or two to decide to come with me. On close inspection of the door, it looked like it had been jimmied open. Moe's kitchen sink had been full of dirty dishes the last time I was here, but now all the cupboard doors were open. Someone had been looking for something.

"What a mess," Peggy said.

The other rooms in the house were in much the same condition. There had been scattered papers in the living room before, but now someone had cut open the upholstery on the sofa and chair. The radio had been pushed over and smashed. A bookcase had been toppled over, and books were scattered nearby.

I assumed the second floor would be the same. I needed to take a look anyway. Peggy followed me up the stairs. The medicine cabinet in the bathroom had been emptied onto the floor. The bedroom was in the same condition as the living room. The mattress was ripped to shreds. Moe's suits and pants had been pulled from the closet, and the pockets had all been turned out.

The second bedroom looked as if Moe had used it as an office. The only furniture was a battered desk, a small bookcase, and a file cabinet. The file drawers were all open and the papers were scattered everywhere. The same with the desk drawers.

Peggy said, "Now what? Whoever was in here probably found what he was looking for."

I thought for a minute. "Not necessarily." I started gathering up all the papers. "There could be something in these."

"That's a lot to go through."

"We'll take them with us."

"Isn't that stealing?" Peggy asked.

I raised an eyebrow. "Moe isn't going to miss them. He would want me to take them if it leads to whoever killed him."

"You're right." Peggy began picking up papers.

Ten minutes later, we had gathered them all up. There was one more place I needed to check—the basement. I paused at the cellar door.

"You don't have to go down there," Peggy said.

"Yes, I do. Pop would go down."

"But you're not your father. You don't have to prove anything to me."

"I know that. I just don't want to miss anything. You wait here." I handed Peggy the stack of papers I was carrying and went down the stairs. I avoided looking at the spot where I'd found Moe.

The basement was the neatest room in the house. The coal furnace took up a good bit of the space. A laundry sink was nearby, and beside it was a toilet, a commonplace item in many of these houses. I'd heard them referred to as Pittsburgh toilets, but in reality they were all over Western Pennsylvania. A broom leaned up against one wall. Other than that, the cellar was empty. I had turned to head back upstairs when I spotted something under the steps. I ducked underneath. It looked like a camera. It was just out of reach, so I got the broom and used it to slide it out.

The camera was smaller than the one Matt used to take photos for the *Herald*, and I wondered if it could be the one Moe had borrowed from him. Except for a few scuffs, it appeared new. I couldn't tell if there was film inside or if Moe had taken any pictures. I'd let Matt figure it out.

I went back upstairs and showed Peggy what I'd found, and we headed back to work.

*　*　*

When Matt came in from his assignment, Peggy sent him in to see me. The camera was sitting on top of my desk, and he rushed over and picked it up.

"I can't believe you found it," he said. "I thought I'd never see it again and have to shell out thirty-eight bucks for a new one."

"That's a lot of moolah. Must be some camera."

"It's the latest model. Kodak Vigilant Six-20. It's easier to carry around than the beast I use here. Where did you find it, anyway?"

"At Moe's. There are a couple of scratches on it."

"As long as it works, I don't mind that." Matt looked it over carefully. "Seems all right. There's no film in it. Moe must have gotten the pictures he wanted."

If he did and I located them, maybe that would help me unravel what he was working on. The other possibility was that the killer had made off with either the film or the photos. "Where would Moe have taken the film to be developed?"

"When I gave him the camera, I offered to develop them," Matt said. "But he turned me down. Said he had other plans. He could have taken it to Thrift Drug like everyone else in town."

I shook my head. "I'll check with them, but I don't think he'd take a chance on going there. I have a hunch that Mildred looks at all the photos when they come in."

"Good point. If the photos were of a compromising nature, he'd want to be discreet. There's a place I know in Butler that will process anything, no questions asked. I can check them if you'd like."

"I'd appreciate it," I said.

He went to the door and turned. "Why are you so hep to know what Moe was up to?"

Matt would keep it under his hat, but the fewer people who knew Moe's death hadn't been an accident, the better—at least until I knew more.

"I feel like I let him down." It wasn't a lie. "If he really was onto something, I want to know what it was."

Matt nodded like he understood. "I'll let you know if I learn anything."

*   *   *

Ken was going to a baseball game that night, so Peggy and I made plans to go through the papers we'd taken from Moe's. We decided to meet at her house, away from the prying eyes of my mother and sister.

Peggy lived in what everyone considered the ritzy neighborhood. The houses were large, as were the incomes needed to maintain them. She never flaunted the fact that her father owned the Progress Savings and Loan. Her parents didn't either. They had money but were as down-to-earth as anyone could be. Heck, my mother was more of a snob. Peggy could have gotten away with never working a day in her life, but her parents insisted she earn her keep. I think it was the fact that they had lived through some tough times during the Depression. They had worked hard and insisted their daughter do the same. They donated to many worthy causes and single-handedly funded the new pipe organ at Saint Michael's. Their only splurge was their membership to the Tall Pines Country Club, where they went every Friday evening.

The Reardons' house was a beautiful red-brick Georgian with white trim and a few black accents. It didn't have a front porch, but there was an enormous flagstone patio in the back. I went right in as usual. We'd long ago stopped ringing each other's doorbells.

"I'm in the kitchen," Peggy called out.

I went down the hallway to the kitchen at the back of the house. The Reardons' kitchen looked much the same as ours, only bigger—white cabinets and sunny yellow walls. I set the folder containing Moe's papers on the table.

Peggy placed a plate of oatmeal cookies on the table. "Mom made these today. She only used half the sugar, but with the raisins, they're sweet enough."

I picked one up and sat down.

"Do you really think we'll find anything?" Peggy joined me at the table.

"Only one way to find out," I said with a mouthful of cookie. I opened the folder and passed half the papers to Peggy. "We'll divide and conquer."

Because the papers had been scattered everywhere, nothing was in order. Notes were mixed in with various receipts and newspaper clippings. I recognized some notes Moe had taken for articles he'd written for the *Herald*. One piece of paper had women's names on it with telephone numbers. The name *Sylvia* had a heart drawn next to it. He apparently hadn't invested in a black book. I added the paper to the trash pile, then changed my mind and put it aside.

"That's not trash?" Peggy said. "It looks like a list of Moe's conquests."

"It's possible Moe bragged to one of the women what he'd been working on. I know it's unlikely, but I should check anyway. I'll start with Sylvia." I pointed to the heart. "Moe must have liked her."

Peggy slid a paper in front of me. "How about this?" It was a torn piece of a calendar page. It contained squares for the third, the tenth, and part of the eleventh of May. The eleventh was the last day I'd seen Moe. The only block that wasn't blank was the one for the eleventh, where Moe had scribbled *TAB 10 AM*.

"What the heck does that mean?" Peggy asked.

"Maybe he was meeting someone with the initials *T. A. B.* at ten AM? See if there are any more scraps in your pile." I sifted through the papers in front of me, looking for more calendar pieces. We both came up empty.

"Now what?" Peggy said.

I had no idea. We searched the rest of the papers for anything else, but the calendar scrap was the only clue, if you could even call it that. It could mean nothing at all. Why did Moe have to be so cryptic? The paper with the names and telephone numbers caught my eye again, and I picked it up. "Look at this." I pointed at a name on the list. "Tina. Maybe that's the *T* on the calendar. Moe was supposed to meet her at ten."

"That makes sense," Peggy said. "Well, as much sense as anything else. Are you going to call her?"

I looked at my watch. Nine thirty. "Do you think it's too late?"

"Nope." She pulled me up and led me to the telephone in the hallway.

I dialed the number and got a busy signal. "Drat." I waited a few minutes and tried again with the same result.

"Try Sylvia," Peggy said. "There has to be some reason there's a heart next to her name."

Sylvia's telephone rang and rang. I hung up. "I'll try again tomorrow, and call Tina and the others on the list."

We went back to the kitchen, and I put all the papers back in the folder. Peggy wrapped a few cookies in waxed paper for me to take home. We chatted a few more minutes, then I headed home, disappointed we hadn't accomplished as much as I'd hoped.

* * *

Saturday mornings were almost always spent helping my mother clean the house. Katherine had worked the three-to-eleven-PM shift at Tabor, so we left the vacuuming until she woke up. Lily's job was cleaning the bathroom, which she complained about end-lessly. Come to think of it, I had done the same and been more than happy to pass it on to her when she was old enough.

While I dusted the tables in the living room, I tried to put together the two puzzle pieces I had—the women's names and the scrap from the calendar. It was possible neither one meant anything. From what I knew of Moe, he'd dated a lot of women. It made sense he'd kept a list of names and telephone numbers, but why wouldn't he keep them in a telephone book? I wouldn't have taken the chance of losing the numbers. What did the heart next to Sylvia's name mean? I couldn't imagine him settling down with one woman. This was going nowhere. I sighed loudly just as Katherine entered the room.

"Dusting isn't my favorite thing either," she said.

"It isn't that," I said. "I can't figure something out, and it's driving me crazy. Did you sleep well?"

Katherine sat in one of the wing chairs and lit a cigarette. "Very well. Want to talk about what you can't figure out? Some-times it helps."

"I doubt that you can help with this."

"Try me. I'm a good problem solver."

I wasn't sure how much I could tell her without giving away what I was doing. Chief Turner wouldn't be happy if it got back to him that I still thought Moe had been murdered and was inves-tigating, even though he'd find out eventually when I had more evidence. I didn't want it blabbed all over town, and I especially didn't want the killer to know what I was doing.

It seemed Katherine could see I was struggling with what to say. "I can keep a secret, if that's what you're worried about. It won't leave this room."

I put the rag down and took a seat in the other chair. "You remember that one of my reporters was found dead?"

Katherine nodded.

"I'm trying to figure out what he was working on. He often chased what he thought were big stories, but this time I think he really was onto something."

"Why do you think that?"

Lily burst into the room. "You're awake! Can we listen to some records?"

Mom was in the room before Katherine could even think about answering. "Lily Marie, Katherine just got up. She hasn't even had coffee yet. I'm sorry she keeps bothering you," Mom said to Katherine.

"It's no bother," Katherine said. "She's just enthusiastic about music. It's always nice to listen with someone who appreciates it."

"See?" Lily said. "I'll even get Katherine a cup of coffee."

Katherine smiled. "That would be lovely, Lily."

"If you're sure you don't mind," Mom said. "I'll go fix you something to eat."

"That's really not necessary," Katherine said. "I can fend for myself."

Mom insisted on making her breakfast and went to the kitchen.

Katherine stood. "I'd better get those records. We can talk later if you want."

"Sure." It was just as well. I doubted she'd have been able to help me anyway.

* * *

86

I had an appointment at Ava's beauty shop after lunch. I was overdue for a trim, and Ava made sure I knew it.

"You should have come here a week ago," she said. "Look at these split ends." She held a length of hair straight out from my head. "I'm going to have to cut off half an inch."

"That's fine," I said.

"You need to take better care of your hair. One hundred strokes every night to get the oil to the ends."

I rolled my eyes at a woman under the hair dryer in the next chair, and she smiled. "If I took the time to do that, I'd never get anything else done." It was a chore putting a few pin curls in every night.

"I'm not a miracle worker," Ava said. "I can only do so much."

"I'm sure you'll work wonders. You always do." I figured it might a good idea to butter up the person holding scissors in her hand.

Ava sighed. "I'll try my best."

While she cut, I got an earful of the latest gossip, which frankly didn't amount to much. Apparently no one was sleeping with anyone they weren't supposed to at the moment. Ava had my hair cut and set in record time. She worked as fast as she talked.

"Let me get Sylvia out from under the dryer, and then we'll put you under there."

Sylvia? It couldn't be, could it? That would be way too much of a coincidence.

Ava turned the hair dryer off and raised the hood.

"Excuse me," I said. "Your name is Sylvia?"

"Yes, it is. Sylvia Fontaine." She was pretty in an unconventional way. Her green eyes were too wide set, and her nose was slightly crooked. She held out a slender hand.

I shook it. "Irene Ingram."

"It's a pleasure to meet you," Sylvia said. "Your name sounds familiar. Have we met before?"

Ava broke in. "Irene is the editor of the *Progress Herald*."

"The *Herald*. Huh. So you work with Moe Bauer."

I noticed she didn't use past tense. "Yes, I do."

Sylvia's eyes narrowed. "Well, tell that two-bit, no-good jerk who thinks he's God's gift to women that I never want to see him again."

It looked like I'd definitely found Moe's Sylvia.

Chapter Nine

Gas Rationing Begins
Restricted to 3 Gallons/Week With A-Card
—*The Progress Herald*, May 16, 1942

Ava and I exchanged glances. She opened her mouth to speak, and I put up my hand to stop her. "I have some bad news, Sylvia," I said.

"What? That Moe is two-timing me? I should have known."

"That's not it." There was no easy way to say it.

"Oh, for heaven's sake," Ava said. "Just tell her."

The way Sylvia felt, she might be glad. "Moe is dead."

All the blood seemed to drain from Sylvia's face. She raised a hand to her mouth and muttered, "No. That's not possible." She burst into tears.

I hadn't expected that.

Ava patted her shoulder. "There, there."

Sylvia stopped crying after what seemed like an eternity. She retrieved a handkerchief from her pocketbook, dabbed her eyes, and blew her nose. She looked at me. "He's really dead?"

I nodded.

"I don't understand. We had a date on Monday night, but he never showed up. He had lots of girlfriends before me, but he said I was his only one. When I couldn't even get him on the telephone, I thought he'd lied to me and gone back to his old ways—that he'd dumped me for some other girl."

That sort of explained the heart next to Sylvia's name on the list. But why did he keep a list like that at all if he'd found true love? Moe had always said he liked playing the field and would never settle down. Maybe the others were backup in case things didn't work out.

"What happened to him? I need to know," Sylvia said.

I told her about finding him at the bottom of his cellar steps. I left out how I thought he'd gotten there.

"Poor Moe," she said. "Poor, poor Moe." Her eyes glistened with tears again. "I'll never forget him."

I imagined she wouldn't. I had a lot of questions to ask her, but I needed to do it elsewhere. I didn't want Ava broadcasting everything we said. What had happened here just now would be spread all over before I even got home. There was one thing I could ask, though—about next of kin.

"As far as I know, Moe's parents are dead. He was an only child. That's really all I know. He never mentioned anyone else."

"So you're the nearest thing to a relative that he had."

"I—I guess I am."

I wondered how I could put it delicately that Moe was still in the county morgue. I settled for asking about a funeral.

"I'll have to think about that," she said. "Maybe you could help me with planning something."

"I'd be happy to." I wasn't really happy about it, but it would give me a chance to talk to her further. I told her I planned to mention a prayer service to Father O'Connor after Mass tomorrow.

"That would be kind, but Moe wasn't exactly the praying sort."

We agreed to meet to drink a toast to Moe that evening at a place near her apartment. She lived two miles away, so I would have to take out Pop's car again.

After that, Ava put me under the dryer. I pretended to read an old *Photoplay* while Ava combed out Sylvia's golden-blonde hair. She and Ava chatted and laughed like nothing was wrong. By the time Sylvia left, she seemed fully recovered from the shocking news of Moe's death. I couldn't help but wonder how much of her sorrow had been an act.

* * *

When I left Ava's, I stopped at Thrift Drug. I bypassed the lipsticks and went straight to the counter where I could check on Moe's photos. The clerk was a kid I didn't recognize. "Where's Mildred today?" I asked.

"She doesn't work on Saturdays," he said. "Can I help you?"

"I hope so. I'm the editor of the *Progress Herald*—"

The kid stood up straighter and puffed out his chest. "I bet you're here to do a story on me and my buddies. We joined up and are leaving next month right after graduation. We're going to whip those Nazis. They don't stand a chance."

I suddenly felt much older than my twenty-two years. He didn't look old enough to even be working here, let alone join the army. There were so many blue stars hanging in windows already. I only hoped not too many of them had to be changed to gold. "That would make a great story. I'll get one of my reporters to follow up," I said, trying to let him down easy. We already had a column about local boys in the armed services, so all it would amount to would be adding their names, their branches of service, and who their parents were. "That's not why I'm here right now, though."

The boy went back to his former slouch.

"One of my reporters might have left some film here to be developed. Would you check on that for me?"

"Sure thing. What's the name?"

"Moe Bauer."

"He didn't," the kid said.

"You didn't even look."

"Don't have to," he said. "Mr. Bauer came in this morning asking for his photos."

"Mr. Bauer did? That's impossible."

He ignored my comment. "He said his wife dropped off the film and he wanted to pick up the pictures. I checked, and there was nothing. Told him his wife must have gone somewhere else. You should have a talk with him. He wasn't real nice when I told him that."

My heart beat a little faster. Moe must have put Matt's camera to good use. "What did this Mr. Bauer look like?"

The boy shrugged. "I dunno. Ordinary. Taller than me."

"What about hair color, eye color? What was he wearing?"

"I dunno. Brown, maybe? He wore a hat. I didn't pay attention to what he was wearing, and I sure didn't look at his eyes."

I was disappointed, but I shouldn't have expected a kid to notice details. "Well, thanks anyway. If you see him again, would you call the *Herald*?"

"Sure thing. But if Mr. Bauer works with you, why don't you just ask him yourself?"

"I would if I could," I said. I left the poor boy scratching his head.

My last stop before heading home was the *Herald*. Donny hated when I went in on Saturdays, as it was the one day where he felt like he was in charge. He undoubtedly had everything under control, but I needed to check for myself. Pop always did. Funny, Donny never complained then.

Most of the time at least one reporter was in the newsroom working on something for Sunday's or Monday's paper, but it was empty right now. There was no telephone ringing, no click-clack of typewriter keys, no shuffling papers. I stood in the middle of the room for a moment and enjoyed the silence, then checked the wire for any important news—especially war news—that needed to be added to the morning edition. All was quiet for now.

In my office, I closed the door and retrieved the list of women's names and telephone numbers from my pocketbook. Running into Sylvia had been a lucky break, but I still needed to call the others.

Twenty minutes later I'd informed several distraught women that Moe would not be calling them. I'd saved Tina for last, hoping that she was the *T* in Moe's message *TAB 10 AM*. It turned out she wasn't. Her initials weren't even close. I was back at the start. I hoped Sylvia would be able to tell me something when we met later.

There was a noise outside my door. I got up as quietly as I could and swung open the door. Donny stood there with a guilty look on his face. "You're really making a habit out of eavesdropping," I said.

"I wasn't," he said. "I heard talking and wanted to make sure you were all right."

"Right."

"It's true!"

"Why didn't you just come in?"

He stammered something unintelligible.

I sighed. Loudly. "Donny, you don't have to spy on me. If you want to know something, just ask."

He stuck out his chin and folded his arms over his chest. "Fine. I'll start with why are you here? You don't have to check up on me. I know how to run this paper."

"You know your job. You don't know how to run the paper."

"Says you."

It was like arguing with a three-year-old. "I almost always stop in on Saturdays. And Sundays. Pop did too. You know that as well as I do. Especially with the war going on, I need to check the wire daily. I can't afford to miss important news."

"I already checked it," Donny said. "There was nothing that needs to be in tomorrow morning's edition. Everything is as it should be, and it's printing as we speak."

"Thank you." It was hard getting those words out.

Instead of telling me I was welcome, he said, "See? I know what I'm doing. I could easily do your job. And I could definitely do Moe's."

I regretted thanking him. The saying that you can catch more flies with honey apparently didn't apply to my cousin. "Is there anything else?"

He didn't hesitate. "Who were you talking to?"

I was tempted to tell him to mind his own business, but then I'd never get him out of my office. "I was calling some of Moe's lady friends to tell them the bad news."

"Oh. I thought it would be something more exciting."

"It wasn't a pleasant task." I could tell he was itching to ask what Moe had been working on and whether I'd found any clues as to who had murdered him. Donny was the last person I wanted to discuss it with. I had accomplished everything I intended to, so I told Donny I was going home and suggested he do the same. For once he didn't argue with me.

*   *   *

I telephoned Peggy right after dinner to tell her I'd found Sylvia and was meeting her for a drink in a little over an hour. She and Ken had planned on taking in a movie, but she insisted they tag along instead. She didn't think it was safe for me to go alone. I wasn't thrilled with the idea. I didn't want to take the chance of two extra people spooking Sylvia. I kept thinking about how her demeanor had changed from being tearful and heartbroken over Moe to laughing and talking with Ava. Maybe that was just the way she dealt with tragedy, but it seemed odd to me. Peggy and I finally settled on taking separate cars, and she and Ken would sit at another table.

Lily had gone to a friend's and Mom to her bridge club. Katherine was working the three-to-eleven shift, so I locked up the house when I left. Just about everyone in town used to leave their doors unlocked, but with so many new people in the area, the chief had convinced most to lock their doors when no one was home.

I got Pop's Pontiac out of the garage and drove through downtown, then west on Fremont Street. Two miles later I pulled into the parking lot of the Roadhouse, a country and western bar. I'd never been here before, and I hoped cowboy boots weren't a requirement. I'd hate to get thrown out for wearing loafers.

Ken pulled in right behind me and parked several spaces away. I waved to him and Peggy and headed for the entrance. A cloud of cigarette smoke drifted out when I opened the steel door. I wasn't all that familiar with country and western music, but the voice coming from the jukebox sounded like Gene Autry. It took a moment for my eyes to adjust to the dim lighting. The Roadhouse wasn't crowded—Progress wasn't exactly the ideal spot for this type of bar. Anyone looking for just a shot and a beer would go elsewhere if they had a choice. It smelled like cigarettes and stale beer, and it sure didn't look like a place Moe would spend any time in. I didn't know Sylvia, but it didn't seem like her kind of place either.

I spotted Sylvia sitting in a booth at the far end of the room. I took a few seconds to study her. She definitely looked out of place here. She wore an emerald-green dress that my mother would have a heart attack if I wore—which I wouldn't, because I didn't have the figure for it. Sylvia did, though. The dress hugged all the right places, judging from the ogling she was getting from a couple of men seated at the bar. Moe certainly would have appreciated it. I made my way over.

"I wasn't sure you'd show up," Sylvia said as I took a seat. Her words were a bit slurred—she wasn't on her first drink.

"I wouldn't do that. What are you drinking? I'll buy." I heard Peggy clear her throat as she and Ken sat in the booth behind me.

"I appreciate that." Sylvia waved to the bartender, and he came over. "I'll have another bourbon."

The bartender turned to me. "How about you?"

"Just some water, please."

"We don't have water," he said.

I wasn't going to argue that everyone had water. "How about a Coke, then?"

"A Coke. No rum?"

"Nope."

"Nothing in it?"

"Just some ice. And I'm buying this round."

"Suit yourself."

I heard him ask Peggy and Ken what they wanted to drink. They ordered Cokes as well. The bartender went back to the bar, shaking his head and mumbling to himself. Apparently ordering something without alcohol in it was a rare occurrence.

Sylvia finished the drink she had in front of her. We made some small talk until the bartender returned. "I probably shouldn't have another. This is my third, but what the heck. This is for Moe, right?"

I raised my glass. "To Moe." We clinked glasses.

"Moe was the best," she said. "Never met anyone like him. He was such a gentleman."

"He was?" I guess she'd forgotten how she'd thought he'd stood her up.

"Treated me like a queen. Brought me flowers all the time." Sylvia sipped her drink. "It was almost like we were married. I'd cook dinner while he sat on the sofa with his tablet, writing notes for his articles."

"He wrote at your place?"

"Not always. Sometimes at his house. I still have his notebook."

My pulse quickened. This was good news. "Moe told me he was onto a big story. Did he talk to you about it?"

"Nah. We didn't do much talking, if you know what I mean."

Now that sounded more like Moe. "He didn't mention a big story?"

"He might've. I guess I didn't pay that much attention." She took another drink. The more she drank and talked, the more she slurred her words. "He did say once that something was going on somewhere and he was going to put a stop to it."

That was descriptive. "What was going on?"

Sylvia finished her drink. "I dunno. Something."

"Try to remember," I said. "It's important."

"I can't. How about I give you his notebook? I'll go get it." She stood and swayed.

I jumped up and grabbed her by the arm before she fell and sat her back down. "I'll go with you. You're not in any condition to go by yourself." I went over to the bar and paid for our drinks, including the two Sylvia had consumed prior to my arrival. I helped her to her feet and she swayed again.

Ken stood up. "Excuse me, but it looks like your friend is having a little trouble. Would you like some help?"

"I don't want to bother you," I said.

"It's no trouble at all," he said. "My fiancée and I would be happy to help."

"We would," Peggy said. She put out her hand. "I'm Peggy, and this is Ken." They were giving an Academy Award–winning performance. I'd never known they had it in them.

I handed Sylvia her pocketbook, and the three of us managed to walk the half block to her apartment building. At least I hoped it was her building. Her directions weren't all that clear. Her apartment was on the second floor, and I had to fish in her purse for her key. It turned out I didn't need the key, however. Her apartment door was wide open.

Chapter Ten

**FDR Signs Legislation Creating Women's Army
Auxiliary Corps**

—The Progress Herald, May 16, 1942

"Why is my door open?" Sylvia said. "I always lock it."

"Are you sure?" I asked. "Maybe you forgot."

"I wouldn't forget that." She lurched toward the open door.

Ken pulled her back. "Let me go first, just in case you did." He entered the apartment with the rest of us close behind.

To say Sylvia's apartment was a mess would be an understatement. Sylvia sank to her knees. "Oh no. No. No. No."

The place hadn't only been tossed. It had been destroyed. In the living room, the cushions from the sofa and chairs had been sliced open, the insides pulled out and strewn on the floor. A bookshelf had been knocked over, knickknacks and vases shattered. The few books Sylvia owned had pages torn out and scattered everywhere. The kitchen area was in the same disarray—cupboard doors open and dishes thrown everywhere.

"Why?" Sylvia moaned. "Who would do something like this?"

I had a pretty good idea. Not who, but why. Moe had definitely been onto something. Whoever had killed Moe and broken into his place somehow knew he'd spent time here. But how? I hadn't known about Sylvia until I'd found the list of phone numbers. If the killer had found that list at Moe's, he wouldn't have left it behind. And why wait until tonight to come here? Someone had to have known Sylvia and Moe had been seeing each other. Besides Peggy and me, the only person who came to mind was Ava. Ava would never intentionally put anyone in harm's way, but she might have gossiped to the wrong person.

Sylvia pushed herself to her feet. "I'd better check the bedroom." She staggered, and I took her by the arm.

"I'll help you," I said.

We went down a short hallway. We passed a small bathroom where the contents of the medicine cabinet had been emptied out onto the floor. Sylvia gasped when we reached the bedroom door. The bedclothes had been removed from the bed, and the mattress was in the same condition as the sofa cushions. Clothes had been pulled from the dresser drawers and the closet. She sank down onto the floor and burst into tears. It was several minutes before I got her to calm down.

"We need to call the police," I said.

"What good is that going to do?" She sniffled. "They'll take one look at me, pat me on the head, tell me they'll take care of it, and not do a damn thing. Meanwhile, I have this to deal with. I can't afford to replace all this." Tears filled her eyes again. "I don't know what I'm going to do."

"I still think we should call the police."

"No."

"Let us help you clean some of this up, then."

She nodded. "I would appreciate that."

For the next hour Peggy, Ken, and I helped Sylvia clean up what we could. Almost everything was beyond repair and would end up in the garbage. The percolator, two coffee cups, and two drinking glasses had survived the onslaught, so Peggy made coffee while we finished up.

"Is there somewhere you can stay tonight?" I asked while we sat on the floor drinking our coffee.

"I can stay with my sister in Butler for a while, but it's too late tonight. I'll sleep here on the floor. I have to be at work in the morning at seven."

"Nonsense," Peggy said. "You can't sleep on the floor. You're coming home with me. You can go to work from there."

"I don't want to be any trouble," Sylvia said. "I'll be okay here."

Ken said, "That's not a good idea. Your lock is broken. You're going to have to have your landlord replace it."

Sylvia shook her head. "I'll do it myself. If I tell my landlord, he'll raise my rent or throw me out."

"Then stay with Peggy tonight," I said. "Get a new lock from Markowicz Hardware tomorrow."

"I'll help you install it," Ken added.

Sylvia started crying again. "You are the nicest people I ever met. I don't know how to thank you."

"It's wartime," Peggy said. "We all have to stick together."

I helped Sylvia gather up some things and put them in an overnight case. "I'll let you know what Father O'Connor says tomorrow about a prayer service for Moe."

Sylvia stopped packing. "I almost forgot why we came here. You wanted Moe's notebook."

"That's not important now."

"That's why someone tore this place apart, isn't it?"

"I think so." I considered telling her Moe had been murdered, but what would it accomplish? It was bad enough that this had happened. We finished packing in silence. It was more evident now than ever that I'd never know what Moe had been working on. I'd never know who'd killed him.

* * *

I talked to Father O'Connor after Mass on Sunday morning about some kind of service for Moe. Since Moe wasn't Catholic—at least as far as I knew—a funeral Mass was out of the question. Father offered to say a few prayers if I could gather Moe's friends together. I decided the best place was at the *Herald*. We set it up for Wednesday. I'd have to find some way to get in touch with Sylvia if she wouldn't be staying with Peggy again. I should have gotten her sister's phone number. I hadn't even found out where she worked. Some reporter I was.

After brunch, I sat with Mom and Lily in the living room listening to the radio while they read the *Herald*. Lily was disappointed Katherine had gone out. She had said she was meeting a friend, and I wondered if it was the same person she'd gone to meet after the telephone call she received during dinner the other night. It was none of my business, but I was curious all the same.

Lily had been reading my article about Oveta Culp Hobby, the newly appointed director of the WAACs. She waved the paper in the air. "If we're still at war in a few years, I'm joining the WAACs."

"I thought you were going to work at Tabor like Katherine," I said.

"I changed my mind," she said. "The WAACs are much more important than making nuts and bolts."

"That's not true," I said. "If someone isn't making nuts and bolts, not to mention trucks, tanks, and airplanes, the armed forces wouldn't have anything to fight with."

Lily said, "But it's so exciting to see women in uniform. Maybe by the time I join, we'll even be able to fight." She jumped out of her chair and made like she was shooting a machine gun.

My mother put the Lifestyle section of the paper on the end table beside her. "That will be enough of that, Lily Marie. You won't be doing either of those things. I don't know what the world is coming to with women in factories and in the service. Women are not meant for those kinds of jobs."

"Mom, you are so old-fashioned," Lily said. "Girls can do anything that boys can do."

"Of course they can," I said. "If it weren't for women pitching in for the war effort, we'd be in trouble."

"Women working like that is a brief exception," Mom said. "We all have to make sacrifices. It's only for wartime. Mark my words, when the men return, all those women will be more than happy to get back to homemaking and raising their children. That's what we are meant to do." She looked at me. "When you marry Bill, you won't have to work at the paper. You'll be able to stay home and raise your children."

"What if I don't want to quit the paper? I can work and raise children at the same time."

"You'll change your mind. You wait and see."

I doubted it, and I also doubted my mother would ever change hers. It was almost the middle of the twentieth century, and she acted like she was back in the nineteenth.

Lily plopped back into her chair. "I'm not going to waste my life being stuck at home. I want to make a name for myself. Get out in the world. Have fun. Look at Katherine. She's done all sorts of things. I don't want to be stuck in this little town all my life."

Mom stood up. "I am not going to listen to any of this foolishness. I'll be in the kitchen."

I couldn't remember if I'd felt the same way at fourteen. I had already been writing articles for the paper at her age. Lily needed an outlet besides school and listening to Sinatra records.

"She's impossible." Lily swung her legs over the arm of the chair.

"She's from another generation when duties between men and women were more cut-and-dried. Things change slowly."

"I don't like it."

I smiled. "Neither do I, kid. But that's the way it is."

Lily swung around and put her feet back on the floor. "But you run the *Herald* now. That's progress. You get to boss everyone around."

"I don't exactly boss everyone around. I read and edit their articles and assign them to cover what needs to be in the paper. And even that doesn't always go over well. They're used to Pop being in charge. They still think of me as Pop's little girl."

"At least you get to do something. All I do is go to school, friends' houses, and the movies." She sighed. "I want to do something important."

"What would you like to do?"

"That's just it. I don't know. I'm not good at anything."

I got up, sat on the arm of her chair, and put my arm around her. "You're good at lots of things. You get great grades. What's your favorite subject?"

"I have two favorites. Promise you won't make fun?"

"Why would I do that?" I asked.

"Because girls aren't supposed to like it."

"Let me guess," I said. "Math."

Lily smiled. "That's it! I love figuring out problems, the Pythagorean theorem, x and y, pi, square roots—"

"Hold it right there." I laughed. "You lost me already. It was never my best subject." If anything, it had been my worst. I'd scraped by with a C minus.

"It's my best subject," Lily said. "I pretend I don't like it so no one will make fun of me."

"Oh, Lily. Never hide how smart you are. Your true friends already know you've got brains, and who cares about anyone else? I used to get ribbed all the time because I could diagram every sentence my English teacher gave us and I got As on every composition."

"Really?"

"Really. I don't think I'd be able to do my job now if I hadn't gotten used to the criticism."

"Wow," Lily said. "I didn't know that."

I was glad I seemed to be making an impression. "You said you had two favorite subjects. What's the other one?"

"Art," she said. "I like to draw."

"I don't think I've ever seen anything you've drawn—at least not lately."

She got up. "Wait here. I'll be right back." She ran up the stairs and returned a minute later with a sketch pad. "I keep this under my bed." She handed it to me.

Lily's sketches were marvelous. There were drawings of the outside of our house, the garden in back, and Mom standing at the kitchen stove. There was one of Pop in his chair by the radio, the ever-present cigarette in his hand. I teared up a little at that one.

"I miss him too," Lily said.

I laughed at one of me hunched over a typewriter. "Do I really look like that when I'm working?"

"I may have exaggerated that one a little."

There were lots of drawings of Frank Sinatra. They were almost as lifelike as photographs. I was amazed. How could I have not known she was so artistic? "Lily, you have a real talent here."

She shrugged. "They're okay."

"They're better than okay. They're absolutely wonderful. They sure don't belong under your bed. Why haven't you shown me before?"

"I don't know exactly. I guess I wasn't sure they were good enough."

"Well, they are." I had an idea of how Lily could put both her talents to good use. "I just thought of a way for you to put some of your skills to work for the war effort."

"How?"

I told her about my upcoming meeting with Mayor Young on Tuesday to talk about plans for the scrap drive. "I'll tell him we need to put some posters around town to let everyone know how important this is. And maybe even some posters for the town's victory garden."

Lily grinned. "What about some with calculations of how much metal goes into certain things like bullets, or guns, or even airplanes?"

"Exactly what I was thinking!" I had another thought. "Why don't you come up with something like that for the *Herald*? With some drawings to go with it."

"Are you serious? They'd be in the paper?"

"Of course I'm serious," I said. "I can't guarantee everything you do will be published, but yes, some of them will be in the paper." I hoped I wouldn't regret it. I could almost hear Donny whining about nepotism. Kind of ironic considering he was related too.

Lily leaped up and gave me a hug. "I'll start right now. This is swell! You're the best sister in the world."

She grabbed her sketch pad and flew up the stairs as the front door opened. Katherine came into the living room.

"What was that whirlwind?" Katherine asked.

"I gave Lily a pep talk. She was feeling like she wasn't doing anything useful, like working in a factory or joining the WAACs."

Katherine sat on the sofa and lit a cigarette. "What did you tell her?"

I told her about Lily's artwork and explained my idea.

"That sounds perfect."

"I hope so," I said. "How was your date?"

She blew out smoke. "It wasn't a date. I just had to meet with someone." She reached into the pocket of her slacks. "Here." She passed a piece of paper to me. "Before I forget again. It's the names of three girls who will talk to you about working at Tabor. Speaking of which, I'd better change and get ready for work." She ground out her cigarette in the ashtray.

I looked at the three names. Betty Riley, Vivian Anderson, and the last one was very familiar—Sylvia Fontaine.

"Wait," I said to Katherine, who was on her way out of the room. "I know one of these women."

Katherine turned. "Which one?"

"Sylvia Fontaine."

"She's a nice gal," Katherine said. "A little snooty until you get to know her. How do you know her?"

I mentioned I'd found her name on a piece of paper at Moe's. "I ran into her by accident yesterday at Ava's hair salon. It turns out she'd been keeping company with Moe." I told Katherine what had happened last night.

"That's terrible!" Katherine said. "What did the police say?"

"Nothing. She refused to call the police. She said if her landlord found out, she'd be out on her keister."

"Don't you find it odd that she wouldn't want to find out who broke in?"

I nodded. "I do, but I can see her point."

"I guess." Katherine took a seat again. "Yesterday you started telling me about something you thought your reporter was working on. Could the break-in at Sylvia's have something to do with that?"

"You should have been a reporter," I said with a smile. "It has to be connected. Sylvia told me Moe had left a notebook there, and now it's gone. And the way her apartment was torn apart, it was obvious they were looking for something."

"Sylvia doesn't know what he was working on? Or what was in the notebook?" Katherine asked.

"She claims she doesn't. She said she only knew something was going on somewhere and he was going to put a stop to it."

"Was your reporter's place broken into as well?"

"Yes."

Katherine was quiet for a moment, then said, "This might be a strange question, but have you considered that maybe your reporter's death wasn't an accident?"

"Why would you ask that?"

"Maybe I read too many detective novels, but the fact that he and Sylvia were seeing each other, both places were broken into, and he was working on something big—it makes sense that someone would try to stop him."

For someone who wanted to be a singer and worked in a factory, she was awfully perceptive. Or she knew more than she was letting on. I'd told her only bits and pieces, yet she'd come to the same conclusion I had. "That doesn't mean he was murdered," I said. "According to the police and the coroner, it was an accident."

"But you don't think that," she said. "I can see it in your face."

I hesitated. I liked her well enough, but I didn't know if I could trust her. It wasn't just the crazy stories she'd told Lily about knowing Sinatra. My reporter's instinct told me there was more to her than met the eye. I just didn't know what.

Katherine said, "What happened to make you think his—what was his name? Moe? What makes you think his death wasn't an accident?"

It was possible I'd regret it later, but I told her about the note Moe had left for me, the scrap of calendar that said *TAB 10 AM*, and my theory that *TAB* was someone's initials.

"Maybe *TAB* isn't a person's initials," Katherine said. "It could be something else, like a place."

"That's what I'm afraid of," I said. "It could be anything. Initials made the most sense, but I've come up empty."

"Is there anything I can do to help?"

"I honestly don't know. At least not yet. But thanks."

Katherine nodded and went upstairs to change for work.

As I sat in the living room, something suddenly dawned on me. It was possible I'd been looking at this all wrong. What if Moe had written *TAB* as short for *Tabor*? It made perfect sense.

I sat up straighter. Could Moe have had an appointment with someone at Tabor at ten AM on Monday the eleventh? That morning I'd sent him to interview Sam Markowicz and Ava. He hadn't talked to either of them. But if he'd had an appointment at Tabor, why hadn't he just mentioned it instead of letting me send him off to Sam's? I tried to recall what he'd said—something about needing to see "old man Markowicz" anyway. But he hadn't seen him. And he'd never come back to work. Had he met with the person who'd killed him? First thing in the morning, I'd call the Ironworks and set up my own appointment with Wilfred Tabor. It was a good place to start.

Chapter Eleven

Oveta Culp Hobby Sworn In as Head of WAACs
—The Progress Herald, May 17, 1942

"Mr. Tabor's secretary said he can see you at nine this morning," Peggy said.

I had come in to the paper at seven and was on my second cup of coffee. As soon as Peggy arrived, I'd filled her in on my theory. "I hope this pans out," I said.

"It makes sense to me. I don't know why we didn't think of it before."

I asked her if Sylvia was still staying at her house.

Peggy shook her head. "She left for her sister's after work yesterday. Did you know Sylvia works at Tabor?"

"Katherine told me yesterday. Sylvia's one of the girls she asked to talk to me about working in the factory."

"Small world," Peggy said. "I wonder why Sylvia didn't mention it last night."

I had been thinking the same thing. Sylvia knew I was editor of the *Herald*. "Maybe Katherine didn't mention my name when she asked her about an interview. Sylvia had a lot to drink, and with the break-in and all, I guess it could have slipped her mind."

There was a knock on my office door, and Frank Mitchell came in. "Am I interrupting?"

I waved him in. "Not at all."

Peggy excused herself, closing the door on the way out.

Frank half sat on the corner of my desk. "Remember that new aircraft called a helicopter being developed for the army?"

"Sort of," I said. "Wasn't there some kind of demonstration of it last month?"

"Yep. It's called the XR-4. Developed by a guy named Sikorsky. It just flew from Bridgeport, Connecticut, to Wright Field in Ohio. Over seven hundred miles. It'll need to be tested some more, but the army is gonna buy some. Probably need some modifications and won't go into service for a while, but they could put them to good use."

"Seven hundred miles is pretty impressive," I said. "Are you going to write something up?"

"I sure am."

"Good," I said. "By the way, Father O'Connor is stopping by on Wednesday to say a few prayers for Moe right after lunch. I'd like it if everyone is here, if you don't mind passing that on."

"Don't mind at all. That's a nice thing to do. Moe was an okay guy. A little too big for his britches sometimes, but okay."

I nodded. "Do you have any idea what story he was chasing?"

"Nope. Wish I did."

"Why?"

Frank grinned. "Because I'd be sure it was my story now."

"Even if you'd have to fight Rex over it?"

"I could beat Rex every day and twice on Sunday," Frank said, still grinning.

I laughed. "I bet you could." Frank was ten years younger and fifty pounds lighter than Rex.

He stood. "I'd better get back to work, or the boss will dock my pay."

"And don't you forget it."

He went out the door, then poked his head back in. "You're all right, you know. For a girl."

I tossed a pencil at him, but he ducked and closed the door. I was still smiling as I grabbed a notepad and a couple of pencils to take with me to see Wilfred Tabor. I'd never win over Donny or Rex, but at least Frank was getting used to the idea that I was in charge. It was something at least. I'd take it.

* * *

"Thank you for seeing me, Mr. Tabor." I took a seat in the chair across from his mahogany desk and took my notepad and a pencil from my pocketbook.

"Certainly." Wilfred Tabor leaned back in his green Naugahyde chair and removed his glasses. "What can I do for you, Miss Ingram?"

"I'd like to write an article about some of the women working in the plant. I'm planning to focus on what it's like for them to work in jobs that have traditionally been held by men."

Tabor took a handkerchief from his pocket and rubbed the lenses of his glasses. "That sounds interesting. Will you show the Ironworks in a good light? I wouldn't want anything printed that doesn't."

"I'll do my best," I said. He really didn't have any say in the matter. I'd write the facts, even if they were negative. The *Herald* wasn't Tabor's or anyone else's propaganda machine. "I'd also like to ask you a few questions."

"I'll be happy to answer them." He returned his glasses to his face and folded his hands on his desk.

I opened my notebook and asked some simple preliminary questions, some of which I already knew the answers to because of the previous article I'd written on the dedication ceremony. I finally got to the point. "How many women are now working in the factory?"

"I'm not sure of the exact number," he said. "But I believe there are around a hundred, give or take."

"How many before the war?" I asked.

"None doing factory work. There were ten girls doing secretarial and other office work."

"That's a big difference," I said.

Tabor smiled. At least I thought it was a smile. His lips barely moved. "We all must do our part and make sacrifices for the war effort. You may quote me on that."

I wondered if his idea of a sacrifice was hiring women. I doubted he meant the women were sacrificing anything. "Do you plan on keeping them on after the war?"

"Oh no," he said. He sounded shocked I'd asked such a thing.

"Why not?"

He gave me a look that pretty much said he thought I was an idiot. "That wouldn't be right. Not at all. The men coming home will need their jobs back, and the women can go back to whatever it is they did before the war."

He sounded like my mother, except Mom knew exactly what women should be doing—getting married, keeping house, and having babies. "Some of them might want to stay on. It wouldn't be right to just let them go."

"I sincerely doubt that any of them will want to do that. And that's not something I'd allow. We'll need to get back to normal." He leaned back and steepled his hands. "Once you talk to a few of the girls, you'll see that I'm right."

"Maybe."

I had a feeling that wouldn't be the case for everyone. I knew Katherine was here only for the money and would be gone when she had enough saved, but the others might want to make it permanent. Well-paying jobs before the war had been hard to come by, especially for women. Now we had the opportunity to show we could do just about anything a man could do.

Tabor stood. "If there's nothing else, I'll have my secretary show you where you can find the girls."

"Thank you." I pushed out of my chair. "I have one more question, if you don't mind."

"Not at all," he said.

"Did Moe Bauer have an appointment to see you last Monday?"

Tabor was silent a moment too long before answering. "Why do you ask?"

I shrugged. "I thought he mentioned something." I wasn't about to tell him about the scrap of calendar.

"He did not have an appointment," Tabor said. "I believe we're finished here." He buzzed for his secretary.

I seemed to have hit a nerve.

"Miss Lewis will show you out."

"What about my interviews with the women?" I asked.

"We're very busy right now," he said. "It's going to have to wait until another time."

I had an inkling that another time would be when hell froze over. "When might that be? I'd like to have this article finished sometime this week."

"I really can't say, Miss Ingram. Miss Lewis will show you out."

Nothing like getting the bum's rush. Tabor's abrupt change and end to the interview told me he knew something. I needed to find out what Moe had been looking into here.

Tabor's secretary led me down the hallway and past an open office door.

"Miss Ingram!" Arnold Moss called out. Seconds later he was out of his office. "That will be all, Miss Lewis," he said. "I'll take it from here."

She held on to my elbow. "But Mr. Tabor said—"

"Mr. Tabor won't mind if I show Miss Ingram out." Moss smiled at her. "Miss Ingram and I are old friends."

Miss Lewis reluctantly let go of my arm and headed back to her desk. I rubbed my elbow. She had quite a grip.

"If I had known you were coming, I would have met you myself instead of Wilfred. I'm much more congenial," he said.

"I had a few questions to ask him. I was supposed to meet with a few of the women who work in the factory, but Mr. Tabor said it will have to be another time. That everyone was busy."

"Well, he's right about that. We got an expedited order for rivets from Dravo this morning. They want them as soon as we can make them."

If Tabor had known this when Peggy made my appointment, why had he bothered to meet with me? "It would have been nice to know that before I came all the way out here and wasted my time."

"You'll have to excuse Wilfred. He's under a lot of pressure with the increased demand. He isn't used to all that's involved in modern production. He's still in the old-school way of doing things."

"I noticed. When I asked him if he'd keep women on in the factory after the war is over, he looked at me like I had three heads."

Moss laughed. "That's old Wilfred, all right." We reached the front door. "Do you mind me making a suggestion?"

"Of course not," I said.

"Why don't you stop in personnel and get the home numbers of the girls you want to talk to and catch them when they're off duty."

I wished I had thought of that. "Good idea. Thanks."

"How about having dinner with me tonight?"

"No thank you." I raised my left hand. "I'm engaged. I don't go out with other men."

"It's just dinner. I promise I'll behave myself."

I shook my head. "I can't. I don't want to give anyone the wrong impression."

"You don't seem like the type who gives a hoot about impressions."

"Most of the time I don't. But I won't be the subject of gossip, and I certainly wouldn't want word to get back to my fiancé that I'd gone out with another man. You haven't lived in a small town long enough to know that news like that travels like wildfire, whether it's true or not."

He might have tried to press the point, but a man burst through the door that led to the plant. "Mr. Moss, you gotta come quick." He sounded frantic.

"What is it?" Moss asked, already heading that way.

"There's been an accident. One of the machines fell over, and his leg is pinned."

I hadn't been invited, but I followed Moss and the worker into the plant. The noise of the machinery didn't quite drown out the screams of pain and the cacophony of everyone talking at once. Across the room I saw two men trying to lift a large piece of metal equipment off what I assumed was a man's leg. There were too many people around him for me to see who it was. I stayed right behind Moss as he barreled his way forward.

The pinned man was facedown on the floor. Two others joined the attempt to lift the machinery off his right leg.

Moss turned to me. "You shouldn't watch this."

I ignored him. The rescuers were finally able to move the equipment. The injured man writhed in agony as it was lifted from his leg. He cried out as someone rolled him over onto his back.

"Oh my God," I whispered. I recognized the man. It was Benjamin Cline.

Chapter Twelve

Sikorsky Helicopter Flies 700 Miles—Bridgeport to Wright Field

—*The Progress Herald*, May 18, 1942

There was a flurry of activity for the next ten minutes. The nurse who manned the first-aid office ministered to Ben Cline as best she could until the ambulance arrived moments later. Two attendants quickly got him on a stretcher. I heard one of them say they were taking him to Providence Hospital. I retrieved my notepad from my pocketbook and got to work.

Arnold Moss was busy barking orders for everyone to get back to work. Questions for him could wait. The nurse was on her way to the door on the other side of the work space, so I hurried that way. "Excuse me," I called out as she opened the door. She either didn't hear me or didn't know I was talking to her. "Nurse!"

She turned. "Yes?"

I held my notepad in the air. "Do you have a minute to answer a few questions?"

"And you are?"

I identified myself, waiting for the inevitable *Aren't you a bit young to be an editor?* question. Surprisingly, it didn't come.

The nurse put out her hand. "Doris McCarthy." Her handshake was firmer than some men's. Doris was probably around my mother's age. She had light-brown hair and a stocky, no-nonsense build. Her white uniform was crisply starched, and her white oxfords didn't have a mark on them. The only thing that wasn't perfect was her cap. It sat a bit askew on her head, but I was sure she'd fix that as soon as she looked in a mirror. I'd bet a quarter none of the men she treated gave her any lip whatsoever. "What are your questions?" she asked.

I didn't dillydally. She wouldn't have put up with it. "What condition is the injured man in?"

"He'll live. His leg is in bad shape, though. The knee was shattered, and I'm sure other bones were broken as well."

I inwardly shuddered. "Do you know what happened that he ended up with that piece of equipment on him?"

"I'm sorry," she said. "I don't. I was notified after the fact. You should ask some of the people who were on the floor at the time."

"I plan to." I thanked her for her time.

She gave me a crisp nod and disappeared through the doorway. I turned and looked around the room. A few workers stood around talking, but most had already gone back to work. Contributing to the war effort appeared to take precedence over severe injury to a coworker. I didn't see Moss anywhere. I guessed he'd gone back to his office. I'd need to get some kind of quote from him before I left. I asked several people what had happened, but no one seemed to know, other than that the machine had toppled over when Ben Cline walked past it. I didn't think heavy machinery just fell over. It made me wonder whether the previous incident where he'd been beaten up had something to do with it. I hoped I was wrong.

I was about to head back to Moss's office when I saw Sylvia enter through a doorway on the other side of the room, pushing a cart stacked with wooden crates. Her golden-blonde hair was half covered with a bandanna, and her dungarees and smudged blouse were a definite contrast to the dress she'd worn the other night. I made my way over while she unloaded crates and stacked them in a corner. She looked up as I approached.

"Hi, Sylvia," I said.

"Hello yourself. I guess you're here about the accident."

If that's what it was. "I just happened to be here then. I actually came to talk to you, Betty Riley, and Vivian Anderson about working here."

"I forgot all about that," she said. "Bets and Viv are off today. They're working second shift tomorrow."

"I'll try to catch them another time. Do you have a minute?"

"That's about all I have right now. Can we talk while I finish unloading these?"

I'd hoped for more time. "How about we meet later? I don't want to take you from your work, and I have more than a minute's worth of questions."

"Sure. After my shift today?"

We decided on Dempsey's Diner at four thirty. She said she'd call Betty and Vivian from the pay phone on her lunch break and see if they could make it. Before I went to find Moss, I asked her if she knew what had caused the accident.

"No, and I don't want to know," she said.

"What do you mean?"

"I don't mean anything." Sylvia unloaded the last crate and turned to me. "I have to get another load of these. I'll talk to you later."

I watched her push her cart away. Everyone's reluctance to answer a simple question reinforced my idea that the machine falling on Ben Cline's leg might not have been an accident. Determined to find out, I headed back to see Moss.

His door was closed when I reached his office, and I heard voices inside. Naturally, I put my ear up to the door. In only seconds I determined the voices belonged to Tabor and Moss.

"What are we going to do?" Tabor asked.

"You worry too much," Moss said.

"And you don't worry enough. What if—"

"It will be fine. I have everything under control."

Tabor said, "I hope you're correct. I'm going back to my office."

I skedaddled down the hall and around the corner. When I was sure Tabor was gone, I knocked on the frame of the now-open door.

Moss looked up. "I didn't realize you were still here."

"I am."

"Have a seat. I'm sorry you had to see that."

I sank into the chair across from him. "What can you tell me about the incident?"

"There's nothing to tell," Moss said. "From what I've been told, Cline was sweeping the floor, he bumped the machine, and it fell on him."

That must have been some bump. "How many pounds does that piece of equipment weigh?" I knew it was heavy enough that it took more than two people to lift it.

"I don't know exactly," he said.

There were going to be a lot of *I don't know*s in my article at this rate. I stood up. "Thanks for talking to me."

Moss leaned back in his chair. "Do you have to leave already? How about joining me for lunch?"

It was only ten thirty. "I really can't. I'm going to get a statement from Mr. Tabor and get back to the *Herald*."

"There's no need to bother Wilfred right now. He's terribly upset," he said. "I can give you a statement."

"Fine."

He looked up at the ceiling as if the words were written up there. "Tabor Ironworks is deeply concerned about the accident that befell one of our employees. We will do everything in our power to keep it from happening again." His gaze moved from the ceiling to me. "How's that?"

"Perfect," I said, although it sounded like a bunch of baloney. I closed my notebook, said good-bye, and headed back to town.

* * *

I parked the Pontiac in Pop's garage and walked back to the paper. On the way I thought about today's incident and what had happened to Ben Cline previously. It was too much of a coincidence to think it was just an accident. Had whoever beat him up taken it a step further this time? He could easily have been killed. I still didn't know what Moe had been looking into, or if it even had to do with Tabor Ironworks. It sure made sense that it did, though. Tabor had just about thrown me out when I'd mentioned Moe's name.

As I neared Markowicz Hardware, I decided to stop and tell Sam about Ben. The store was empty of customers, and Sam looked up when he heard the bells on the door jingle. He gave me a smile. "What can I do for you today, Irene?"

I hated to be the bearer of bad news. "Nothing."

Sam must have read something in my face. "Is something wrong? It's not your father, is it?"

"No," I said. "Pop is fine, thank goodness."

"Then what is it?"

"I was at Tabor this morning, and there was an accident." There wasn't an easy way to say it. "A piece of heavy machinery fell on Benjamin Cline."

Sam's face turned white. "He's not . . . he's not . . ."

"No, but he's seriously injured. It smashed his leg pretty bad. They took him to Providence Hospital."

"I must get there. I will close the store for today." He pulled off his apron and hung it on a hook beside the counter. "Thank you for telling me."

"I thought you would want to know."

We walked to the door together, and Sam turned off the lights. He suddenly turned to me, angry. "Someone needs to stop these people."

"What people?"

Instead of answering my question, he said, "You will look into this, yes?"

Sam didn't wait for a reply. He was two storefronts away and getting into his car before I even opened my mouth. I would look into it, all right. As soon as I figured out where to start.

* * *

"That's horrible," Peggy said when I told her what had happened.

I was typing a draft of the article with what little information I had. I would need to call the hospital and check on Ben's condition before I could finalize it. "I stopped to tell Sam Markowicz on the way back here, since he knows Ben Cline. He was very upset."

"I can imagine."

"Sam closed up for the day so he could go to the hospital," I said. "He said the oddest thing to me, though."

"What did he say?"

"He told me that someone needs to stop these people."

"What people?" Peggy asked.

"That's what I want to know. I asked Sam the same question, but he didn't answer. I'm wondering if it has to do with Ben Cline's previous trouble at the plant."

Peggy nodded. "That makes sense. How are you going to find out?"

"I'm not sure." I pulled the sheet of paper out of my typewriter and laid it on the desk. "I might start with Chief Turner. I don't think anyone called him about the accident, and he should know, especially if it has to do with what happened before."

"Did you ever tell him about Moe's place being ransacked?"

I shook my head. "No. And I'm not going to. At least not yet. I want to get another look around first. Whoever broke in found what they wanted at Sylvia's, if they'd been searching for his notebook, but maybe they—and we—missed something at Moe's."

The phone rang on Peggy's desk. She wasn't gone a minute when Rex barged into the office. "I heard there was a bad accident out at Tabor. I'm gonna go see what I can find out."

I held up the paper with my draft article. "Already done."

It wasn't often that Rex was speechless. It took him a moment to recover. "How did you manage that?"

I told him.

"How bad was it?" he asked.

"The nurse said his knee was crushed."

"Ouch. Who was it, anyway?"

"Benjamin Cline."

"No kidding! The janitor who got beat up? Talk about unlucky."

"I guess you could call it that."

Rex stared at me. "Sounds like you think it's something else."

I didn't want to tell him what I thought.

"You're thinking someone did it on purpose. Don't go putting two and two together and getting three," he said. "Sometimes an accident is just an accident. Tabor's important to the war effort. They sure as hell wouldn't put up with any nonsense, especially when someone gets hurt."

"You're probably right." I wasn't sure I believed my own words. It was possible it was only bad luck on Ben Cline's part, but what about what Sam had said? I wasn't the only one who thought there was more to it.

"Of course I'm right," he said. "I'm always right."

* * *

I grabbed a quick lunch at Woolworth's, then went to see my future father-in-law. Jimmy Feeney was sitting at his desk, eating something on rye bread that stunk to high heaven. I waved my hand in front of my face. "What in the world are you eating? It smells awful."

He grinned. "But it tastes delicious. Limburger and onion with mustard on rye bread. Nothing like it."

"I hope there's nothing like it. If anyone comes in here, they're going to need a gas mask. We could use that as a secret weapon.

Drop a few bombs filled with Limburger, and the war will be over in a week."

"I'll send that suggestion to the War Department."

"Is the chief in?"

"He is," Jimmy said. "He closed the door. He couldn't stand the fragrance either."

I knocked and entered, quickly closing the door behind me in an attempt to keep the odor at bay. I had a feeling it would be in vain. That stink would penetrate walls better than Superman's X-ray vision.

"You should have called," Chief Turner said. "I would have warned you about that." The window behind his desk was open wide.

"You're going to have to air out the whole station."

"Probably," he said. "But it's Jimmy, so everyone will forgive him, including me. What can I do for you?"

"I was at the Ironworks this morning, and one of the employees was severely injured."

"I hadn't heard. No one called it in. What happened?" He picked up a pencil.

"I'd gone to talk to Mr. Tabor about an article I'm writing. As I was leaving the building, someone hollered that there'd been an accident. When I arrived, a few men were pulling a large piece of machinery off Benjamin Cline's leg."

"Cline?"

"The same one who was beaten up last week. Mr. Moss insists Ben Cline bumped the equipment and it toppled over on his leg. I'm not buying it."

"I assume there were witnesses."

"There had to have been, but when I asked around, no one knew anything. I think someone pushed it onto him."

"Now, Irene—"

"Hear me out. You know what happened to him before, but I'm not sure you know the rest. I ran into him in the hardware store. Sam told him he should tell me the whole story, but he refused. Sam insisted, and Ben said if he did, he was a dead man. And now this. It's not a coincidence."

"How does Sam know Cline?"

"They go to the same synagogue."

"Hmm."

"That's it?" I said. "That's all you're going to say?"

His chair squeaked as he pushed out of it. "For now. I'm going to have a talk with Wilfred Tabor."

"I'm going with you."

He held up a hand. "No, you're not. This is police business."

"But—"

"No buts. After I see Tabor, I'll go and speak with Cline."

"Ben's not going to talk to you. He said he doesn't trust the police."

"We'll see about that. I promise I'll get to the bottom of what's going on. If anything comes of it, you'll be the first to know."

He opened his door, and I prepared to be bombarded with the stink, but it wasn't too bad this time. It had diminished some since Jimmy had finished lunch, cleaned up the area, and propped open the front door. I said so long to Jimmy, and the chief walked me out and drove off in his squad car.

Instead of going back to the paper, I went home and retrieved Pop's car again. Benjamin Cline wouldn't talk to the police, but he might talk to me.

Chapter Thirteen

Red Army Inflicts Toll on Nazis in Kharkov
12,000 Reported Killed

—*The Progress Herald*, May 18, 1942

Providence Hospital was located a mile from the Progress town limits. Built in 1930, it was modern and had everything the Pittsburgh hospitals did but on a smaller scale. It was six stories tall, and the yellow brick with white window trim was clean looking. I parked in the asphalt parking lot and made my way to the front entrance. Inside I crossed the black-and-white linoleum to the reception desk. I asked where I could find Benjamin Cline.

The receptionist paged through the large book of names and room numbers. "Oh, here it is," she said. "Room two-oh-three."

"Thanks." It was only one flight, so I took the stairs and found the room easily. The door was partially open, so I peeked in. The patient appeared to be sleeping. Sam sat in a straight chair beside the bed, and looked up as I entered.

Sam stood. "We can speak in the hallway," he whispered.

"How is he?" I asked.

"Not good. He is sedated at the moment, and they will be taking him to surgery soon." He shuddered. "The doctor said he will lose his leg."

"Oh no." The injury was even worse than I'd realized. "Is there anything I can do?"

Sam shook his head.

"Was he able to tell you anything about what happened?"

"He said he doesn't know what happened. I do not believe he was telling me the truth. He is frightened."

"I don't blame him," I said. "I would be frightened too, if someone was out to get me. He needs to talk to Chief Turner when he's able."

"He will not."

"Then he needs to talk to me."

"He will not do that either," Sam said.

Frustrated, I said, "Well, that's just stupid. There's something going on, and you as much as said so. You asked me to look into this. How can I discover the truth if Benjamin won't tell me anything?"

After a long pause, Sam said, "Benjamin won't talk to you, but I will. This needs to stop, and it will stop with me."

"Thank you. I know it's hard for you."

"I am staying with Benjamin until he is out of surgery. I don't want him to be alone. I will come to see you tomorrow afternoon."

Just then, a nurse and an orderly wheeled a gurney down the hall to Ben's room. I thanked Sam again, and he disappeared into the room with them. As I walked back out to the car, I didn't know whether to be sad or angry. Maybe a combination of both. Whatever was going on, I vowed to make it right.

* * *

I wrote my weekly household article that afternoon for Wednesday's paper, but my heart wasn't in it. Keeping house wasn't exactly a priority in my mind at the moment. My thoughts kept turning to Benjamin Cline. He was going to lose his leg. That was something that happened to soldiers on the front lines, not here at home. It was devastating. How would he get by? He'd no longer have a job at Tabor—at least not the same one. Maybe I could find something here for him to do. He was a proud man, though. He might look on it as pity, which I was sure he wouldn't tolerate. At least Ben had a good friend in Sam. Sam would make sure he was taken care of.

My thoughts were interrupted when Peggy let me know the chief was here to see me. I told her to send him in.

"Are you busy?" he asked.

"Never for you, Chief." I pointed to the chair across from me.

He sat and removed his hat. "When are you going to start calling me Dad? You don't have to wait until the wedding, you know."

Whenever that would be. "I know that. It's just hard to get used to."

"Well, get used to it. I already consider you my daughter. Bill would want you to call me Dad."

I was embarrassed to feel tears forming and blinked them away. "I miss him."

He leaned across the desk and patted my hand. "I know you do."

I cleared my throat. "Did you talk to Mr. Tabor?"

"I did. According to him it was a tragic accident and they will be taking steps to make sure nothing like it happens again. He assured me that Cline's accident today had nothing to do with what happened last week."

"And you believe him?"

He smiled. "I didn't say that. It could be true, but I don't like coincidences. I'll need to get Cline's statement when he's able. He was in surgery."

"I know. I went to the hospital to check his condition and talked to Sam." I decided not to say anything about meeting Sam tomorrow. If Sam had wanted the police to know the information he was planning to tell me, he would have called them. If there was anything the chief should know, I would pass it on after our meeting. "Sam plans on staying at the hospital until Ben's out of surgery."

"That's good." He chuckled. "I should have known you'd beat me to the hospital."

I shrugged. "It's my job."

He stood. "That it is. Promise me you'll stay out of trouble and keep me informed if you learn anything I should know about."

"I will." I felt a little bad for withholding what I knew about the break-in at Moe's house, but I wanted to get in there again. There wasn't much he could do about it anyway. And as soon as I figured out what was going on, he'd be the first to know.

After the chief left, I put the finishing touches on my article about the incident at Tabor. I mentioned that the victim was in surgery and used the quote Moss had given me. Despite being told that the whole thing had been an accident, I ended the article with, "The cause of the incident was undetermined." That wouldn't make Mr. Tabor happy, but that was too bad.

At a quarter to four, I went downstairs to see where Donny was with the layout. I made one suggestion, and he was miffed that I would have the audacity to do such a thing. I ignored his ranting and went back to my office. I wasn't in the mood for an argument. I powdered my nose and reapplied my lipstick, then hoofed it to Dempsey's Diner to meet Sylvia.

*　*　*

I was the first to arrive and took a seat in a red Naugahyde booth. Mr. Dempsey waved to me from behind the counter where he was talking to Dan Petrie, the local garden and feed store owner, who was quickly demolishing a slice of cherry pie.

Dan turned around. "Hiya, Irene. All ready to start planting the victory garden this weekend?"

With everything else going on, I'd almost forgotten about it. The groundbreaking in the park was scheduled for Saturday the twenty-third. I made a mental note to have Matt photograph the event for the *Herald*. "I'm as ready as I'll ever be."

"We should be in fine shape as long as we don't get another frost. Not that that's likely, as warm as it's been," he said. "I'll keep an eye on the weather the next couple of weeks. I can cover the seedlings if it gets too cold."

Sylvia came in just then and headed my way.

"Thanks for that," I said to Dan. "I'll see you on Saturday."

"Big date on Saturday?" Sylvia asked as she slid into the booth.

"Hardly." Dan was a good twenty years older than me and happily married. "The groundbreaking for the victory garden is on Saturday. Dan's supplying the plants."

"Victory garden? I thought those went by the wayside after the last war." She picked up a menu from the holder at the end of the table.

"They're back. Roosevelt is encouraging everyone to pitch in and plant one."

"Where are you planting?"

I filled her in on the plans. "Want to help? We can use all the volunteers we can get."

"Sure. It sounds like it might be fun."

Mr. Dempsey brought over a couple of mugs and a pot of coffee. "What can I get you girls?"

"Just coffee for me," I said.

Sylvia ordered coffee and a sweet roll. "Betty and Vivian should be here any minute." No sooner were the words out of her mouth than two women entered the diner. Sylvia made the introductions.

Betty Riley was a petite redhead about my age. She giggled when she sat down beside me. "I can't believe you're an honest-to-goodness newspaperwoman!" she said.

Vivian Anderson was probably in her thirties. She wore her brown hair in an old-fashioned bun on the top of her head.

Mr. Dempsey returned with Sylvia's sweet roll and took orders from the other two. Once we were all settled, I thanked them for talking to me.

Vivian gave me a simple, "You're welcome."

"Gosh," Betty said. "It's an honor. Imagine little old me being in the newspaper! I can't wait to send a copy to my folks. They'll be so thrilled!"

I opened my notebook on the table. I started with easy questions to get their background. Betty was from a little town near Butler called Chicora. She was actually younger than me—she'd just turned eighteen. Vivian and her husband had owned a farm until last year, when he was killed in a fall. She'd recently sold the farm and moved to Progress.

I asked them what their jobs were at Tabor and if they liked working there.

Betty spoke up first. "I'm a welder, if you can believe it. I love it! It's so exciting. I've never done anything like it before."

"What is there to weld in a plant that makes nuts and bolts?" I asked.

"Oh, you'd be surprised," Betty said. "Sometimes we need to weld two parts together, or something breaks and we need to put it back together."

"So you like working there?" I asked.

Betty said, "I do! It's such meaningful work, thinking little old me is helping to win this war."

Sylvia rolled her eyes. "You're not doing it single-handedly. There are men actually fighting it, you know."

"I know that," Betty said. "But I like doing my part, no matter how small it is."

"Is it that way for you, Vivian?" I asked.

"More or less," she said. "My job is mostly on one of the sorting lines. Sometimes they move me around to other spots. Not quite as exciting."

"But important nonetheless," I said.

Vivian shrugged. "I guess. It gets a little monotonous, but it pays the bills."

"So you're there for the money?"

"Isn't everyone?" Sylvia said. "I sure as hell wouldn't be toting around crates and such otherwise."

Betty sighed. "But Sylvia, what about all those boys fighting to keep us free? Don't they mean anything to you?"

"Sure they do," she said. "But the money is better." Sylvia pointed to me. "Don't quote me on that. I'll be run out of town on a rail."

I asked Vivian why she worked there.

"Frankly, I needed something to do. After Lester died and I sold the farm, I didn't know what to do with myself. I was so used to being a farmer's wife and everything that entailed that I was lost. I didn't have enough to keep me busy, and when the Ironworks advertised for help, I thought I'd give it a try. I've made . . . some good friends there."

"How are you treated by the bosses and the men who work there?"

Sylvia answered first this time. "Most of the men were jerks until they figured out we were pretty good workers after all. Some still don't like us being there. The bosses are all right. Old man Tabor pretty much ignores us."

"What about Moss?" I asked.

"Mr. Moss is so dreamy," Betty said. "He looks just like Gary Cooper."

Vivian said, "He's definitely not marriage material."

Sylvia snorted. "Is any man? They talk a good talk but don't follow through. Something always happens to kill your dreams."

She was talking about Moe. It seemed he'd been fond of Sylvia, but would he have married her? We'd never know.

"Arnold Moss chases anything in a skirt," Sylvia said. "Or slacks, or dungarees . . . and some of the girls fall for his line. He'll never marry any of them."

"You know what they say," Vivian said. "Why buy the cow when you can get the milk for free."

Sylvia laughed. "And Moss is milking a lot of cows."

Betty looked confused. "I didn't know Mr. Moss was a farmer too."

That sent the three of us into fits of laughter. When Sylvia explained it to her, Betty's face turned red as the seat back behind her. It was several minutes before I got the interview back on track. I had them tell me a little more about what they did every day, how they felt about helping with the war effort, and what their plans were when the war was over. It wasn't long before I had plenty for my article. I had one more question that had nothing to do with the article. "What do you girls know about the accident this morning?"

"I heard about that," Betty said. "That poor man. What a terrible thing to happen."

"What happened exactly?" I asked. "Do you know of anyone who actually saw the machine fall on Mr. Cline? I'd like to talk to them."

All three shook their heads, and Sylvia said, "Nope."

"I heard he bumped it when he was sweeping the floor and it fell over on him," Vivian said.

That seemed to be the standard response.

I thanked them for their time and paid the check. On the walk home, something nagged at me. Everyone at the plant I'd talked to so far had denied witnessing the accident, but more than one person had said Ben Cline had bumped the machine while he was sweeping the floor. The sight of him lying on the floor writhing in pain was indelibly etched in my mind. If he'd been sweeping the floor, wouldn't the broom have been on the floor beside him? Someone might have had moved it. Or perhaps it hadn't been there in the first place.

Chapter Fourteen

Man Seriously Injured in Accident at Tabor Ironworks
—*The Progress Herald*, May 19, 1942

Lily was waiting on the front porch steps with her sketchbook when I got home. She jumped up. "Wait till you see what I came up with. Can I go with you to see Mayor Young tomorrow?"

I laughed at her enthusiasm. "Don't you have school?"

"I can skip."

"That's a bad idea. Mom would kill us both."

"But I want to tell the mayor about my ideas."

We walked into the house together. "I'll tell him everything he needs to know."

"That's not fair," Lily whined.

"What's not fair?" Mom said as we entered the kitchen. She was frying up chicken, and it smelled heavenly.

"Irene won't let me go with her to her meeting with the mayor tomorrow."

A chicken thigh sizzled as Mom dropped it into the hot skillet. "You have school tomorrow, Lily. Besides, why would Irene take you to see the mayor?"

"To show him these." Lily waved her sketchbook in front of Mom's face. "Irene said I could make posters for the scrap drive."

Mom gave me a look and raised an eyebrow.

"Lily's drawings are very good," I explained. "I promised I would show the mayor her work and see if we could post them around town."

"But she's just a schoolgirl," Mom said. "Mayor Young probably knows professional artists to make posters."

"How many professional artists do you think live in Progress?" A rhetorical question. The answer was zero. "In my opinion, Lily's drawings are every bit as good as any artist's."

"That's why I have to go to the meeting," Lily said. "Can I go?"

Mom lifted a piece of chicken and placed it on a rack to drain. "I'll think about it. For now, I need one of you to set the table and one to mash the potatoes."

"I get the table!" Lily disappeared into the dining room with the dishes Mom had placed on the counter.

I pulled the potato masher out of the drawer and got milk and butter out of the Frigidaire. I turned off the burner and drained the potatoes.

"How was your day?" Mom asked.

"Busy. There was an accident at Tabor Ironworks this morning." I mashed potatoes while I told her what had happened, leaving out my theory that it hadn't been an accident.

"That's horrible," she said. "That poor man."

"He's a friend of Sam Markowicz. Sam was staying at the hospital with him." I added butter to the hot potatoes and continued mashing.

Mom turned off the burner under the skillet and put the remaining chicken on the rack to drain. "I'll talk to Sarah and see if she knows if he needs anything. That poor man." She shuddered. "How horrible to lose a leg."

I poured in a little milk and told her about meeting the girls from the factory for my article. By the time I'd finished, the potatoes were mashed and Mom had placed the chicken on a platter. We carried them into the dining room. There was no more talk about my day. Lily took over the conversation in an attempt to persuade Mom to let her meet with the mayor. In the end, Mom gave in. It looked like I wouldn't be going to the meeting alone.

* * *

I waited up for Katherine, hoping she'd know more about Ben Cline's so-called accident than everyone else I'd talked to. It was well after midnight and I was falling asleep on the sofa when the front door opened.

Moments later Katherine plopped down onto a chair and slipped off her oxfords. She crossed one leg over the other and rubbed her foot. "My dogs are killing me."

I sat up. "I can imagine."

"Why are you still awake?"

"I wanted to talk to you."

She switched legs and rubbed her other foot. "Let me guess. The accident today."

"Yep."

"I'm not sure I can tell you anything you don't already know."

"You can tell me it wasn't an accident and someone pushed that machine onto Ben Cline."

Katherine stopped rubbing her foot. "Why would you think that?"

I leaned forward. "You know as well as I do that a machine weighing so much it crushes a man's leg and takes four people to lift doesn't just fall over if someone bumps it."

Katherine was silent. She pulled her pack of Chesterfields from the pocket of her slacks and took her time lighting one. Finally she took a drag and blew out smoke. "It could under the right circumstances."

"And what might they be?"

"If the machine was positioned a certain way."

"Like how?" I couldn't picture it.

She leaned back and took another pull on her cigarette before she answered. "It could have been leaning already, and when Cline bumped it, it fell over."

"That's a load of bull," I said. "If it happened that way, it would have fallen away from Ben and not on top of him. And if he thought it would fall toward him, he would have jumped out of the way. The only way it could land on him was if it took him completely by surprise."

"That doesn't mean it wasn't an accident. Maybe he bumped it but it didn't fall right away. Everyone says he was sweeping the floor. He might not have even noticed it."

"I was there right after it happened," I said. "I watched him lying on his face in agony while four men moved the equipment off of him."

"Wait a minute. He was facedown?"

"Yes." I could see Katherine trying to picture it in her head.

"That doesn't sound right."

"Well, he was."

She ground her cigarette in the ashtray and pushed out of the chair. "I'm bushed. I think I'll get ready for bed now."

Puzzled at the abrupt end of our conversation, I turned out the light and sat in the dark, trying to figure it all out. Katherine hadn't been much help. I had expected her to tell me what had really happened. Maybe that was asking too much. I knew she needed this job and had to toe the company line. Everyone told the same story, and Katherine was no exception. None of them could risk being let go. Ten minutes later I heard quiet footsteps on the stairs. I watched from the darkened room as Katherine opened the front door and went out, gently closing it behind her. So much for being bushed.

* * *

In the morning I was tempted to peek into Katherine's room—my former room—to see if she'd come back. I talked myself out of it. What would I say if she woke up—*I forgot this wasn't my room*? I really wanted to know where she'd gone that late at night, especially after she said she was going to bed. I couldn't help but wonder if it had something to do with what we'd been talking about. But why would that have made her lie about retiring for the night? She had to know more than she was letting on. That still didn't tell me why she had left the house.

Lily was eating breakfast when I went downstairs. She was dressed in her Sunday best, and her sketchbook was on the table beside her. I'd almost forgotten she was going with me to meet with Mayor Young.

"I'm all ready to go," she said. "I even made a couple more drawings, and I have all the calculations for how much scrap we need to collect."

I smiled. "You're very thorough."

"I can't wait for the mayor to see everything."

"Keep in mind that he may not like our idea. He could very well have something else in mind." That was one reason I hadn't wanted her to accompany me. If the mayor didn't like it, I'd be able to let her down easy.

"We'll just have to convince him," Lily said.

I crossed the dining room to the kitchen where Mom was slicing a loaf of her homemade bread. "Lily is raring to go this morning," I said, giving Mom a kiss on the cheek.

"She was up at five getting ready," Mom said. "I'm surprised you didn't hear her."

I put a slice of bread in the toaster. "I was up late talking to Katherine. I slept like a rock."

"What were you talking to Katherine about?"

I told Mom I'd wanted to see if Katherine had heard anything else about the accident in case I needed to update my article. I didn't mention Katherine leaving the house late at night.

"Was there anything new?" Mom asked.

I shook my head. "No. I'm hoping Sam will shed some light on it. I'd like to talk to the injured man when he feels up to it." My toast popped up, and I reached for the butter.

"It's so sad," she said. "I can't stop thinking about that poor man. I'll talk to Sarah today and see if there's anything I can do."

Lily burst into the kitchen. "Aren't you ready yet? You'd better shake a leg. You'll be late for work."

"We have plenty of time." I stood at the counter to eat my toast and drink a cup of coffee while Lily fidgeted. I was tempted to eat a second slice of toast but instead took pity on my sister. I gave Mom a kiss on the cheek, and we were off.

* * *

Peggy was already at her desk when Lily and I arrived at the Herald. "Is this our new staff member?" She smiled. "She looks a little young to me."

"For today only," I said.

"I'm going to make the posters for Mayor Young's scrap drive," Lily said.

Peggy looked at me.

"I keep telling her the mayor might say no."

"He won't," Lily said.

Peggy and I headed to the kitchen while Lily settled herself into my office.

"Any news on the injured man?" Peggy poured coffee into a cup and handed it to me.

"I'll check on him in a bit," I said. "Sam Markowicz is coming in to see me this afternoon. He might have some news."

"Why is Sam coming in?"

"At the hospital, he said that Ben Cline wouldn't talk to me but he would. I'm hoping he can shed some light on what's going on."

"How was your interview with the Tabor girls?" Peggy asked.

"Tabor girls. I like that! You just gave me my headline for the article—*Tabor Girls Keep the War Machine Rolling*, or something like that."

Peggy laughed. "Happy to help."

When we got back to her desk, I heard voices and laughter coming from my office. It sounded like Matt and Lily. "Uh-oh," I said. Matt was likely telling her some outrageous story.

Peggy's telephone rang, and she reached for the receiver. "Keep me posted. That sounds like trouble."

I entered my office. Lily was sitting in my chair behind the desk, and Matt was perched on a corner looking at her sketchbook.

He looked up. "How did I get so lucky? Two gorgeous Ingram girls in one room."

"You must need new glasses," I said. "What are you two up to?"

Matt pointed to Lily's sketchbook. "These are terrific. Lily says the mayor is going to use them in his scrap drive campaign."

"We don't meet with the mayor until ten o'clock. He hasn't even seen the drawings yet," I said.

"He'll like them when he sees them," Lily said.

Matt flipped the sketchbook closed. "Of course he will."

I didn't say anything. Lily's mind was set. I really hoped she was right. It had been my idea to show the mayor her sketches, but I wished Lily hadn't insisted on tagging along. I was worried her ideas would be rejected, and then what? She'd be back to thinking her drawings weren't good, when the truth was they were better than good. At least I could use some of them in the paper.

"Can I talk to you for a minute, boss?" Matt motioned toward the door.

I told Lily I'd be right back and followed him.

"I read your article about what happened at Tabor yesterday," Matt said. "It got me thinking."

"Imagine that."

Matt grinned. "Yeah, I do that on occasion." His expression turned serious. "I kind of read between the lines that you don't think it was an accident."

"I said it was undetermined."

"So I guess you don't want to see the dozens of pictures I took at the ceremony last week."

"What good would that do? Ben Cline was injured yesterday."

"Yeah, but you never know what might be in the photographs. I was shooting all over the plant—not just at the ceremony. If someone was giving him trouble, it might be on film."

I threw my arms around him. "You're a genius!"

Matt laughed. "That's a first. But if you're gonna squeeze me like that, you can call me anything you want."

"Don't get used it," I said. "How many photos do you have?"

"Sixty or so. I'll bring them around before the end of the day."

"Thanks, Matt."

"Any time, doll face," he said in his best Bogart voice.

"Get back to work." I grinned. "And if you call me doll face again, you're fired."

"Gotcha, boss."

* * *

"Mr. Mayor, this is my younger sister, Lily." We'd just been shown into Mayor Young's office by Dorothy, his secretary, who was almost as old as he was. She'd been with him for all eight of his terms and was completely devoted to him. Although the mayor had been married for more than fifty years before his wife passed on, there had been a rumor of a romance with Dorothy for years. It was none of my business, but I wondered why they hadn't gotten hitched after his wife died.

Mayor Young reached out his hand to Lily. "It's a pleasure to meet you."

Lily shook his hand. "It's nice to meet you too."

"You look so much like your mother when she was your age," he said.

"Really?" Lily said. "I didn't know that."

"And your big sister resembles your father." He looked at me. "How is Pete these days? Staying safe, I hope."

"Mom got a letter from him a few days ago. He couldn't say exactly where he was, but he's safe so far." I hoped it stayed that way. Covering the war that closely was dangerous—something I tried not to think about.

"And your beau enlisted, didn't he?" the mayor asked.

I nodded. "Bill enlisted right after Pearl. He's training down in Louisiana right now."

The mayor went around his desk and sank into his chair. "What can I do for you girls today?" He pointed to the chairs across from him, and Lily and I sat down.

I told him I was going to write about the scrap drive as well as the town's victory garden groundbreaking that was coming up on Saturday. When he'd answered my few questions, I brought up the idea of posters around town to advertise the scrap drive.

"That's a wonderful idea," he said. "Do you have anything in mind?"

Lily looked at me, and I nodded. "I do, sir." She opened her sketchbook and laid it on the desk in front of the mayor.

He silently paged through Lily's drawings while she tried and failed to sit still. Her fingers drummed a beat on her leg, and she looked like she was going to jump out of her skin. Finally he closed the sketchbook. He stared at Lily for a moment, then smiled. "Looks like you've got yourself a job, young lady."

* * *

Lily was on cloud nine when I walked her home after the meeting. She couldn't stop talking about "finally doing something meaningful." I didn't remind her that her schoolwork was also meaningful.

Mom would be sure she didn't neglect it. It was almost lunchtime, so I made a sandwich and wrapped it in waxed paper to take back to the *Herald* while Lily chattered on and on to Mom about her plans for the posters. I gave Mom a quick kiss on the cheek and headed back to work.

It was going to be a busy afternoon. Roosevelt was awarding Jimmy Doolittle a Congressional Medal of Honor for leading the raid on Tokyo back in April. I was still astounded that any of the crews had made it through alive. Doolittle had definitely earned the medal. I'd assigned Rex to write that article. He'd wanted to go to Washington to cover it, but when I'd told him it wasn't in the budget and he'd have to pay his own way, he'd decided to stay put.

The other big news of the day was that New York was suspending night baseball games. There had been a lot of controversy about cities on the East Coast being reluctant to order and enforce blackouts. The powers that be had finally decided it was better to lose a little business than risk having their cities bombed and boats off the coast torpedoed. Inland cities were getting ready to do the same.

From a block away, I noticed the lights were off at Markowicz Hardware and something red was on the door. As I got closer, the something red became more visible. I gasped when I realized what it was. Someone had painted a swastika on the door.

Chapter Fifteen

New York City to Suspend Night Games

—The Progress Herald, May 19, 1942

I rushed to the door and pulled on it. Locked. Thank goodness Sam wasn't here. I touched the red paint—it was still sticky. Someone had had the nerve to do this in broad daylight. Surely someone had seen it. I thought of Ava right away. She had a clear view of the store from her shop. If anyone had seen it, she had.

Ava was putting a client under a hair dryer when I entered. "Did you see it?" I asked.

She turned on the dryer and put her hands on her hips. "You're going to have to be more specific than that."

I pointed out the window. "Over at Sam's."

Ava went to the window. "Oh my lord. That's terrible!"

"Did you see who did it? The paint is still wet, so it hasn't been long since it happened."

Her face paled. "I might have. I had no idea that's what he was doing. I thought he was just trying the door."

"Who was it? Can you describe him?"

"I didn't pay that close attention. It wasn't anyone I know. I figured it was one of the newcomers to town."

"What did he look like?" I asked. "Chief Turner is going to want to know."

Ava looked at the ceiling like she could see the culprit up there. "It was a man."

"That's real descriptive," I said.

"I'm not finished. He wasn't very tall for a man—maybe my height."

Ava was five foot eight, give or take.

"He was standing at the door, so I only saw his back. He wore dark pants and a dark jacket. And a cap, so I didn't see his hair."

"That's it?" Her description fit more than half the male population.

"If I'd known what he was doing, I would have paid more attention," she snapped. "Why does everyone in town think I know everything that's going on?"

Maybe because you do, I thought. "I'm sorry. I just want to know who is doing these things."

"I wish I could tell you more," she said. "I'll ask around. Maybe someone got a better look at him."

"Thanks. I appreciate it."

I left the salon and went straight to the police department. As usual, Jimmy Feeney was at the front desk.

"Here for the crime blotter?" he asked.

I'd actually forgotten it again. "Sure," I said. "That's not the only reason I'm here." I told him about the painted swastika.

"And you say it's fresh paint?"

"Yep. It's still tacky. Someone had to have seen the guy who did it."

"Does Sam know?"

"I don't know," I said. "His store is closed. I imagine he's still with Ben Cline—the guy who got hurt at Tabor yesterday." Was that just yesterday? It seemed like ages ago.

"The chief is out, but I'll get him on the radio. After that I'll take a walk over and make sure no one tampers with anything."

"Thanks, Jimmy. I'll try to get a hold of Sam." I'd have to call the hospital when I got back to the paper. I turned to leave, and Jimmy called me back. He held up my copy of the blotter. "Sheesh." I took the paper from him. "I'd forget my head if it wasn't attached."

When I left the police station, there was a crowd gathered in front of the hardware store. Maybe not a crowd exactly—it was six or seven people. Roger Eckel, the manager of the A&P, was holding a bucket and a scrub brush. I bulldozed my way past two clerks from Woolworth's. I grabbed Mr. Eckel's arm, and water sloshed out of the bucket, just missing my shoes. "Stop," I said.

He yanked his arm away. "What are you doing? I want to get this off before Sam sees it."

I explained that the police needed to look at it first. "Sergeant Feeney notified Chief Turner, and he's on his way over."

"But what if Sam sees this?" Mr. Eckel asked. "He's had enough trouble."

"I know he has. He'll need to know anyway. The important thing right now is to find the culprit." A few more people had gathered by this time. "Did any of you see who did this?"

I got a chorus of *no*s and shaking heads.

One of the Woolworth clerks said, "I know it wasn't there when I passed two hours ago."

Well, that was something, anyway.

Virgil Curry came forward. "I saw something." Virgil was a veteran of the last war and spent his days on a park bench near the statue of a Civil War soldier on the other end of the square—when he wasn't in the bar, that is. "There was a guy in dark pants looking in the store window at ten o'clock."

Jimmy Feeney arrived just then. The crowd separated like the Red Sea parting for Moses. "Everyone stay back," he said. "This here's a crime scene." He seemed happy to have something to do other than sit behind his desk.

I told him Virgil might have seen the culprit. He gave me a look like he believed all Virgil could see were some pink elephants.

"A man in dark pants," I said. "That's the same thing Ava told me."

Jimmy said, "Tell me exactly what you saw."

Virgil rubbed his unshaven chin. "Well, I was walkin' down the street, heading to my bench. I was going to cross the street and say hello to Sam when I seen the guy looking in the store window. The store was dark, and I figured the guy was looking to see if Sam was inside. I didn't pay no mind after that."

"What time was that?" Jimmy asked.

"Ten o'clock sharp. I like to get to my bench before someone else claims it."

As if someone would have the nerve to sit on Virgil's bench. It didn't have his name on it, but everyone knew he sat there every day.

Jimmy asked him for a description.

"Like I told the girl, he wore dark pants and I think a jacket or dark shirt with long sleeves."

"Was he wearing a cap? Ava thought he was," I said.

Jimmy gave me a look.

"Sorry," I said.

"He did have a cap on," Virgil said. "But he took it off to put his face up to the window."

"Did you see his face?" Jimmy asked.

Virgil shook his head. "Nope. I only saw the back of his head. His hair was blond or gray. Couldn't tell from across the street."

Jimmy patted him on the shoulder, and Virgil went on his way. Jimmy turned to the crowd. "If none of you have anything to contribute, you can leave too."

There were some grumbles, but the group broke up. When it was just Jimmy and me left, I asked him where the chief was.

"He's tied up on an automobile accident. Someone hit a deer and it landed on the hood of their vehicle. He's waiting for the game warden to come and remove it. The driver's lucky it didn't go through his windshield."

"Are you going to be here long?" I asked. "I want to send Matt over to get some pictures."

He nodded. "I'll stay long enough for that, then go and look for witnesses."

*　*　*

Back at the *Herald*, I sent Matt to get some photographs and assigned Frank to follow up on the incident. I was already behind on my daily duties, so I got right to work. Much later I remembered the lunch I'd brought. I'd once gotten sick from a sandwich I'd left out too long. I hated to waste it but I didn't want to go through that ever again. I tossed it in the trash. I scrounged around for a nickel in my pocketbook and got a Hershey bar from the candy machine in the kitchen. I hoped it would keep me going for the rest of the day. I was licking chocolate from my fingers when Donny barged into my office.

"While you were out doing who knows what, I took care of this week's payroll. In case you forgot, payday is Friday."

"I am perfectly aware of when payday is," I said. "You know as well as I do that I prepare Friday's payroll on Wednesday. Not Tuesday. Just like Pop always did."

Donny sniffed and folded his arms across his chest. "I decided waiting until Wednesday isn't efficient. I suggested this to Pete last year."

I clenched my fists. "And what did Pop tell you?"

"He said he had everything under control. He never actually told me no."

"What the heck do you think he meant when he said he had it under control?"

"He didn't tell me I couldn't do it."

I was about ready to explode. It took an effort to keep my voice calm and even. "Well, I'm telling you. I want everything you did on my desk in fifteen minutes."

"But—"

"No buts. You had no authority to remove the ledger from my desk. From now on it will be locked up. Mr. Reardon will be going over every inch of it to be sure you didn't tamper with anything." Peggy's father, the banker, took care of the *Herald*'s financial affairs.

"I would never do that!"

"You stole a ledger from my office."

Donny's face turned an ugly color of pink. "That's not theft! I'm trying to help. Pete would be proud of me."

154

I stood up so quickly Donny took a step back. "My father would be appalled at your behavior. He would fire you on the spot. You're lucky I'm not doing the same. That will change if Mr. Reardon finds anything amiss. Not only that, Chief Turner will be calling on you."

"You can't do that." He was on the verge of tears. "This newspaper is my life. It's all I ever wanted to do."

I sat back down. "Maybe you should have thought about that sooner."

Donny dropped into the chair on the other side of my desk. "I was only trying to help."

I sighed. "Did you ever think of asking me first?"

"You would have said no."

"Probably. I'm not going to change anything Pop put into place without good reason. He kept a certain schedule, and so do I."

"I still say I could do better."

Of course he'd think that. "That's not your call. Pop put me in charge. Not you. And you'd better remember that."

He nodded and pushed out of the chair. "I'll go get the ledger now." He stood there for a moment, possibly waiting for me to thank him. When I didn't, he left.

I'd barely had time to calm down when Peggy poked her head in. "Mr. Markowicz is here to see you."

* * *

Sam was worn out. I could have sworn lines that hadn't been in his face a week ago were etched deeply now. His eyes were bloodshot, with dark circles underneath. I'd never seen anyone look so sad. It broke my heart. I offered him coffee.

"Yes, please. Black," he said. "That's very kind of you."

I went to the door, asked Peggy to bring him a cup, and returned to my desk. "How is Ben?" I asked.

"Physically, the doctor says he will recover, but up here"—Sam pointed to his head—"he is not good. He keeps saying he wished he had died."

"What can I do to help? Would you like me to talk to him?"

Sam shook his head. "He will not talk to you. He will not talk to anyone. He screams at the nurses to leave him alone. They had to give him a shot before I left today to quiet him down."

Peggy brought Sam's coffee and went back to her desk.

He took a sip and made a face. "This coffee is very strong."

"It's probably been sitting in the percolator for a while. I can make a fresh pot."

"No, this is fine." He took another sip.

"Have you been to the store today?"

"Yes. Mr. Eckel was cleaning it off when I arrived." Sam put his cup down on the desk. "I am tired of being intimidated. Sarah is frightened that something will happen to me if I speak up, but I can no longer be silent."

"You're doing the right thing."

He began by giving me some background—the same story the chief had told me when he showed me the sign that had been left in the store last week. "Sarah and I never imagined we'd face the same hatred in America."

I didn't know what to say.

"The message left for me last week wasn't the first incident," he said. "Other members of our synagogue have received similar messages. Some in the mail, some scrawled on their homes."

"Why didn't they report it to the police?"

"What could the police have done? No one saw who did these things. It was always in the dead of night—except recently. They are getting bolder. Benjamin will never be the same."

"Was Ben able to tell you anything about what happened yesterday? Everyone I spoke with said he was sweeping the floor and bumped the machine."

"That is not true," he said. "Benjamin takes great care around the machines. He would not bump them."

"Is that what Ben told you?"

"He is still saying that he doesn't know what happened."

"But you don't believe that."

Sam shook his head. "No, I don't. Benjamin has been having trouble with some men at the factory. He is afraid of them. I am sure one of them did this."

"Who are they?" I asked.

"Benjamin will not tell me."

"Is one of them the same man who beat him up?"

"I believe so," Sam said.

Even though I believed it too, it was still speculation. I didn't have much more to go on than before.

"I should have spoken up sooner." His voice cracked. "If I had, Benjamin would not be hurt and Moses would not be dead."

"Moses?"

"I believe he preferred to go by Moe."

"Moe? Moe who worked here?"

Sam nodded. "Moses wasn't a member of our congregation, but he was Jewish. He told me he had lost the little faith he had a long time ago. I talked to him on occasion and tried to convince him to return. One day I mentioned a note I had received in the mail, and when I told him others had received them as well, he was very interested."

Could this have been the big story Moe was working on? That didn't make sense. I was sure Moe had been looking into something at Tabor. "Was he going to write about it?"

"I do not know. The others would not talk to him."

"I'm a little confused," I said. "What does this have to do with Moe's death or Ben's accident?"

"That is what I want you to find out."

Chapter Sixteen

Tabor Girls Keep War Machine Rolling
—*The Progress Herald*, May 19, 1942

After Sam left, Peggy came into my office and closed the door. "Spill it," she said. "I heard him mention Moe. What's going on?"

I filled her in on the little I knew. Sam hadn't really given me much to go on. At least he'd agreed with me that the chief was wrong and Moe's death hadn't been an accident.

"What are you going to do?" Peggy asked.

I leaned back in my chair. "I have no idea. It's horrible that Sam and the others are being harassed, but I don't think that's all Moe was investigating. There's more going on here than Sam knows. I'm sure of it. At least one of the culprits works at Tabor because of what's happened to Ben Cline. Moe would have written an article right away and exposed whoever it was, and he didn't do that. He must have found something else. Moe would have gone after the bigger story."

Peggy nodded. "But why wouldn't Moe have gone to see Sam when you sent him to cover the robbery that turned out not to be a robbery?"

"I don't know. Maybe he knew who was doing it and went to see him instead?"

"That makes sense."

"And don't forget the note he left for me, that if something happened to him it wasn't an accident. This has to be much bigger than what Sam is talking about. I need to talk to Ben Cline."

"Didn't Sam say he won't talk to anyone?"

"He did," I said. "But that's never stopped me before."

* * *

My cousin returned the ledger, and I warned him once again of the consequences if anything was amiss. I spent the rest of the afternoon proofing articles, including Rex's on the Doolittle medal. He'd done a bang-up job, not only writing about the ceremony but also giving a summary of the raid itself and a little information on the other crew members involved. Ken's article about New York suspending night games was good as well. I wrote up a short piece on the incident at Sam's and picked out a couple of Matt's photos to go with it. Frank was still interviewing some of the townsfolk for the follow-up, and we'd run his piece tomorrow.

On the walk home I thought some more about Moe and the little bit Sam had revealed. I felt like I was spinning my wheels. I wasn't getting anywhere at all. I really didn't know much more than I had days ago. I went over everything I did know.

Last Monday, someone had left the message on cardboard in Sam's store. I'd sent Moe to talk to Sam and Ava. He didn't talk to either one. The police blotter showed a fight between Ben Cline and some nameless person at Tabor. Moe didn't show up for work. I found him at the bottom of his cellar steps. He had left a note for me saying his death wasn't an accident. Peggy and I went to his house—it had been tossed. We found a scrap of calendar with *TAB 10 AM* written on it and a list with some women's names on it. One of the names was Sylvia, who'd turned out to be Moe's girlfriend. Sylvia's place was ransacked and Moe's notebook stolen. A piece of equipment fell on Ben Cline's leg. Sam had revealed other harassment and the fact that Moe was also Jewish.

I turned the corner onto my street. There was a huge chunk of this puzzle missing, and I was at a loss to piece it together. I needed to make a plan. First would be talking to Ben Cline, if I was able. I wasn't hopeful he'd tell me anything, but I had to give it a try. Second would be going through Moe's house with a fine-tooth comb. I had to have missed something. Moe had hidden the note he'd written me in one of the books in his desk. If he had been so careful to hide a mere note, it was possible he'd hidden something important, especially if he'd known he was in danger. I just had to figure out where. I couldn't help but wonder if the notebook he'd left at Sylvia's was a ruse. If he truly cared about her, would he have put her in danger by leaving any evidence he had there? Moe had been a rogue, but he wasn't a jerk.

As I stepped onto the porch, the sound of Frank Sinatra singing "Blue Skies" came through the open living room window. It immediately put me in a better mood. Inside, I found Lily sprawled out on the living room floor, drawing on a large piece of butcher's paper. "Where did you get that?" I asked.

"Mom and I picked up a few things at the A&P this afternoon. The butcher knows someone who works in the mayor's office and heard I was making posters for the scrap drive. He gave me a whole roll of paper."

Word certainly got around quickly.

"And before you ask," Lily said, "before she left for work, Katherine said I can play her records any time I want to."

That reminded me I would need to wait up for Katherine again. She might know who had been harassing Ben Cline. I was also curious about where she'd gone last night after she'd told me she was going to bed. Maybe she'd meant bed in someone else's house, in which case it was none of my business, but I wouldn't mind hearing the details anyway.

After dinner I helped Mom clean up while Lily went to a friend's house to find out what schoolwork she'd missed that day.

"Is there any news about the man who was injured yesterday?" Mom asked. "I didn't want to mention it in front of Lily."

"Sam came to see me this afternoon. He said he's doing well physically, but not mentally."

"I imagine that will take some time." She rinsed a plate and put it in the drainer. "I went to visit Sarah Markowicz today to see if there was anything I could do."

I picked up a dish and dried it. "That was nice."

"It was the oddest thing, though. Didn't you say that fellow went to their synagogue?"

"Yep."

"Sarah swears she doesn't know him. She even seemed put out that I went to see her. I kept asking her if something was wrong, but she said no. Something wasn't right."

"When I ran into her at Woolworth's the other day, she said the same thing. She's frightened. There was another incident at the hardware store today. Someone painted a swastika on the door."

"Oh my. That's horrible!"

I finished drying the dishes and hung the damp towel on the oven handle. "That's not all. Sam said there have been other incidents with members of their community."

Mom drained the dishwater out of the sink and dried her hands on her apron before taking it off. "What does Walt say about it?"

"They haven't reported it to the police. I have no idea why, other than maybe they hoped it would just go away."

"Walt needs to know," Mom said. "Are you going to talk to him?"

"I hadn't thought about it, but yes, I will." We moved to the living room and turned on the radio. I hadn't mentioned that I didn't think Ben Cline's injury was accidental or that I thought Moe had been murdered. I considered telling her, but she would only worry. She had enough to fret about with Pop being away, and I didn't want to burden her further. We spent a quiet evening chatting and listening to the radio. It felt almost normal, like before the war. It made me miss Pop and Bill all the more.

* * *

I was getting a piece of Mom's icebox cake, which was still delicious even with half the sugar, when Katherine came in around midnight.

"I was wondering who was raiding the icebox," she said as she entered the kitchen. "I half suspected it was Lily."

"Want a piece?" I asked.

"I'd love one." Katherine pulled a chair out from the kitchen table and wearily sat down. She pulled her ever-present Chesterfields from the pocket of her dungarees and lit one.

I got another plate down and put a piece of cake on each one, then poured two glasses of milk.

"Thanks. I was so busy tonight I never got dinner," she said.

"There's leftover roast in the Frigidaire, if you want a sandwich."

"This will do for now. If I'm still hungry, I'll make one."

We didn't talk until we'd both finished our cake. "Why so busy?" I asked. "Because of that new order?"

"Yeah. There's a real push to get it done early. The company gets a bonus if they do."

I drank the last of my milk. "So will they be early?"

Katherine shrugged. "I'm not sure. We had some problems today, but I'm hoping they get them worked out."

"What kind of problems?" I got up and took our dishes to the sink.

"One of the forming machines had something wrong with it. One of the engineers was still trying to figure it out when my shift was over." She lit another cigarette. "Have you heard any more about the guy who was hurt yesterday?"

I leaned against the counter. "I was just going to ask you if you had heard anything more about why that machine toppled over on him."

Katherine studied her fingernails. "No one's changed their story, if that's what you mean."

"I heard he was being harassed."

"Who told you that?"

"A good friend of his. He also said it's happened more than once."

Katherine was silent for a moment, still looking at her hand. "He was in a fight. Nothing more."

"He was beaten up."

She stood up. "Leave it alone, Irene."

"Why?" I asked. "Why won't you tell me what's really going on?"

"It's for your own good. Just leave it alone." She turned quickly and left the kitchen.

I was more confused than ever and more sure that something strange was going on at Tabor. I went up to bed, but I didn't sleep. For the life of me, I couldn't figure out why Katherine was covering up whatever was going on. She'd been helpful when I talked to her about Moe, but now she was shutting me out. Was it possible she was in on it? Was she involved in the harassment of the Jewish community? I found it hard to believe. But I really didn't know her, other than what she'd told me. It could all be lies. After all, she surely didn't know Frank Sinatra, and her story about being a singer was most likely hogwash. I was going to have to keep a closer eye on her.

Chapter Seventeen

Doolittle Receives Medal of Honor for April Raid on Tokyo
—*The Progress Herald*, May 20, 1942

Father O'Connor arrived at the *Herald* at nine forty-five in the morning to say a few prayers for Moe. I couldn't help but think that Moe would have had a laugh over a Catholic priest saying prayers for him. Or anyone saying prayers for him, for that matter. Although I'd mentioned it to Sylvia, I doubted she would show up. She was likely working today. So far it looked like it would just be the staff.

"Thank you so much for coming," I said to Father O'Connor.

"It's my pleasure." He spoke with a brogue. He preached a good sermon, but I suspected the brogue was the main reason his congregation hung on every word. He was soft-spoken and reminded me a little of an Irish Bing Crosby. "What can you tell me about Moe?"

"His given name was Moses. Moses Bauer. He was a good guy. We clashed once in a while because he sometimes didn't do what I asked him to. He was always chasing a new tip, hoping it would lead to a big story."

"Was he a religious man?" Father asked.

"I'm afraid he wasn't. I only found out yesterday that he was Jewish but had turned away even from that faith. If I'd have known earlier, I wouldn't have troubled you."

"It's no trouble at all. I'm happy to do this."

Precisely at ten, Rex, Frank, Ken, Peggy, Matt, Donny, and a couple guys who worked the printing press gathered together. Father O'Connor said a few inspirational words, followed by some traditional prayers. It was over in ten minutes. After Father O'Connor left, I went into my office and closed the door.

I sat and stared into space, drumming a beat with a pencil on my desk blotter. It had been a week since I'd found Moe lying at the bottom of his steps. What had I accomplished? I was no further along in finding out who had killed him than I had been when I found his note. I needed to make some kind of plan. I stopped drumming and grabbed a piece of paper to jot down the ideas I'd come up with on my walk home the day before.

I felt better now that I'd put my plan in writing. I pushed the note aside, opened my desk drawer, and pulled out the draft of an article I'd been working on. I loaded a new sheet of paper into my typewriter and got to work.

* * *

I was leaving the *Herald* to get lunch when Frank called me over to his desk. "You need to see this," he said.

I changed direction. There was a copy of the *New York Times* open on his desk. "Reading the competition?" I teased. We were hardly competition for anyone, especially the *Times*.

Frank pointed to the headline of an article on page four— *'New Order' Dead Listed at 400,000.*

I skimmed the article and looked at Frank. "Why did they bury this on page four?" I asked. "This should be front-page news." The article, written by a United Press correspondent, stated that Hitler's firing squads had killed 400,000 Europeans, including 100,000 in the Baltic States, 100,000 in Poland, and 200,000 in Russia, many of whom were Jews. In the process they had looted more than $36 billion.

"Apparently the city's new blackout and the Russians flanking Kharkov take priority," Frank said. "I'm gonna follow up on this."

"I'd appreciate it." I didn't care that he hadn't asked if he could follow up. He probably wouldn't have asked Pop either. I knew his piece would be good and thorough. And unlike the *Times*, I'd put it on the front page. He was already dialing the phone when I left and went home for lunch.

Mom was at a garden club meeting, where they were finalizing their involvement with the victory garden festivities for Saturday, so I made myself a sandwich with leftover roast beef. When I finished eating, I took Pop's car and headed to Providence Hospital. I figured now was as good a time as any to see Ben Cline.

* * *

I stopped at the nurses' station to see how Ben was doing. The charge nurse told me he was doing well physically but wasn't taking losing his leg very well. I couldn't say I blamed him. I didn't think anyone would take it very well.

"A visitor is just what he needs," she said. "Are you his girlfriend?"

"Can we have a few minutes undisturbed?" I didn't exactly lie, but she could think what she wanted.

"You can have all the time you want," she said.

His door was partially open, but I knocked anyway.

His eyes were closed, and he didn't open them when he barked, "Go away."

"No can do, Ben."

"Get the hell out before I call for my nurse."

"Your nurse says I'm just what you need." I pulled a straight chair over to his bedside. "She thinks I'm your girl. She's not going to throw me out."

He opened his eyes and glared at me. "You're wasting your time. I'm not talking to you."

"Fine. I'll just sit here and keep you company." He closed his eyes, and after five minutes passed I thought he'd fallen asleep until I saw a tear slip down the side of his face toward his ear. I reached over and touched his hand.

"Please go away," he said. "You can't help me. No one can help me."

"That's not true, Ben. Sam wants to help. I want to help if you'll let me. I can't do that if you won't tell me what really happened."

"I can't."

"You mean you won't."

"That's right." He opened his eyes again. "I won't."

I tried another tactic. "The harassment isn't going to stop unless someone speaks up."

"I don't know what you're talking about."

"Sam told me what's been going on."

Ben winced as he turned a little in bed to face me. "You don't get it, do you?"

"Get what?"

"You're either naïve or plain stupid," Ben said. "I don't know which is worse."

It was the first time I'd been called either. I didn't much like it. "I'm definitely not stupid. Naïve, maybe. All I know is that public knowledge of what's been happening is the best and the only way to stop what's been going on."

"You really are stupid," he said. "These people can't be stopped. Publicity only makes them more determined. More angry. More deadly. You're making it worse, and you'll end up getting us killed."

"That's not—"

"Get out." He pressed his call button. "Get out or I'll have you thrown out. Your choice."

I stood, knowing he would do just that. The nurse came in, and as I started down the hall, I heard him tell her to keep me away from him.

I drove away from the hospital feeling miserable. I'd only wanted to help. Had I made it worse by printing articles about the messages left at Sam's or about Ben's accident? I didn't see how that could be, but was I wrong? I'd thought that the more people knew, the better. I wanted my readers to sympathize with their plight. I hadn't considered that it would make the perpetrator angry enough to want to hurt them further. I needed to talk to someone about it. In ordinary times, that person would be Pop, but he was far away. I'd go to the second-best person—my future father-in-law.

*　*　*

Jimmy wasn't at the front desk. I saw the chief through his open office door. He was sitting at his desk, reading what looked like a report. I knocked on his doorframe.

He looked up and smiled. "Come on in."

I took the seat across from him. "Where's Jimmy?"

"I gave him the day off. He and the missus went to Pittsburgh to visit her sister, who just got a dog. I'm pretty sure Jimmy was more excited about seeing the dog than his sister-in-law."

I managed to give him a half smile.

The chief pushed his stack of papers aside and leaned forward. "What's wrong? You don't seem like yourself."

"I just came from visiting Ben Cline. I'm afraid I've made a mess of things."

"I doubt it," he said. "Tell me about it."

I told him what Sam had revealed yesterday and Ben's accusation today that I was making things worse. "Am I?" I asked. "Will I make it worse if I write about the harassment? The last thing I want is for anyone else to get hurt."

"Irene, sometimes things have to get worse before they get better."

"So I am making it worse."

"That's not what I'm saying. You can't just stop writing the news because you think it might hurt someone. Your job is to report what's happened and let people decide for themselves. Reporting on these anti-Semitic acts might make the culprits angry, but it will make more people sympathetic to our neighbors who are targeted because of their faith. We don't condone that here in America, and we especially don't condone it in Progress. The more people are aware, the more they can watch out for things like this and put a stop to it."

"Maybe."

"Look at yesterday," the chief said. "Look at how everyone gathered in front of Sam's. At how Roger was ready to scrub the paint off the door before Sam saw it. That's what we do around here. We take care of each other. No one I know is going to let some bully have his way for long."

He was right. I was doing what I was supposed to do. Pop wouldn't have let someone else dictate what he printed in the paper. If he saw something was wrong, he'd do whatever it took to make things right. And that was exactly what I planned to do. "Thank you," I said. "I guess I just needed a little reassurance."

He leaned back in his chair. "Tell me more about what Sam said about Moe."

I did. "I wonder if Moe had figured out who was behind it."

"He never said anything? Gave you any kind of clue?"

I shook my head. "I wish he had. I really wish he had. Maybe he'd still be alive." The words were out before I could stop them.

"His death was an accident," the chief said. "There's no proof it was more than a fall down the stairs. Don't look for trouble where there isn't any."

I wouldn't convince him otherwise—not yet anyway. I wouldn't have had time anyway—a call came in, and he had to leave. I walked out with him.

He put a hand on my shoulder. "I know that whatever you write will be fair. We can't tolerate this type of thing in Progress."

"I'll do my best," I said. "Thanks, Dad." Calling him Dad came out naturally. I hadn't thought about it or planned it.

He gave me a huge smile. "It's about time you called me that."

It was. It finally felt right.

*   *   *

Matt was waiting for me when I got back. "Sorry it took so long, but here are the pictures I took at Tabor last week." He dropped three large manila envelopes on my desk. "I realized I still hadn't developed some of them, so I did that last night."

"Wow," I said. "That's a lot of pictures. It will take me a while to go through them all. Do you mind if I keep them for a few days?"

"Keep them as long as you need. I'll just file them away when you're done."

"Thanks."

We chatted for a minute. I filled him in on the schedule for the victory garden groundbreaking on Saturday and told him what I wanted in the way of photographs. After he left, I got caught up on a couple of articles, including one reminding everyone of the groundbreaking. I read through the articles the other reporters had turned in. They rarely needed my touch on them, and these were no exception. I passed them on to Peggy to send down to Donny.

After that, I tackled the payroll. I hadn't followed through on having Mr. Reardon check the ledger, but Donny didn't know that. I'd see if anything was amiss first. I was happy to see everything was in order. I hated to admit it, but Donny had done a good job on the entries. I didn't want to reward him for doing it behind my back, but I needed to consider passing this off to him. I would still write the checks, of course, but it wouldn't be the worst thing in the world if he did some of the accounting. Pop had always done everything himself, but I wasn't Pop. He liked the administrative end of things, and most of his writing involved editorials. I'd rather be out and about, writing about whatever came my way. We couldn't afford to add an accountant to the staff, but if Donny took over those duties, I'd have more time for other things. Like finding Moe's killer and finding the person responsible for putting Ben in the hospital. I'd give it some serious thought.

At the end of the day, I picked up the three envelopes containing Matt's photos and closed my office door. Peggy was getting ready to leave too. She pointed to the envelopes. "Taking work home?"

"Not exactly." I told her what they were. "If I get a chance, I'll take a look at them later."

"Mom and Dad are out again tonight," she said. "Why don't you bring them over? I'll help you go through them. Not that you need an excuse to come over."

"That would be great." It would be much easier with two of us, plus I wouldn't have to explain to Mom or Lily what I was doing. We decided on seven thirty. I walked home feeling much better than I had earlier today. I hadn't made any progress with my investigation, but that could change tonight. Peggy and I had put our heads together before, resulting in us finding Sylvia. Maybe we'd have even better luck tonight.

Chapter Eighteen

Liberty Ship Sunk in Caribbean Sea by German Sub
—*The Progress Herald*, May 21, 1942

I emptied the first envelope onto the Reardons' kitchen table. There were dozens of photographs in different sizes. Peggy and I sorted them into three stacks according to size. I pulled the stack of the largest photos toward me and quickly flipped through them. These were all from the dedication ceremony, some of which had been featured in the *Herald*. I passed them to Peggy.

"I saw these already," I said. "See if you notice anything."

While Peggy did that, I picked up the next stack. These were all five-by-sevens of the ceremony. Some were duplicates of the larger photos. I put a few aside that I wanted to take a closer look at.

"This is a nice one of Arnold Moss," Peggy said, holding up a photo. "He's a handsome man." She grinned. "Don't let Ken know I said that."

"My lips are sealed. The problem is he knows he's handsome. He should try a little humility once in a while. Maybe I should give him that picture. He could hang it on his wall and admire himself."

Peggy laughed. "Of course, someone might throw darts at it while he's not looking."

I picked up Moss's photo. "That's not a bad idea."

"What? Throwing darts at it?"

"No. Giving him the photo."

"Why in the world would you want to do that?"

"It would give me another chance to go inside the factory without Mr. Tabor throwing me out on my keister. Moss likes me, or at least he pretends to like me. It would be a goodwill gesture."

Peggy rolled her eyes. "It'll make him more persistent. He'll think you like him."

"Maybe I need to make him think that. I don't see any other way to get in there and try to find out what's really going on."

"He'll never give up trying to get in your bed if you do."

"I'll consider it one more sacrifice toward the war effort."

"Irene!"

"I'm not going to sleep with him! I'm already taken—and happily so. He can try all he wants, and I'll keep turning him down." I grinned. "That can be *his* sacrifice for the war effort."

Peggy held up a photo, laughing. "Here's a really lovely one."

I grabbed for it. "Gimme. That one is going in the trash." It was the one where Matt had caught me by surprise and almost blinded me. I definitely had that wide-eyed deer-in-the-headlights look.

My so-called best friend held it out of reach. "I think I should post this in the newsroom."

"If you do, you're fired."

"Meanie." She stuck her tongue out at me, and we dissolved into fits of laughter.

Once we recovered, I put the photos—minus the one of me that would never see the light of day again—back in their envelope and emptied the second one on the table. While I sorted them, Peggy went to the Frigidaire and returned to the table with two bottles of Coke. It was a nice treat. We went through the photos one by one, and just when I thought this was a pointless exercise, something caught my eye. "Hey, look at this." I passed the picture to Peggy.

"Is that Katherine?" she asked.

"I'm positive it's her. And the other girls are Sylvia and Betty—I talked to them about working at the factory." They were standing in a corridor with two men. They appeared to be engrossed in conversation. "I wonder who those men are." It didn't matter, but I was curious.

"Maybe they're in some of these other pictures."

We found another one of Katherine with Sylvia and Vivian Anderson and Arnold Moss, of all people. My guess was he was telling them what a great guy he was and that one or even all of them should have a drink with him. When we finished, I put Katherine's pictures aside, and Peggy put the rest back in the envelope. Then I dumped out the last one.

I began sorting and picked up one of the small photos. As I went to put it on the stack, I took a second look. One of the men in the picture looked a lot like one of the two in the photo with Katherine. But the thing that really struck me was that the other man might be Ben Cline. They looked angry, and although it was hard to tell from a picture, they appeared to be arguing. I asked Peggy if she had a magnifying glass.

"I think so. Why?"

I told her.

"My dad has one in his desk." She disappeared for a minute and came back with a magnifying glass.

I held the glass over the photo. It was definitely Ben Cline, but I wasn't sure about the other man. I compared his image to the similar-appearing man in the picture with Katherine. It sure looked like the same guy, but in this picture his fists were clenched and his mouth was twisted. Was this the person who had been harassing Ben and the others? I picked up the photo of Katherine and the girls with the two men. In this one, he seemed relaxed and had a smile on his face. I had to find out who he was. Katherine would know. I guessed I'd be waiting up for her again tonight.

*　*　*

When Katherine got home, we sat at the kitchen table and I passed the photographs to her. "I was going through all the pictures Matt took at Tabor and thought you might like to see these."

"Yikes," she said. "These sure don't show my best side."

I doubted she had a bad side. I pointed to the two men she and the girls were with in one picture. "Who are those guys?"

"That's Richard Adler, and that one is John Smith."

"What are they like?"

I expected her to say they were good guys or something to that effect. Instead she asked, "Why do you want to know?"

I pointed to the man in the photo with Ben Cline. "I think this is Richard Adler. It looks here like he's angry with Ben Cline."

She peered at the picture. "It does look that way."

"Does this Adler get angry often? Does he have a problem with Ben?"

Katherine leaned back in her chair and stared at me. "What are you getting at?"

"I'm trying to figure out who put Ben Cline in the hospital. When I mentioned that he was facedown the other night, I could tell you thought the same way I did—that it wasn't an accident."

"I never said it wasn't." Katherine took a Chesterfield out of the pack and lit it.

"You didn't have to. You abruptly ended our conversation and went upstairs to bed."

"I was tired."

"I heard you leave the house not ten minutes later. Where did you go?"

"I couldn't sleep, so I took a walk."

"Oh, come on. You didn't even have time to brush your teeth, let alone put on a nightgown and get into bed. What's going on? Did you meet someone? Are you protecting this Richard Adler?"

"I'm not protecting anyone. What I do with my time is no one's business. I'm not discussing this any further." Katherine stubbed out her cigarette so hard the ashtray almost tipped over. She stood up. "For your own sake, drop it. It won't help anyone if you keep pursuing this. People could get hurt, including you." She left the kitchen and went up the stairs.

Was that a threat? Or just a warning? Either way, it made me more determined than ever to find out what was going on at Tabor. Mom might have been right about Katherine. She was trouble.

* * *

Needless to say, I didn't sleep well. I kept replaying everything in my mind, going all the way back to the mysterious phone call Katherine had received shortly after she arrived. She'd gone out right afterward. Then on Sunday, she'd met with someone. At the time, I'd thought it was a boyfriend, but what if it was something else? Something sinister? It was possible. It was also possible she was frightened like Ben was, but she seemed more angry than frightened. In any case, she was certainly hiding something.

Peggy was already at work when I arrived, and I pulled her into my office and shut the door. I told her that Katherine had identified the two men in the photo.

"That's great," Peggy said. "What did she say about them?"

I tossed the packets of photos minus the ones I had in my pocketbook onto my desk. "Not much except for their names." I filled her in on Katherine's reaction to my questioning.

"Wow. What do you make of it?"

"That's just it." I slipped into my chair. "I don't know whether it was a threat or a warning. Neither one makes any sense to me. She's been friendly up until last night, and I don't understand the change. Sure, she's been secretive about where she goes or who's telephoning her, but why wouldn't she be? She's only known me a little over a week—I'm practically a stranger to her. And she's been really good with Lily, letting her borrow records. I honestly don't know what to think."

Peggy half sat on the corner of my desk. "She seemed nice enough when we went to the Starlight, but you're right, you don't know much about her. What are you going to do?"

I hadn't known until that very minute. An idea suddenly came to me. "My afternoon is clear, isn't it?"

"Yeah. So far, anyway."

"Good. I have a plan."

After telling Peggy what I was thinking, I organized a few things I wanted to do that morning, then went to the kitchen and poured a cup of coffee for myself and one for Peggy. She was at her desk going through some ads that local businesses had sent in. Much of our revenue came from ads. Although our circulation was growing, the money from that wouldn't cover all the bills. I left her to it.

While I sipped my coffee, I checked the war news from the wire. Not exactly good news from yesterday. The Japanese had completed their takeover of Burma. I was sure most Americans didn't even know where that was. I certainly wouldn't have known before the war began. If nothing else, everyone was getting a geography lesson almost daily.

On an even sadder note, the last of the residents of Japanese descent had been removed from San Francisco. Most of the time I agreed with Roosevelt's policies, but not this one. It was wrong to remove people from their homes and send them away. Many of these people had been born in this country and were loyal citizens. Some of them spoke no Japanese—all they knew was English. They were losing their homes, their businesses, their livelihood, their friends—everything they'd ever known. Why should they be punished because of their ancestry? It made no sense to me. It didn't to Pop either. He had gotten a lot of flak when he wrote an opinion piece against it when the order first came out. A few people he'd known for years and thought were his friends were vehemently in favor of Roosevelt's decree, almost to the point where they believed the only good Japanese was a dead one. Pop said if they felt that way, they'd never been real friends anyway.

I decided a new editorial was in order. I loaded a sheet of paper into my typewriter. The words came as fast as my fingers could type, putting my thoughts of the last couple of minutes down on paper. It was the first editorial I'd written since Pop had put me in charge. When I read it over, I couldn't help thinking he'd be proud.

I got up and took the article out to Peggy. "Tell me what you think of this," I said.

Peggy read more slowly than I did, and I impatiently tapped my foot. She looked up. "Go and get another cup of coffee. That tapping is driving me crazy. It'll take me twice as long to read this with you standing there hovering."

"I'll get one for you too." I took both cups to the kitchen and returned a few minutes later.

"Are you sure you want to stir this up?" Peggy took the cup I handed to her.

"Positive. It's what Pop would do."

"If you're sure. It's really good, and I agree one hundred percent. But we might lose a few customers over it."

"I'll take the chance," I said. "I can't let it go, just like I can't let the recent incidents with Sam and Ben go."

Peggy nodded. "I'll take it down to Donny for tomorrow's paper. Or would you rather put it in the weekend edition?"

"Let's do the weekend. Circulation is higher for that one." I smiled. "More people to want to tar and feather me."

"Don't joke about that!"

"Who's joking?" I went back to my office to finish my other tasks.

* * *

After lunch I headed up the street to Thrift Drug. Chances were the clerk who had been working the other day was in school, but I hoped he was there. If I showed him the picture of Richard Adler and John Smith, he might recognize one of them. I was disappointed that Mildred was working instead. I liked her well enough, but she wouldn't be able to help.

"Hi, Mildred."

"Hello, Irene. What brings you in? I don't think I have any photographs here for you."

"Yeah, I know. I actually had a question for the kid who was working here last Saturday."

"Oh, that would be Mikey. Is there a problem?"

"Not at all." I didn't want to explain the whole thing. "He said he and his friends were joining the service after graduation, and I wanted to get some more information."

"That's so nice of you!" She looked at the calendar hanging on the wall behind her. "Mikey's working later today. He'll be in at four. Should I tell him to contact you?"

"I'll just stop back. Thanks."

My next stop was Ava's. She said she hadn't gotten a good look at the man who had painted the swastika on Sam's door, but seeing a picture might jog her memory.

Ava was in the middle of giving Mrs. Miller a permanent wave, and the place stunk to high heaven. "I'll be with you in a minute, Irene," she said.

I waited by the door, hoping I wouldn't pass out from the fumes. Five minutes later Ava came over. "How can you breathe that in all day?" I asked.

Ava shrugged. "You get used to it. When are you going to let me make you a blonde?"

"No thanks," I said. "I'll keep my natural color."

"Your loss. What can I do for you, then?"

I told her and showed her the picture of Richard Adler and John Smith. She studied it for a minute or two and finally shook her head.

"I'm sorry. I just can't tell if either of them is the person I saw. I only saw him from the back."

That was strike two. I stopped at home to get Pop's car and headed to my third stop, hoping it wouldn't be strike three. When I pulled up to the Tabor offices, I was surprised to see Chief Turner's car and an ambulance there. I quickly parked in a spot marked GUEST and went inside. No one was in the lobby, so I headed toward Wilfred Tabor's office at the end of the hall. As I got closer, I heard voices and hysterical crying. I hurried up.

Mr. Tabor's secretary, Miss Lewis, was sitting behind her desk, sobbing. Something terrible must have happened.

"Miss Lewis," I said. "What's going on?"

She sobbed louder and pointed to her boss's office. Two ambulance attendants stood in the doorway, and I spotted the heads of my future father-in-law and Arnold Moss. I walked that way and saw Doc Atkins. That could mean only one thing. Someone was dead.

Chapter Nineteen

Largest Contingent of U.S. Troops Arrives in Ireland
—The Progress Herald, May 21, 1942

I squeezed between the two ambulance attendants and got a glimpse of Wilfred Tabor and blood before the chief spotted me. He pointed to the attendants. "Get her out of here."

A hand clamped down on my shoulder, and I was unceremoniously guided out of the office and plunked into a chair near Miss Lewis.

"You shouldn't go in there," she said. "It's . . . it's . . . horrible." She shuddered. "Poor Mr. Tabor."

I hated to admit it to myself, but I was a little shaken after seeing the blood on the floor. "What happened?"

Miss Lewis shook her head. "I don't understand it. Why didn't he say anything? Why didn't he tell me?"

Something told me Miss Lewis was much more than Mr. Tabor's personal secretary. I touched her arm. "He meant a lot to you, didn't he?"

She delicately dabbed at her nose with a handkerchief. "We were very close. I've worked for him for over twenty years."

"I can see how much you cared for him."

"Oh, I do. I did. He was a wonderful man. So kind. So considerate."

It hadn't been considerate when he just about threw me out of his office.

Miss Lewis began crying again. "I don't know why he did this. I could have helped him. I could have saved him."

I felt a lump in my throat as I realized what she meant. "How could you have saved him?"

"Something must have been troubling him. He hadn't been himself for months. He was even short with me, and that had never happened before. I thought it was just the pressure of all the new production with the war and all. I should have asked him, talked to him about it. I just never thought . . ."

Chief Turner came out of Tabor's office and motioned to me. I got up and followed him a few feet down the hall.

"You shouldn't be here, Irene."

"I came to talk to Mr. Tabor," I said. "I didn't know something had happened to him."

"You should go back to work."

"I'm working now," I said. I doubted he would have told Pop to go back to the paper. As awful as it was, I still had a job to do. "What happened to Mr. Tabor?"

"It appears he took his own life. It must have happened late last night. His secretary found him. He had planned to come in late this morning, so she didn't think anything of it. When she needed a file from his office, she took her key and unlocked the door. He was on the floor, still holding the gun he'd used."

My stomach churned. How terrible. "No one saw or heard anything? No one thought to check when he was late coming in?"

"I don't know that yet. I'll be talking to anyone who was working last evening. I don't know any more than that." He excused himself and went back to work.

I went outside and sat in the car for a while. I hadn't really known Mr. Tabor aside from the few interactions we'd had. Other than how he'd behaved at my last visit, he seemed like a good person. I couldn't even imagine what must have gone through his mind. What would happen to the company now? Who would be in charge? That was an important thing to know.

I got out of the car and went back inside. I expected Arnold Moss to still be with the chief, but he was sitting in his office, talking on the telephone. He saw me approaching and told whoever he was talking to that he had to go.

"It's a sad day, Irene," he said.

"Yes, it is. I'm sorry to bother you, but I do need a statement. Unfortunately, this will be big news."

Moss nodded. "Of course. Have a seat."

I took my ever-present notebook and pencil out of my pocketbook. "What can you tell me about what happened?"

"What did Chief Turner tell you?"

"He told me he was investigating."

Moss leaned forward and folded his hands on his desk. "Nothing to investigate, in my opinion. It's obvious what happened. Wilfred couldn't take the stress anymore."

"Did you know he was so despondent?"

"Don't you think I would have stopped him if I thought that?" He didn't wait for an answer. "Looking back now, there were signs. I missed them. Hell, everybody missed them. Even Miss Lewis. He worried over the most minor things, like if the employees enjoyed working here. I told him you can't worry about that when you're running a business—especially when we're getting by on the slimmest of margins. You can't make everyone happy, no matter how hard you try."

"That's a rather callous attitude," I said.

"It sounds that way, but it's business. I like to see happy faces as much as the next guy, but it's not like the old days, especially now."

I understood that. Sort of. "So Mr. Tabor didn't like change?"

"No, he didn't," Moss said.

"Can I get a quote from you for the paper?"

He thought about it briefly. "How about this? Wilfred was a good man. He lived and breathed this place, and the Ironworks will never be the same without him. He will be sorely missed, but we will do our best to carry on without him."

I'd give Moss one thing. He was good at coming up with quotes. He knew exactly what to say. "Who will take over for Mr. Tabor?"

Moss seemed surprised by the question. "I will, of course. That's what Wilfred wanted. Is there anything else?"

It appeared I was being dismissed. "As a matter of fact, there is." I put my notebook away and retrieved two photographs from my pocketbook. I passed the picture of Moss that Peggy and I had joked about across the desk. "I found this in some pictures our photographer took and thought you might like to have it."

"That's a pretty good picture of me," he said. "I might get this framed and hang it on the wall."

Wait until I tell Peggy.

"Thank you, Irene." He smiled. "Are you doing anything this evening?"

He never gave up, even after today's tragedy. "I am. I'm going home and having dinner with my mother and my sister. Besides, won't you be a little busy with the aftermath of Mr. Tabor's death?"

"I would make time for you."

"I'm sorry, but no." I passed the other picture to him. "Who is this man with Ben Cline?"

He studied the picture for a moment. "I don't know. He looks familiar, so I assume he works here. Cline is the janitor, right?"

"Yes. He's the one who got hurt and had to have his leg amputated."

Moss slid the picture back to me. "Terrible thing to happen." He stood up. "I have to get back to work, if there's nothing else."

I was happy to leave. It would be different here now that Mr. Tabor was gone and Moss was in charge. Tabor Ironworks would never be the same. I had a feeling Moss would change things dramatically. I wasn't sure that would be for the better.

* * *

I went back to the *Herald*. After I informed the staff of what had happened, I closed myself in my office to write the article on Mr. Tabor's death. I planned to keep it general and simply state that he had been found deceased. I wouldn't even hint that it had been by his own hand. There were some things people had no right knowing. There would be gossip, but I was sure Arnold Moss would quickly put a stop to it. It might be bad for business.

When I finished the article, I sat back and rubbed my temples. I hadn't accomplished a single thing I'd set out to do today. I was at a loss for what to do next. I thought I'd narrowed down who had targeted Sam and Ben, but I had no proof. Arnold Moss wouldn't be much help. He wouldn't do anything that would affect his bottom line. If he'd recognized Richard Adler in the photo, he'd given no sign of it. He'd barely recognized Ben Cline. I had hoped Katherine would have helped with that, but not after last night. I didn't want to think she was involved, but I had to admit it was a possibility. Short of charging into the factory and confronting Adler and John Smith, I was out of ideas.

I was no closer to finding Moe's murderer than I'd been days ago. I still needed to go back to his house and search again. Since I had no plans after dinner, tonight might be a good time. I got up, opened my door, and asked Peggy what she was doing later.

"I told Ken I'd go to the Progress High baseball game with him. Why?"

"I want to take another look at Moe's. See if there's anything we missed."

"You shouldn't go by yourself," she said. "I can cancel with Ken. He won't mind."

I shook my head. "No, you go to the game. Maybe Sylvia would come with me. There might be some things she wants anyway." I had no intention of calling Sylvia. Even if I wanted to, I didn't have any way to reach her. I couldn't do a thorough search with her looking over my shoulder.

"Where are you going?" Donny asked, making me jump.

"Nowhere you need to know about," I said, annoyed that he was listening in on our conversation again.

"Sheesh. I'm just asking. I could go with you."

"You don't even know where I'm going. Or do you?"

He didn't answer the question. "I need your article on old man Tabor."

I retrieved it for him. As he walked away, I winked at Peggy. "I think I'll skip going over there tonight. I'm kind of tired. The chance of finding what Moe was working on is slim anyway."

Peggy caught on. "Good idea."

As soon as Donny was gone, I said, "That should keep him out of my hair."

"You hope. He needs more to do. He's always lurking around and listening in on everyone's conversations."

"It's not just me?"

Peggy shook her head. "He reminds me of the tattletales in school who were always listening for things to tell the teacher."

"But who's he going to tattle to? I'm the boss."

"Good question. Do you think he's writing to your dad?"

"If he was, Pop would put a stop to it. I think he's just nosy. He wants to be a reporter. He's thinking if he gets a big scoop, he'll make a name for himself. The problem is he's not a good writer. The article would sound like it belongs in one of those pulp rags. But I agree he might need more to do." I told her my idea of letting him do some of the accounting.

"Can you trust him with that?" Peggy asked.

"I was worried about that when he took it upon himself to start the payroll this week. I planned on asking your father to look at the ledger, but I checked, and Donny actually did a good job with it. Maybe he wouldn't be such a pain in the rear if he had more responsibility."

"It's worth a try."

Peggy's phone rang, and I went into my office and grabbed my pocketbook. I had one more stop to make before calling it quits for the day.

* * *

Mikey, the clerk, was on his knees stocking the soap shelves when I returned to Thrift Drug. He looked up when I said his name.

"It's Mike," he said. "I'm a little too old to be called Mikey. Mildred is my next-door neighbor, and she still thinks I'm six."

I smiled. I had wondered about that. "Mike it is, then. I don't know if you remember, but I was in last week asking about some photos."

"I remember." Mike straightened up a row of Lifebuoy. "You're the newspaper lady. You were supposed to send someone to talk to me and my buddies."

"Yes. Someone will. It's been a busy week." I'd send Ken to get the information. "If I showed you a picture of who might have asked about those photos, would you recognize him?"

He gave me a puzzled look. "I thought you said the guy worked for you."

"Well, he did . . . he does, but he wasn't the one who came in. And I'm trying to figure out who it was. Would you take a look?"

"Sure." He stood, and I handed him the photo of Katherine, Sylvia, and Betty with Richard Adler and John Smith.

He pointed to Katherine and whistled. "She's a looker. I wish she'd have stopped in."

I didn't mention that she was too old for him.

He studied the picture and pointed to John Smith. "It might have been that guy, but I dunno. He wasn't dressed like that, and he wore a hat."

"Have you seen either of them in here since then?"

"I don't think so. Wait, let me see that again." He took another look. "That other guy was in here with a lady, but not the ones in the picture."

"Can you describe her?"

"I'm not very good at that. Let's see. She was older. Older than you but not real old."

That really told me a lot. That would be a third or more of the town.

"She wasn't pretty like the girls in the picture. And she wore her hair kind of old-fashioned."

"Old-fashioned? Like how?"

"Pulled up on top of her head and twisted into a little ball."

"A bun?"

"I guess that's what you call it."

"Thanks, Mike. You've been very helpful. I'll be sure to send a reporter to talk to you soon."

I left the store convinced I was on the right track. I didn't have any proof yet, but I believed Richard Adler and John Smith were the ones targeting Sam and Ben, and if Moe had photographs to prove whatever was going on at the Ironworks, they were also responsible for Moe's murder. Thanks to Mike, I now knew there might be a woman involved. A woman who wore her hair in a bun. I knew of only one who wore her hair that way—Vivian Anderson.

Chapter Twenty

Last Japanese Evacuated From San Francisco
—*The Progress Herald*, May 21, 1942

I was surprised to see Katherine sitting with Lily on the front porch when I got home. I hadn't realized she wasn't working today. Lily was stretched out on the floor with her sketchbook in front of her. Katherine laughed at something Lily said—I couldn't hear what it was. Lily jumped up when she saw me coming.

"Katherine let me draw her picture."

"She improvised quite a bit," Katherine said. "I don't own a dress like that."

Lily shoved her drawing in front of me. It was a picture of Katherine in a long slinky gown standing in front of a microphone. She wore a flower in her hair and elbow-length gloves. "Very nice," I said.

"And don't worry," Lily said. "I have most of the posters ready for the scrap drive and a couple of small ones for the *Herald*, if you still want to put them in."

"Of course I do," I said. "I'll take them with me tomorrow."

She closed her sketchbook. "I'd better go in and start my homework before Mom finds out it's not done yet." She ran into the house.

"Did she just volunteer to do homework?" Katherine asked.

"She did."

"Irene, I want to apologize for how I acted last night. I was tired and frustrated and I took it out on you. I shouldn't have snapped at you like that. I get caught up in my own problems and forget that you've lived here all your life and are only trying to help people who are your friends and neighbors. I would do the same thing."

I wasn't sure whether to believe her or not. I didn't think her attitude last night had been due solely to her being tired. I took a seat in the chair beside her. "Frankly, what you said sounded like a threat."

"I certainly didn't mean it that way."

"Then tell me what's going on."

"There's something—"

Mom peeked out the front screen door. "Dinner's almost ready."

Katherine stood. "We'll talk later."

"Wait." I got up too. "Did you hear what happened today?"

She shook her head. "In town?"

"At the plant. Wilfred Tabor is dead. His secretary found him this afternoon."

"That's terrible," she said. "Did he have a heart attack?"

"Chief Turner is investigating, but it appears he took his own life. They found a gun in his hand."

Katherine turned white and dropped into her chair. "Oh my God."

Her reaction caught me off guard. "What is it?"

She shook her head.

"You're not telling me something," I said. "What is going on?"

She took a deep breath, and the color returned to her face. She pushed out of the chair. "Tell your mother I'm sorry, but I can't stay for dinner."

"Are you going to tell me what's going on?"

"I can't. Not now." She went inside and grabbed her handbag from the table in the hall. "I don't know when I'll be back." She hurried to her car, which was parked on the street, and sped off. Seconds later the only sign of Katherine was the dust swirling through the air.

What in the world was that all about? One minute it seemed like she was ready to talk, and the next minute she was speeding away. She'd seemed fine until I told her about Mr. Tabor's death. I didn't understand her reaction to the news. It was sad that he'd died, but Katherine was taking it almost as hard as Miss Lewis had. Something wasn't adding up.

Lily came to the door to say that dinner was on the table. "Where's Katherine?"

"Your guess is as good as mine."

* * *

All through dinner, Lily kept speculating on where Katherine had gone. I was mostly silent and happy to escape when it was over. While Lily helped Mom in the kitchen, I hollered that I was going over to Peggy's, picked up my pocketbook, and left. I wasn't going to Peggy's, though. I was heading to Moe's.

It was a brisk fifteen-minute walk to his house. The yard was a little more unkempt than it had been last week. The front door was locked, so I went around to the back where I'd entered the last time. The kitchen reeked of old garbage and spoiled food. If there was evidence in here, I'd need a gas mask to look for it. Since I didn't have a gas mask, I propped open the door and cracked the window. The previous intruder had already made a mess of the cabinet and drawer contents, so I didn't feel bad doing another search and messing it up more. Most of the cabinets were empty. It looked like Moe didn't believe in having more than a set of four dishes, all of which were dirty. There was one pot in the sink where the remains of whatever Moe had heated up last were growing something unintended. A cast-iron skillet on the stove was one of the few clean items.

There was a box of corn flakes in one cupboard. I took it down and looked inside. It was half-full, and I shook it to see if anything was hidden among the flakes. Nothing. I closed it and put it back. The next cupboard contained salt and pepper shakers and an empty sugar bowl. The only thing under the kitchen sink was a box of Lux soap and a dishrag.

Like almost every kitchen, this one had a junk drawer, but someone had already dumped the contents out onto the enamel top of the kitchen table. There was a pair of scissors, some tangled string, and a few pencils. I went through the silverware drawer, which at the moment held only a few clean items. The rest were in the sink.

I climbed on a chair and ran my hand across the top of the cabinets, but all I found was a lot of dust. I saved the icebox for last. Moe must have lived on corn flakes or ate out a lot, because the only thing in it when I got the nerve to open the door was a half-empty quart of milk. I assumed it was sour, but I wasn't about to verify that.

Finished with the kitchen, I moved on to the living room. There weren't many places to check here. Whoever had broken in had done a pretty good job of tearing things up. The bookcase that had been toppled over the last time I was here had been moved and was now lying on its back. The books were still scattered on the floor. I doubted I'd find anything in the books, but considering Moe had left me a note in one at work, I had to check. It took ten minutes to flip through two dozen books, partly because I had to read the dust jackets on several of them. There were no notes.

I went upstairs to Moe's office. Peggy and I had been through it already, but we might have missed something. There was a smaller bookcase here that had been knocked over. These books were mostly for reference, so it didn't take long to go through them. I came up empty once again. I sat down at Moe's desk to think. If I were going to hide something important, where would I put it? I scanned the room. There were no pictures on the walls, but Moe hadn't been the type to waste time decorating. I was at a loss.

I turned back to the desk and opened a drawer. Peggy and I had checked them all, and so had whoever had broken in, so I didn't know why I was doing it again. Suddenly I remembered something I'd seen in a detective movie. For the life of me, I couldn't remember the name of the movie, but the detective had found an envelope taped to the bottom of a drawer. I pulled the drawer all the way out and flipped it over. Nothing. I did the same thing to the remaining drawers and ended up disappointed.

When I replaced the bottom drawer, it stuck halfway in. I pulled it out, tried again, and the same thing happened. I slid the drawer out and placed it on the floor. Down on my hands and knees, I reached into the opening to see what was holding it up. There was something stuck in the drawer slide. I yanked on it and it came loose. It was three pages folded in quarters that appeared to have come from a notebook. Moe's stolen notebook, perhaps?

Excited, I sat back down in the desk chair. I'd started to unfold the paper when I heard a noise downstairs. I froze and listened. A cupboard door slammed closed. I stood and looked for a place to hide. Moe's bedroom closet. I slid the papers into my pocketbook and tiptoed to the next room, thankful that the floorboards didn't squeak. Once in the closet, I left the door open a crack to get a view of the hallway.

I heard footsteps on the stairs and backed up farther, wishing Moe's clothes hadn't all been tossed on the floor. The closet smelled like the aftershave he'd worn. My heart pounded so hard I could have sworn whoever it was would hear it. I breathed deep and slow to stop the pounding.

I'd almost managed to calm down when I got a glimpse of the intruder—my cousin Donny. I burst out of the closet, the door slamming into the wall. It gave me some satisfaction that he yelped and jumped a good foot in the air.

"Irene! You just scared the hell out of me. What are you doing here?"

"The better question is, what are you doing here?"

"You told Peggy you were going home. I didn't think you'd be here."

"You don't have permission to be here," I said. "You're breaking and entering."

"So are you."

"No, I'm not." Why was I arguing with him? "Really, why are you here?"

He crossed his arms over his chest. "For the same reason you are."

"I doubt that."

"I want to find what Moe was working on," Donny said. "Then maybe I'll have a chance."

"For what?"

"You know I want Moe's job. If I come up with a big story, you won't have any choice but to give me the job."

He sounded so pitiful that I almost felt sorry for him. "Donny, your talents lie in other areas. The *Herald* needs you right where you are. You're good at what you do."

"I know I am," he said. "But I want to do more."

"This is not the time or place to talk about this."

"There never seems to be a good time."

He might be right about that. Ever since we were kids, I'd avoided him as much as possible. He didn't make it easy to be nice to him when his attitude alternated between *Woe is me* and *I'm the greatest in the world*. But maybe I was being too hard on him. "We'll talk at the paper tomorrow."

"I don't believe you."

"I have an idea for something you can do."

"A reporting assignment?"

I didn't want to give him false hope, but I wasn't going to discuss it now. "We'll talk about it tomorrow."

Donny sighed. "Have you found anything?"

"No, I'm afraid not," I lied. "I was about ready to leave when you showed up."

"This place gives me the creeps."

"Me too," I said. "Let's get out of here."

* * *

Lily met me at the door when I got home to show me the drawings she had done for the *Herald*. One was a smaller version of the scrap drive poster she was making for the mayor. Two others encouraged people to plant victory gardens, and one was about rations. I hadn't realized she understood rationing better than most adults.

It drove me crazy that I didn't have the opportunity to even take a glance at the paper I'd found in Moe's desk. I sat in the living room with Mom and Lily, half listening to the *Kraft Music Hour*. My thoughts bounced around like the pinball in the machine in the arcade at Kennywood Park that Bill had insisted on playing on one of our visits there. I tried not to get my hopes up that there would be something of significance in what I'd found, but I couldn't help it. What if it was only paper Moe had stuffed in a drawer and it had somehow gotten stuck in the slide? I pushed that possibility out of my mind. If Moe had had the foresight and been worried enough to leave me the prior note, he had to have left something else. And this might be it. It had to be.

Mom and Lily finally went up to bed at ten. I waited long enough to be sure neither of them would be back down before I retrieved the paper from my pocketbook. I spread the pages out on the kitchen table. At first glance they didn't reveal anything I'd hoped for.

At the top of each page was a range of dates followed by rough columns of what looked like gibberish, and not entirely due to Moe's atrocious handwriting. There were letters and numbers, but none of them made any sense. Nothing was in any kind of alphabetical or numerical order. The first page had *4/19 to 4/25* written at the top. Underneath it was *L5 B628 3S A*. Below that was *L14 R353 2S S*. Each successive entry began with *L*, followed by letters and numbers. Page two was dated *4/26 to 5/2*, page three *5/3 to 5/9*. They had similar entries, all beginning with the letter *L*.

It appeared the *L* was important, but what did it stand for? I ran through a bunch of words in my mind: *level, land, limit.* None of those fit. It had to have something to do with Tabor Ironworks. I thought for a moment before I came up with the right word. *Line.* That was the only thing that made sense.

If I remembered correctly, Tabor currently had twenty-two production lines, up from their prewar ten, plus lines for packaging, shipping, and who knew what else. I looked at each page to see exactly what numbers followed the *L*. The numbers were out of order, but all of the twenty-two production lines were accounted for on every page. The *L* definitely stood for the production lines. So what did the other numbers mean? Some of the entries seemed incomplete, with zeros in the second column and dashes in the third column, whereas the others had *1S, 2S,* or *3S.*

Katherine came into the kitchen just then. I'd been so engrossed with my task I hadn't heard her come home. "That doesn't look like fun," she said.

"It's not." It was too late to hide the papers from her. I still didn't trust her, but she might be able to help.

She took a glass from the cupboard and filled it with water from the tap. "I'm sorry I ran off before. I was so shocked about Tabor's death, and there was someone who needed to know about it."

"Wouldn't a telephone call have been enough?"

"I'm afraid not." Katherine took a seat at the table. "I had to do it in person." She took a sip of water. "I know you have questions, and I've not been very forthcoming."

I didn't say anything. When Pop taught me about interviewing someone, he'd told me that people are uncomfortable with long silences and will sometimes tell you things they might not if you keep asking questions.

"I didn't mean what I said last night to sound like a threat," she said. "But I'm worried for your safety."

"Why?" I asked, before I remembered I was supposed to stay silent. *Sorry, Pop.*

"There's a lot I can't say," she said. "But something is going on at Tabor."

"I know that much."

Katherine lit a cigarette and took a slow drag. "I haven't been entirely truthful with you. I was sent to Tabor to see what's going on."

I rolled my eyes. "So now you've gone from being friends with Frank Sinatra to being a spy?"

"I'm not a spy. Not even close. But I do know Frank. That's the truth."

I didn't know what to believe.

"It's a long story," she said.

"I'm not going anywhere."

She took another pull on her Chesterfield and blew the smoke toward the ceiling. "Are you sure you want to hear this?"

I nodded. "I really do."

"Not long after Pearl, I started singing at some dive club in New York City, making peanuts. At the end of March, some guy approached me and said he'd pay me two hundred dollars to deliver a package for him. Two hundred is more than I made in six months. I knew I should question what was in the package, but all I could think about was the money. My rent was overdue and I barely had enough to buy groceries. If I took the gig, I could send some home to my mother, pay off a few bills, and catch up on my rent. Except it didn't work that way. Five minutes after I delivered the package, I was swarmed by agents and handcuffed."

I tried not to look shocked but apparently didn't succeed.

Katherine gave me a grim smile. "It's not only a long story, it's a sordid one."

"I'm sorry. What happened next?"

"I was given the option to cooperate or probably go to prison for a long time. I chose the former."

Chapter
Twenty-One

Tabor Ironworks President Dies Tragically
—The Progress Herald, May 22, 1942

I f given that choice, I would have done the same. Most people would. "What was in the package?"

"The agent showed it to me, but I still don't know. Documents of some kind and all in German. The only German word I know is *prost*. I'm sure that wasn't anywhere in those papers. It took several days to convince him I was just a singer and not smuggling something for the Nazis. That's when they made the offer."

"And they sent you here?" I asked. "Why?"

"Do you remember the Duquesne Spy Ring?"

"Of course I do. It was in the paper and on the radio daily." The members of the notorious spy ring had been recruited by Germany and taken various positions to gather information and possibly commit sabotage in the event of war with the United States. In January of this year they had been convicted and sentenced.

"That was the largest group," Katherine said. "There are smaller groups, mostly connected to the German American Bund, that the government has been keeping an eye on. Most of these men—and some women—have been living in this country for years but are still loyal to their homeland."

I was starting to get the picture. This had to be what Moe had discovered. It would have been the story of a lifetime for him. "So they think some of these men are working at Tabor?"

Katherine crushed out her cigarette in the ashtray. "They're sure of it. Someone informed the Pittsburgh office that there was a shipment of rivets heading to Dravo that were . . . I'm not sure of the right word . . . they were bad."

"Do you know who squealed?"

"I think we both have an idea of who it was."

"Ben Cline."

She nodded. "It's no coincidence that someone beat him up and then either pushed that machine on him or tampered with it in some way that it fell."

"He could be in danger. I need to tell the chief."

"It's been taken care of. One of the orderlies at the hospital isn't really an orderly. He's watching Mr. Cline."

My head hurt. This was almost too much to take in. "Wait a minute. I thought he was targeted because he's Jewish. Ben attends the same synagogue as Sam Markowicz, who owns the hardware store. He said others have gotten anti-Semitic messages as well."

"I don't know how or even if it's related. The only way we'll know is to catch these people," Katherine said.

I rubbed my temples. "I really wish you had told me all this earlier."

"I wanted to, but I couldn't. Mr. Tabor's death was the last straw. I told the agent I'm working for that I was going to talk to you. I haven't been able to give him anything of substance yet. I reminded him I wasn't trained for this crap. I'm a singer, for God's sake. He wasn't happy, but he didn't stop me."

"Maybe if we put our heads together, we'll figure it out."

Katherine sighed. "Part of me wishes I'd never agreed to this."

"You didn't have a choice. All you did was make a dumb mistake. They shouldn't have put the screws to you like that."

"It's water under the bridge now." She pointed to the papers I had spread out. "What's all that?"

I told her I'd found it stuck in Moe's desk drawer and what I'd come up with so far.

"Let me see." She pulled her chair closer, and I turned the papers around. She studied them for a minute. "The *L* is definitely *line*." She put her finger on the second entry on the first page. "This one. *L14* followed by the *R353*. The *R* could stand for *rivets*, but I don't know what the number means. It seems low, so it can't be the number produced."

"What about the other letters and numbers?" I asked.

Katherine stared at the page for a good two minutes. "I have no idea." She leaned back in her chair. "I know one way to find out."

"How?"

"Get myself assigned to one of those lines."

* * *

Despite talking until well after midnight with Katherine, I was up before Mom and Lily. Katherine was back on the daylight shift and had left early to see about changing her assignment. I had tried to talk her out of it. She was adamant about it, which made me worry all the more. I was angry that she had been put in that spot in the first place, all because of a momentary lapse in judgment.

I was the first one to arrive at the *Herald*. After putting a pot of coffee on to percolate, I went to my office to mull things over. I felt like I was close to a breakthrough and frustrated that I couldn't quite put it all together. I went over everything in my mind.

If Moe's papers were what Katherine and I thought they were, everything led to Tabor Ironworks—Ben Cline getting beaten up, the machine falling on him, Katherine being sent there because of reported sabotage. How had Moe found out? Had Ben talked to him? Then there were the anti-Semitic messages. How were they connected?

I wondered if Moe's notebook that had been stolen from Sylvia's contained more than these cryptic notes. There might have been more, but as careful as Moe had been with what I'd found, I doubted anyone would have been able to make heads or tails of it. I still didn't know what had happened to the photos Moe had taken when he borrowed Matt's camera. If he had taken them out of town to be developed, there was no telling where they were. If they had been found, they would have been destroyed by now.

Thinking about photos, I suddenly remembered what Mike at Thrift Drug had told me. One of the men—Richard Adler—had been in the store with a woman who wore her hair in a bun. It had to be Vivian Anderson. No one else wore their hair that way in this day and age. When we met at the diner, Vivian had struck me as a practical, down-to-earth person. Maybe she and Adler were just friends, but he seemed like odd company for her to keep. I needed to ask Katherine about it. Or Sylvia, but I had no idea when she was working.

I also needed to talk to Ben Cline again. If he was the one who had blown the whistle to the feds, he might be able to decipher

Moe's notes. I had to figure out how to talk to him without being thrown out of the hospital.

That would all have to come later. I heard staff beginning to arrive. Right now, I had work to do and a paper to run.

* * *

The morning flew by with getting articles written, editing six articles by Rex, Frank, and Ken, and proofing ads that Peggy had put together for the weekend edition. It was almost lunchtime when I asked Peggy to send for Donny. After our conversation at Moe's house, it was time to give him more responsibility. If nothing else, it would free up some of my time and hopefully get him off my back about doing some reporting.

Peggy raised an eyebrow. "You're going to do it? Give him the payroll?"

This was the first chance we'd had to talk. I hadn't told her yet that I'd gone to Moe's house. "Yeah."

"Are you sure? I don't know that it's a good idea."

I filled her in on running into Donny at Moe's and how my cousin wanted to do more.

"Well, the worst that can happen is he messes it up and you're back to doing it yourself," she said.

"Unless you want to take it over."

"No way. I have enough trouble keeping things straight with ads and subscriptions. I don't need Rex and Frank badgering me about their paychecks. Donny can have it." She leaned over my desk. "Did you find anything at Moe's?"

"A couple sheets of paper in the back of a desk drawer that didn't amount to anything." I felt terrible not telling my best friend my theory or about Katherine, but we had decided last night that the fewer the people who knew about the papers, the better. Moe had gotten killed because of what he had found out. Katherine had sworn me to secrecy about her reason for being at Tabor. If anyone caught wind of it, she might very well be the next victim.

"That's too bad," Peggy said. "What are you going to do next?"

I shrugged. "I'm not sure."

"I'll try to think of something. In the meantime, I'll go get Donny."

Donny was all smiles when he entered my office instead of his usual dour, petulant self.

"Have a seat," I said. "I have a job for you."

"I knew you would finally see it my way. I'll be just as good as Moe. Even better."

Uh-oh. This was not good. "It's not a reporting job."

His face fell. "But you said—"

"I never said anything about you taking over for Moe. All I said was that we'd talk."

"Yeah, about a reporting job. I told you that's what I wanted." He was back to being petulant again.

"I have something more important in mind."

"I don't believe you."

"You say that an awful lot," I said. "Will you let me finish?"

Donny leaned back and crossed his arms over his chest. "Fine."

I told him what I had in mind. "I was pleasantly surprised you did such a good job with the payroll ledger."

He uncrossed his arms. "You want me to take care of the payroll?"

I could see he was warming to the idea. I played it up some more by telling him it was the most vital job there was. Everyone who worked here needed money, from the paperboys to the people down in the basement printing the paper.

"Will I be writing the checks as well?"

I'd known he'd ask that and had planned ahead. "No. Not yet, anyway. Pop has me as the only signer—besides him, of course. We can't change that with Pop overseas. Maybe when he comes back."

He nodded. "I understand. I have to say you surprised me, Irene. I never thought I'd get to do anything but lay out the paper. Thank you."

I almost fell out of my chair. My cousin, the perpetual pain in the butt, had actually thanked me.

"I won't let you down." He got up.

"I hope not," I said. And I hoped I was doing the right thing. More importantly, I hoped Pop would think I was.

*   *   *

After lunch, I had wanted to get out of the office briefly to at least try to see Ben Cline again, but it wasn't to be. News came over the wire that Mexico had declared war on Germany, Italy, and Japan. It was all hands on deck to get articles written for the weekend edition. I called Pop's friend in the War Department to get a quote. I sent Rex out to get some man-on-the-street reactions, and Frank talked to Mayor Young. We could have just used the Associated Press article, but our readers liked it when we got the local angle too. Donny wasn't happy he would have to rearrange things, but when I made the comment that maybe he was too busy to take on another duty, he shut up.

Later in the afternoon Matt came into my office. "Busy day, huh?" he said.

"Sort of."

"I wanted to check and see what time you wanted me for the victory garden thing tomorrow."

"I plan on getting there about nine. Frank is covering it too. The mayor is supposed to break ground at ten, but he'll probably give a speech first. I hope there's a good turnout. And I hope the rain stops." It had been drizzling all day.

"I wouldn't worry about the turnout. I'm pretty sure the whole town will be there. No one's gonna want to look like they don't want to do their part for the war."

"You're probably right," I said. "My mother said the garden during the last war was the talk of the county."

I opened the bottom drawer of my desk and pulled out the envelopes containing Matt's photographs. "I kept a few pictures. I hope you don't mind."

He took the envelopes from me. "Don't mind at all. Did they help?"

"I'm not sure yet. Time will tell."

"It's a shame about old man Tabor," he said. "He seemed like a jake kind of guy. Why do you think he did it?"

"I wish I knew. He had so much going for him."

Matt nodded. "Maybe the stress of running the place and the increased demand from the government got to be too much."

"Maybe."

After Matt left, I thought more about Mr. Tabor. Matt's question was a good one. Why would Tabor kill himself? He'd had everything. His company was successful, even more so with the extra production. And after adding Arnold Moss to be in charge of production, he should have been under less pressure, not more. Another thought popped into my head. Could Tabor have found out about the sabotage? Maybe it had been too much for him, thinking his company would be ruined if word got out. I wasn't sure that made sense. As far as I knew, he was an upstanding citizen. Like Matt said, he was jake. If he'd been worried about bad press, he would have gone to the authorities to report it. No, he couldn't have known about it, not unless . . . I didn't even want to consider the possibility, but the thought nagged at me. What if he *had* known and his death wasn't a suicide at all? What if he'd been murdered?

Chapter
Twenty-Two

Mexico Declares War on Germany, Italy, and Japan
—The Progress Herald, May 23, 1942

That wasn't possible. It just couldn't be. Miss Lewis had told the police his door had been locked and she had found him when she unlocked it. She could have been mistaken, but knowing the little I did about her, that wasn't likely. The chief would have found some evidence that Tabor hadn't shot himself. It was a ridiculous notion. I was letting my imagination run wild.

Peggy peeked in at the end of the day to ask if I wanted to go get a drink with her and Ken, but I told her I still had a few things to do to get ready for tomorrow. A drink sounded great after the long day, but I wanted to get home. I was anxious to hear how Katherine had fared at work and if her request to be put on a production line had been granted.

On the walk home, I saw that Markowicz Hardware was open, so I decided to make a quick stop and see Sam. No one was in the store at the moment, and Sam was sorting screws and putting them into boxes according to size.

"Hello, Irene," he said when he looked up. "I have to sort these almost every day. No one puts them back in the correct boxes. I do not know why. The boxes are marked."

"Some people just don't care, I suppose."

"Perhaps you are right. Or they might be in a hurry, or thinking about something else." He straightened up. "No matter. What can I do for you?"

"Nothing," I said. "I'm on my way home, and I wanted to see how you were doing."

"I am fine. Do you have any news?"

I felt bad telling him I didn't.

"I understand," he said.

I asked him how Ben was.

"Benjamin was released from the hospital today."

"Already? I thought he'd be there a while yet."

"He insisted on leaving." He smiled. "And Sarah and I insisted he stay with us. He is still weak, although he will not admit it."

"Has he said any more about what happened to him?"

"No. He is very stubborn."

That was an understatement. I wondered if Ben was still in danger. I didn't know how one of the agents would be able to watch him now.

"Benjamin does not like the idea, but there will be someone from the hospital coming to see him every day to change his dressing and see if he needs anything."

"That's good. I'd like to stop and see him sometime this weekend." Ben wouldn't dare try to throw me out of Sam's house. Sarah would never stand for it.

Sam smiled again. "That would be just the medicine he needs. Come anytime you'd like."

*　*　*

I smelled tuna casserole the minute I entered the house. Some people don't like it, but it happened to be one of my favorites, at least the way Mom made it—noodles, tuna, mushroom soup, and lots and lots of cheese. My mouth watered. I dropped my pocketbook in the hallway and went into the kitchen. I gave Mom a kiss on the cheek. "That smells heavenly."

Mom smiled. "It will be ready soon."

"What can I do to help?"

"You can heat the green beans."

I got the can opener out of the drawer. "Where's Lily?"

"She went to Cindy's house. She's staying there overnight and will meet us in the square in the morning."

We chatted about my day while we finished getting dinner together. I was setting the table when Katherine came in.

"How was your day?" I asked her.

"Not too bad. I did get reassigned. We'll have to talk about it later." She went upstairs to clean up and change.

Eating dinner seemed to take forever. Mom filled us in on some activities she was arranging for wives and mothers of the men in the service. Even though Pop was a correspondent and not in the service, they considered Mom to be one of them. Correspondents were often on the front lines and in just as much danger as the soldiers. I tried not to think about that. I was happy Mom had those women for support. She had tried to get me to join them. I appreciated it, but my time was better served making sure the *Herald* was still around when Pop got back.

I was helping Mom with the dishes when Katherine asked if I wanted to join her for a walk. Mom said she'd finish, since we were almost done. The rain had stopped, but it was chilly, so I lifted a sweater from the coatrack in the hallway, and Katherine and I headed out.

"That was the longest dinner ever," I said as we started down the street.

Katherine laughed. "Not quite the longest. You haven't suffered through a meal with a bandleader and a couple of musicians vying to top each other with the most outrageous story. Come to think of it, I'd probably win that one now. The trouble is no one would believe me."

"I'd back you up." I pulled my sweater tighter. I hoped the chill in the air didn't mean rain for tomorrow. "What happened today?"

"It was mostly uneventful," she said. "The foreman put me on line fourteen. Vivian Anderson was on the line with me. I didn't see Adler or Smith."

I was disappointed. "So nothing happened?"

"I didn't say that."

We reached the park behind Progress Elementary School and sat down on a bench. "Well?"

"There was another accident this afternoon. There's a section in the plant where they coat the bolts and rivets in this hot—I don't know exactly what. Aluminum, maybe? One of the cables that holds the buckets of this hot liquid snapped. Fortunately, the bucket was almost empty at the time, or a lot of people would have been hurt. It's going to set back production for a few days until they get it repaired."

"Do you think it was sabotage?"

"Maybe. They're supposed to check the cable to see why it snapped. Those cables are an inch thick. I don't understand how it would break like that or even what someone would have to do to one to make it break. Or how anyone could do it without being seen."

"But it's not impossible," I said.

"No, it's not." Katherine lit a cigarette.

"I forgot to tell you something last night." I told her about showing the clerk at Thrift Drug the pictures and how he'd recognized Richard Adler. "He said Adler was with a woman who wore her hair in a bun."

"Well, that's interesting."

"I thought so," I said. "The only person I've ever seen around here who wears her hair that way is Vivian Anderson. Do you think she and Adler are seeing each other? Could she be involved in this?"

"We're not even sure Adler and Smith are involved yet. But now that I'm working beside Vivian, I can try and find out."

"Please be careful."

"I will." She smiled. "That's exactly what Frank told me when I got into this mess."

"Frank? Sinatra?"

"Of course."

I still wasn't sure I believed she knew him. "You do know he's married, don't you?"

"We're just friends. We see each other on the rare occasions we're in the same city and talk on the telephone sometimes. There's no hanky-panky involved. I think that's why we got to be friends. After he got it through his head I wasn't going to sleep with him, he relaxed. There are more than enough women who will hop into bed with him. I don't need to be one of them."

"This is none of my business, but why didn't you ask him for help when you needed money instead of delivering that package from a stranger?"

Katherine dropped her cigarette stub onto the ground and crushed it out with her foot. "This probably sounds dumb, but I didn't want him to know. I didn't want him to think I wasn't successful and was only friends with him because he's Frank Sinatra. He was really mad when he found out what happened."

"Couldn't he help you out now?"

"And do what?" She laughed. "Believe me, he offered. The last thing I needed was for him to be arrested for offering someone a bribe—or worse. I told him in so many words to stay out of it. I got into it myself and I'll get out of it myself. I think he respects me for it."

"It's good to have a friend like that."

"It is."

We sat in silence for a while. I finally pushed off the bench. "We'd better get back before Mom sends out a search party."

Katherine got up. "We certainly wouldn't want that."

On the way home I mentioned that Ben Cline was out of the hospital and staying at the Markowiczes' and that I planned to stop and see him sometime this weekend. With the event in town tomorrow and articles that would need to be written about it, I hoped I'd be able to fit it in. Katherine offered to go with me if we could do it after she got home from work. We made a tentative plan for tomorrow evening.

I went up to bed early, happy to have a room to myself for a change. As much as I loved my younger sister, sharing a room with her wasn't always easy. I wrote a quick letter to Bill to put in the mail in the morning. I drifted off to sleep thinking about him and what our life would be like after the war was over.

* * *

Mom gave me a look of disapproval when I entered the kitchen for breakfast. "Is that what you're wearing?"

"Yes. What's wrong with it?" I planned on helping to dig and plant vegetables, so I was wearing dungarees, a red blouse, and saddle shoes with white anklets. My hair was tied back with a scarf. Mom, on the other hand, wore a lemon-yellow cotton dress. Freshly starched.

"It's not very ladylike, or befitting of your position as the editor of the *Herald*."

I was amazed she'd actually mentioned my title for a change. "I can't very well dig and plant wearing a dress, or even nice slacks. I can get these dirty and not worry about it."

Mom handed me a plate of scrambled eggs and toast. "Should you be digging instead of covering the event for the paper?"

I buttered a slice of toast. "I can do both, and Frank will be there too."

"I don't know what your father would think about that."

I rolled my eyes. "Pop would do the same thing I'm doing. He'd be the first one in there with a shovel." Mom didn't reply because she knew it was true. Pop would have gotten more information planting vegetables alongside the others than he would have going around asking questions. I planned to do the same. "What will you be doing?" I asked my mother.

"I'm in charge of the lemonade stand."

That explained the yellow dress, a color she rarely wore.

"All the proceeds will go to the families in need," she said. "It was Ava's idea. She'll be at the booth with me."

I wondered if Ava would also be wearing yellow. That would not be a good contrast with her bright-red hair. Of course, clashing colors had never deterred her before. "I'll stop by to get a quote for the paper. Maybe Matt can take your picture."

Mom patted her hair. "That would be nice. It's for such a good cause. So many families are having difficulties because a loved one is off fighting the war."

I finished gobbling down my breakfast and put my plate in the sink. "That might be my quote right there." I kissed Mom on the cheek. "I'll stop by anyway."

After the chill the previous evening and my worry that it might rain, the morning turned out to be warm and sunny. It was only eight thirty and I had planned on getting there at nine, so I took a walk around the square. I chatted with those who arrived early. Roger Eckel and two of his stock boys were hanging red, white, and blue bunting around a small stage beside a cordoned-off area where the garden would be. Members of the Progress High School marching band were practicing off to the side of the stage. I couldn't tell what the song was, but I was sure it was something patriotic. I hoped the mayor hadn't invited Evelyn Quinn to sing the national anthem. Evelyn imagined herself another Kate Smith. The famous singer wasn't my cup of tea, but Evelyn wasn't even the tea leaves left in the bottom of the cup.

I spotted my future father-in-law across the square. He was coming down the steps of the police department accompanied by a young man I didn't recognize. I crossed the grass toward them. The chief—Dad—was pointing in various directions, and the man nodded at each one. At one point Dad slapped him on the shoulder and they both laughed. When the chief saw me, he waved.

"Good morning, Chief. I mean Dad," I said when I reached them.

He smiled. "Rally, this is Irene Ingram. She's engaged to my son, and she's the editor of the *Progress Herald*. Irene, this is Rally Johnson, our new patrolman."

New patrolman? I knew the chief had been interviewing candidates and he'd eventually hire someone to take Bill's place while he was away, but it hit me like a ton of bricks. It made Bill's absence all too real. All I could manage to say was, "Rally?"

Rally grinned. "Yep. My given name is Elmer, so you can see why I don't use that. I'm not sure where Rally came from, but I've been calling myself that since I could talk."

Rally was tall, maybe the tallest person I'd ever seen. He had to be at least six five. His hair was rust colored and his face was covered with freckles. I held out my hand. "Nice to meet you."

"Likewise," Rally said. "And before you ask, I did play basketball in high school."

I asked him where he was from.

"I grew up in a town near Pittsburgh called Clairton."

He was probably about the same age as Bill and me and I wanted to ask why he hadn't joined up, but it was none of my business.

The chief said, "Rally doesn't start until Monday, but he wants to get to know the town, so he's tagging along with me." He turned to his new officer. "I need to talk to Irene for a minute, if you don't mind."

"Sure thing, Chief. I'll take a walk around."

"I'm sorry that took you by surprise," the chief said. "I know Rally's dad. The kid wanted to join the army, but he's color-blind. He took it bad. He got a job in the coke works, but he's not cut out to work in the mill. I told his dad I'd give him a chance here and see what happens. I meant to tell you the other day that I'd hired someone but had other things on my mind."

"Like Tabor's death."

He nodded. "That's another thing I wanted to talk to you about." There was a long pause before he continued. "Don't take this the wrong way, but I don't want to see any of this in the paper."

"Any of what? I've already written about Tabor's death."

"Not this you haven't."

I had a funny feeling in my stomach. "What don't I know?"

He lowered his voice so no one would overhear. "The bullet that killed Tabor was shot from too far away. His death wasn't suicide. It was murder."

Chapter Twenty-Three

Japanese Land in Leyte Gulf, Occupy Leyte and Samar
—*The Progress Herald*, May 22, 1942

So I hadn't been wrong.

"You don't seem surprised," the chief said.

"I'm not. Not really. Tabor had everything to live for. Why would he kill himself when everything seemed to be going his way?" I didn't expect an answer, so I continued. "Is there a reason you don't want this in the paper?"

"I don't want anyone at the Ironworks knowing there's an investigation going on. At least not yet. I don't want the killer spooked into leaving town."

One big fact puzzled me. "Wasn't Tabor's door locked? Miss Lewis said she unlocked it to go in to get something and that's when she found him."

"She might have been confused. She was pretty shook up."

I asked if he'd heard about the accident at the Ironworks yesterday.

"Yep. It's good no one was hurt this time."

Ava Dempsey was heading our way. The chief said, "I'd better go find Rally."

I smiled. "Afraid of Ava?"

"You bet I am."

"Bye, Dad," I said. It felt a little more natural this time.

He walked away with a smile on his face.

"Hi, Ava," I said when she reached me.

Ava resembled a black-eyed Susan. Her dress was a golden yellow and she'd dyed her hair black. "Who was that young man with Chief Turner? I've never seen him before."

For once I knew something she didn't. "That was Rally Johnson, our new police officer."

"I wondered when the chief was going to wise up and get some help," she said. "He was being run ragged."

"He still has Jimmy."

"Like I said, he needed more help. What were you two talking about? It looked important."

Ava was the last person I'd tell anything to. "Nothing important. We were just shooting the breeze." I could tell she didn't believe me. I changed the subject. "What can you tell me about your lemonade stand? I'd like to write something up, and I'll send Matt around later for a picture."

* * *

Unfortunately, Evelyn Quinn sang her version of the national anthem. Before anyone's eardrums recovered, Mayor Young got up to speak. His speech was long and rambling, and he talked more about riding with Teddy Roosevelt in the Spanish-American War than the current war. I'd probably get booted out of town if

I told anyone I thought it was time for a new mayor, but it really was. Eight terms was more than enough. My thoughts wandered midspeech, and I noticed Sylvia had been talking to me only when she tugged on my arm. She was with Betty Riley.

Sylvia smiled. "Where were you off to? Dreaming about your fiancé?"

"Something like that." I couldn't tell her I was actually trying to figure out how someone had managed to kill Tabor without anyone seeing them. Through a locked door no less, if Miss Lewis had been correct. "Are you two here to help plant the garden?"

Betty giggled. "I'm not dressed for digging. I'm just going to watch." Betty looked downright summery in a cute little shorts outfit and wedge sandals. Some of the women around us were giving her disapproving glances, and Mrs. Crenshaw elbowed her husband when she caught him ogling.

Sylvia wore dungarees but looked glamorous anyway. It might have been because of the sunglasses and the way she'd tied her scarf around her head. I needed to get a scarf-tying lesson from her.

"I'm ready to pitch in," Sylvia said. "When is the windbag going to be finished?"

I laughed. "Don't let anyone hear you call him that. Don't you know he rode with Teddy Roosevelt?"

"Well, la-di-da," Sylvia said, laughing along with me. "So did my grandfather. I wonder if they knew each other."

Betty said, "I thought the president's first name was Franklin."

Sylvia and I laughed harder, and a couple of people shushed us. I motioned for the girls to follow me. I had already gotten the gist of the speech, and Frank was around somewhere, hopefully listening to the rest. Between us we'd get a quote or two to use. We moved to the shade of the town's hundred-year-old oak tree.

Betty shivered. "It's chilly in the shade. I should have brought a sweater."

"Maybe if you had actually worn some clothes, you wouldn't be cold," Sylvia said.

"You sound like my mother," Betty said. "I'm going to stand in the sun." She moved away from us.

"I heard about the accident yesterday," I said. "I'm happy no one was hurt."

"I was surprised no one from your paper showed up. I thought for sure I'd see you."

"I only found out last night when Katherine told me. They must want to keep it quiet, especially after Mr. Tabor's death."

Sylvia nodded. "I guess that kind of thing isn't good for the bottom line."

I wanted to ask her about Vivian but wasn't sure how to do it without raising suspicion. It would be better to wait. "Have you moved back into your apartment yet?"

"Not yet. To tell you the truth, I'm kind of spooked to move back in. I'm still staying with my sister. I'll need to buy some new things too, since they ruined everything. Have you made any progress tracking down whoever did it?"

"No, I haven't." It wasn't entirely a lie. I had a few leads and a theory, but that was it. I couldn't even ask her about the notes I'd found because of my promise to Katherine. "I'm not giving up, though."

"I didn't think you would. You reporters are like a dog with a bone. That's the way Moe was." She sighed. "I sure miss him."

I was glad she'd brought him up. I asked if she knew who Moe's landlord was, because someone needed to do something with his house. She didn't, and she suggested I watch his mail. Sooner or later he'd get a late-rent notice. I was embarrassed I hadn't thought of that. I hadn't even thought to check the stack that had been dropped through the mail slot in his front door. I'd have to do that as soon as possible.

Mayor Young had finished his long-winded speech by this time, and the high school band began playing "You're a Grand Old Flag." At least that's what I thought it was. I told Sylvia I'd see her later and headed toward the garden area. I met Frank and Matt on the way.

"Hi, fellas," I said. "Enjoying yourselves so far?"

"I'd rather be sitting on my duff listening to a Buccos game," Frank said. "How about you, Matt?"

Matt grinned. "I dunno. I'm getting some great shots of some good-looking dolls. There were a couple I'd like to get to know better."

I tried to look mad. "And how many of these pictures is the paper paying for?"

"None, I swear," Matt said. "Don't worry, I'm getting plenty for the paper."

"That reminds me," I said. "I promised Ava you'd get one of her."

He groaned. "Why'd you go and do that? I'll never get away from her."

I gave him a big grin and slapped him on the shoulder. "We all have to do our part for the war effort."

Frank laughed. "Better you than me, buddy. I'm off to get a quote from the mayor. I think I slept through his speech."

I shook my head and kept walking. Dan Petrie stood with a dozen people and was passing out shovels. Peggy and Ken were among them.

"This is going to be so fun," Peggy said.

Ken put his arm around her shoulder. "You might ruin that manicure."

"I don't mind. It's for a good cause."

"Listen up," Dan hollered. "The six of you I gave shovels to—you're the first crew. You don't have to dig deep. Just turn over the soil and break up the big clumps. The next six people will rake it out. After that I'll make the rows where we'll be planting. I need a dozen volunteers to plant the vegetables in the rows and a few more to mark what they are."

"Wow, he really has this planned," Peggy said.

"First crew, get to work!"

Ken said, "That's us. See you later, Irene."

While they turned over the soil, I walked over to Dan and volunteered to plant. "You can do some green peppers," he said. "I've already assigned tomatoes, carrots, potatoes, and squash. This is a great turnout. I was worried no one would show up."

"It looks like everyone in town wants to help." I was already composing an article in my head. "What's next after planting?"

"We'll have to water everything—and every day until the plants are established. Sam Markowicz supplied us with some hoses. I was worried we'd have to run them across the street, but there's a water hookup near the fountain over there." He pointed to the fountain in the middle of the square. "After that, we just have to keep up with weeding, and before you know it, we'll have some tasty produce."

"You make it sound easy."

"It is. Especially with this many people."

I wondered how many would lose interest after today. I hoped the fact that the government was encouraging everyone's participation would make a difference. So far, almost everyone was contributing to one thing or another, whether it was dropping off tin cans at the A&P or saving their bacon grease and cooking fat. I expected the upcoming scrap drive would have good participation as well.

Dan stepped over the rope around the edge of the garden to supervise the diggers, and I went to check on Mom and Ava's lemonade stand. Ava was off to the side chatting with a couple of women. They must have been admiring Ava's new color, because she was beaming and kept patting her curls.

Lily and her friend Cindy were behind the booth with Mom. Lily ran out to greet me when she saw me.

"The mayor said my posters are being printed and they'll be hung up around town as soon as they're done," she said. "Can you believe it? I'm going to be famous!"

I laughed and gave her a hug. "That's wonderful. I'll make sure Donny puts one of your drawings in the *Herald* this week."

Lily made a face. "Donny's a creep. He won't like it."

"Doesn't matter, kiddo. I'm the boss, remember?"

Mom held out a glass of lemonade for me. "It's on the house."

I took the lemonade and pulled a nickel out of my pocket. "That wouldn't be fair." I dropped the nickel into the jar on the table. I said hello to Lily's friend. Cindy blushed and mumbled something that might have been hello. She was as shy as Lily was outgoing. They made the perfect combination. If anyone could get Cindy to come out of her shell, it would be my sister.

"Walt stopped and introduced the new officer," Mom said. "Did you know about that?"

I shook my head. "I only found out this morning. I'm glad he has some help, but it will feel strange seeing someone else in uniform."

Mom reached out and patted my arm. "Don't you worry. This war will be over before you know it and Bill will be back home."

I swallowed the lump in my throat. I wasn't as sure as she was. I remembered all Pop's reasons that it wasn't going to be quick. The Japanese would rather die than surrender. Bill thought he'd be going to Europe and not the Pacific, but Hitler wouldn't be surrendering anytime soon either. I finished my lemonade and handed the glass to Lily, said good-bye, and moved on. Thirty minutes later I ended up back at the garden, where the group raking out the soil was finishing up.

Dan Petrie motioned to me. He showed me a dozen green-pepper plants and pointed to the far side of the garden. "You and your partner will plant these over there."

I was about to ask who my partner was when Sylvia sidled up to me. "Hey, partner," she said.

We chatted for a minute or two before Dan gave us both spades and the box full of pepper plants. We were the last ones given plants, and the people already planting carrots and potatoes seemed to be vying to see who could finish first. Dan caught wind of what they were doing, and I couldn't help laughing when he told them it wasn't a race and there was no prize for finishing first. They slowed down.

Sylvia and I worked quietly, digging holes with our handheld spades, gently placing each plant in a hole, putting the dirt back, and tamping it down. I put the last plant in the ground and patted down the dirt. I got up from my knees and stretched. "I'll give the tools back to Dan if you take the box," I said to Sylvia.

"Sure thing." She picked up the box and stepped over the rope.

I was a few seconds behind her when I heard angry voices coming from behind some bushes not far from the garden. I'm not ordinarily an eavesdropper, but I took a few steps closer to try to make out what they were saying. I stopped suddenly when I realized the voices weren't just angry. They were arguing in German.

Chapter Twenty-Four

Groundbreaking for Progress Victory Garden Huge Success
—The Progress Herald, May 24, 1942

I dropped the hand spades, and they clanked together when they hit the ground. I picked them up and rushed to the other side of the shrubs, but the men were gone. The noise must have scared them off. I scanned the area, but there were too many people milling around. Whoever it was had blended into the crowd. I asked several people if they had seen two men near the bushes, and they looked at me like I was nuts.

Virgil Curry was sitting on his bench near the Civil War memorial, and he waved me over. "I heard you ask about two men near the bushes. I seen them."

"Where did they go? What did they look like?"

"They went that way." He pointed toward a side street.

I took off running, hoping to catch them. The street was empty when I reached it. "Dammit." I rarely swore, but no other word would do right now. I went back to Virgil's bench and sat down.

"No luck?" he said.

"No luck. Did you get a good look at them?"

Virgil shook his head. "They was moving pretty fast. One of 'em looked a little familiar, but I don't know where I seen him before."

I wanted to scream, *Think!* but I knew it wouldn't help. "Does he come to the park? The bar?"

"I dunno. Maybe." He smiled all of a sudden. "He was wearing a cap! I seen that cap before."

A man wearing a cap and speaking German. "Was it the guy you saw by Sam's store the day a swastika was painted on his door?"

Virgil snapped his fingers. "That's it! That's who it was. He wasn't wearing dark pants today, though. They were tan. And no jacket."

"What about the other guy?"

Virgil squeezed his eyes shut as if that helped him think. "He was taller." He paused. "That's all I remember."

"Thank you, Mr. Curry. You've been a big help."

He smiled, pleased with himself. "I ain't no Mr. Curry. I'm just Virgil. Glad to oblige, Miss Newspaper Lady."

I walked away thinking Virgil Curry was more observant than a lot of people who had all their wits about them.

Realizing I was still holding the digging tools, I went back to the garden where Dan was watering the newly planted vegetables. Much of the crowd had dispersed by this time.

"I thought you absconded with my tools," he said with a grin. "I was just about to report you to Chief Turner."

"Sorry about that. I saw something I wanted to follow up on. I didn't think I'd be so long. Need some help watering?"

"Sure. Now that the excitement is over, everyone is leaving. That other hose is hooked up. All you have to do is turn it on."

I picked up the second hose and turned the nozzle until the right amount of water came out, somewhere between a mist and a deluge.

"Looks like you've done this before," Dan said.

"Mom's always had a little garden in the backyard—a few tomato and pepper plants. And green onions. Pop loves green onions. I learned at an early age not to drown the plants."

Dan laughed. "A good lesson."

Matt came by and snapped a picture of us watering. "I'd better see this in the paper," he said. "Caption—'Fearless leader is all wet.'"

"Ha-ha," I said. "How about 'Fearless leader waters staff photographer.'"

"You wouldn't."

"Oh, wouldn't I?" I started moving the stream of water toward him.

"I'm outa here." He left quickly.

Once the garden was watered, I helped Dan roll up the hoses. I did a final walk around the square, hoping to see anyone fitting Virgil's description of the men, with no luck. I was disappointed, but overall it had been an enjoyable day. I headed home tired and dirty.

* * *

After a bath and a quick dinner of sandwiches, Katherine and I headed to Sam's house. Mom insisted I take one of the apple pies she'd baked yesterday.

The evening was cool and pleasant. It was a little too far to walk, so I offered to drive. On the way I told her about the chief saying Mr. Tabor had been murdered. She was about as surprised as I had been when the chief told me. We decided we wouldn't mention it to Ben and that I'd be the one to question him so as to not give away the fact that Katherine wasn't an ordinary factory worker.

Sam lived three miles out of town in a neighborhood of small homes that had originally housed the workers of a mine that had closed fifty years ago when the coal had been depleted. The current residents were a mix of locals and immigrants who had seen the writing on the wall and left Europe in the thirties. Although old, most of the houses were well kept. Some had picket fences lining the front yards and freshly planted flower and vegetable gardens. The Markowicz house was one of these.

Sam and Sarah were sitting on their front porch when I pulled up. Sam stood when Katherine and I got out of the car. Katherine passed the pie to me as we went up the walk. "I hope we're not intruding," I said.

"Not at all," Sam said. "I told you to visit anytime."

Sarah pushed up from her rocking chair and smiled. "You are welcome here always."

I gave her the pie. "Mom baked this yesterday."

"Your mother is always so kind," she said. "Tell her thank you. I owe you both an apology for lying to you about knowing Benjamin. I was afraid. I am still afraid, but knowing you are helping us makes it easier."

"There's no need to apologize. I understand." I introduced Katherine as a friend who was working at Tabor and staying with us. Any other explanation would have been too long. And now that I knew her story, she was becoming just what I'd said.

"Any friend of the Ingram family is a friend of ours," Sam said.

Sarah said, "I am glad you both have come to see Benjamin. He could use a visit from some pretty girls."

"How is he doing?"

Sarah sighed. "Physically, he is getting better. His mood is another thing."

"He will be angry you have come," Sam said. "He will tell you to leave. This is our house. Don't listen to him."

Sarah and Katherine went inside. I followed, but Sam touched my arm.

"Wait," he said.

I stood by the door.

"Have you found out anything? Sarah is very worried."

"Nothing definite, but that's one reason we're here. I found some notes that Moe had written, and I'm hoping Ben can decipher them."

"Why would Benjamin be able to do that?"

I didn't want to get into details at the moment. "It's a long story, and if it pans out, I'll fill you in. It may be nothing." I didn't believe it was nothing. Not by a long shot.

Sam nodded, and we went inside.

"Your home is lovely," Katherine said.

The living room was small but warm and inviting. The style was too old-fashioned for my personal taste, but it fit Sam and Sarah.

Sarah took the pie to the kitchen while Sam led us down a short hallway to the second of two bedrooms and knocked on the door.

"What now?" Ben's response was muffled through the closed door.

"You have visitors."

"Tell them to go away."

"I will not," Sam said. He opened the door.

Ben was sitting up in a chair beside the bed with a blanket covering his lap. His crutches were beside him, leaning against the wall. "Get out. I don't want to see anyone, especially her." He pointed to me.

Sam ignored him. He backed out and closed the door behind him.

"It's nice to see you, Ben," I said.

He made a sound of disgust. "A guy can't get any privacy anywhere." He looked over at Katherine. "Don't you work at Tabor?"

At last. A little interest in someone besides himself.

Katherine gave him a warm smile. "I do. I'm so sorry about your accident."

"You're the only one, then."

"That's not true." Katherine sat on the edge of the bed. "Lots of people are concerned for you."

"I'm sure," he said.

"It's true," I said. "The people who work at Tabor are very concerned."

Ben snorted. "Concerned for themselves. Concerned for keeping their jobs."

This was getting nowhere. "Then how about doing something so they can keep their jobs."

He didn't respond.

I opened my pocketbook and took out the papers I'd found at Moe's. "I found these in Moe Bauer's house."

There was a short pause before he asked who Moe was.

"You know perfectly well who he was. You were working with him."

An expression of fear flitted across Ben's face. "That's ridiculous."

"You were attacked both times because you were feeding information to Moe. Your being Jewish was only part of it."

"Then how do you explain the messages sent to Sam and a couple others?" Ben asked.

"I can't. Not yet anyway."

There was a long pause, then he said, "If I tell you, I'll be signing my own death warrant."

"Think about the reason you told Moe in the first place," I said. "And the reason you told the FBI about the bad rivets."

He looked surprised. "How did you know about that?"

I shrugged. I couldn't say Katherine had told me. "I'm a reporter, remember? I asked a few questions and put two and two together."

He laid his head back on the chair and closed his eyes. "How do you know I can trust your friend here?"

"I trust her." I couldn't have said the same a couple of days ago.

After a moment he opened his eyes and held out his hand. "Give me those papers, and I'll tell you what you want to know."

He winced as he shifted in his chair and opened them up on the table beside him.

"Does it hurt much?" I asked.

"What? My leg? Or maybe I should say where my leg used to be? Of course it hurts. It hurts like hell."

He made it sound like I was stupid for even asking such a question. Maybe I was. "I'm sorry," I said.

"That and a nickel will get you a cup of coffee. How about shutting up so I can study these." It didn't take him long. "What do you know about production lines?" He looked at Katherine. "You probably know some."

"Not as much as I should," she said. "I'm usually on a packing line. I go to wherever I'm assigned and do what I'm told."

"Okay. Tabor Ironworks has twenty-two production lines, making everything from nuts, bolts, and rivets to various items for any business that needs metal parts. Lines one to three are nuts, four to ten are bolts, eleven to eighteen are rivets, the last few are for other items. I see all of this because I'm mostly invisible. No one pays attention to the guy with the broom."

"Someone paid attention," I said.

"Anyway, Tabor uses the cold-forging method for all but the largest bolts and rivets, and the process is similar for each. To make a long story short, steel coils come in from J&L in Pittsburgh; the coils are straightened, cut to size, and formed in machines. There's another machine that is supposed to catch any that aren't formed right and separate them from the good ones."

"What about the numbers on that paper?" I asked.

"You're really impatient, aren't you?" Ben said. "I'm getting there."

"Sorry."

"One night I saw someone grab a handful of bad bolts and toss them on the belt with the good ones. I didn't say anything, but the next night it happened again. I reported it to the foreman. The guy who did it must have been fired, because I didn't see him around anymore. I forgot about it. The next week I was on the first shift and noticed rivets on the belt that didn't look quite right. I told the guy working that section of the line, and he told me they were fine and to mind my own business. Right after that I was jumped and beaten up."

I opened my mouth to ask another question, but Ben shut me up with a look. I'd let him finish.

"I started taking notes—secretly, of course. I'd jot down the line number, a *B* or an *R* for bolt or rivet, the box number they ended up in, and what shift." He pointed to the first line on page one. "*L5* is the line, the *B* stands for bolt, *628* is the box number, and *3S* is third shift."

I didn't tell him Katherine and I had figured some of it out— the line number and the *B* or *R*. We'd been right in thinking the *628* wasn't the actual number of bolts. But we hadn't known it was a box number. "What about the *A* or *S* at the end?"

"They're the initials of who worked those lines on those shifts."

Katherine and I exchanged glances.

Ben confirmed what we were both thinking. "Richard Adler and John Smith."

Chapter
Twenty-Five

Smaller Unions Combine to Form United Steelworkers of America

—*The Progress Herald*, May 24, 1942

"Why are they still working there?" I asked. "Why wouldn't the foreman have them fired like the first time?"

Ben leaned back in his chair, exhausted. "Because it was my word against theirs. When the foreman checked, there were no bad parts in the boxes. Somehow, they switched boxes or . . . I don't know what. I haven't figured it out. I know what I saw. I finally reported it anonymously to the FBI. They never did anything about it."

I wished I could tell him about Katherine. I still didn't understand why Adler and Smith hadn't been stopped yet if the feds had their names.

"I knew Moe through Sam," Ben continued. "If the government wasn't going to stop them, maybe the press would. We met a couple times, and I told him what I knew. At our last meeting he told me there were more involved and he thought he knew who the ringleader was. Then he turned up dead."

"I think Moe met with that person on the day he died," I said.

Ben nodded. "I think so too. The next day I found a note in my lunch box in the break room saying the same thing could happen to me. I don't remember much about what happened to me, but I know it wasn't an accident." His face suddenly twisted in pain. "I think it's time for some medicine."

Katherine stood. "We've taken too much of Mr. Cline's time. We should go."

"We'll let you rest now," I said. "Thank you for talking to us."

He warned us to be careful and to please keep his name out of it. I told him I'd do what I could.

I had so many more questions, but they'd have to wait. Katherine was quiet on the way home. I finally asked her what she was thinking. It was getting dark, but I saw her wipe a tear from her cheek.

"I'm tired," she said. "I'm tired of nothing being done. I don't understand why they haven't gone in and arrested Adler and Smith. They could have done it weeks ago when Ben called them."

"I thought the same thing, but Ben did say that Moe told him there might be others. And there's the ringleader."

Katherine took a handkerchief from her pocketbook and dabbed under her eyes. "I just want this to be over with. I don't care if there are others. If they arrest those two, it might scare them away."

"Or it might make them bolder. They could take more drastic action than the acts of sabotage they've performed so far. We need to figure out who else is involved and put a stop to it once and for all."

* * *

Sunday morning was quiet as usual. Mom, Lily, and I went to Mass, and Mom made breakfast when we got home. Katherine was working the day shift again. She had gone straight upstairs when we returned home the night before, saying she just wanted to go to bed.

Our yard needed some attention, so I got Pop's lawn mower out of the garage and cut the grass. I enlisted Lily to rake up the clippings and helped her dump them in the corner by the back fence where we had started a compost pile. While we did that, Mom weeded the flower beds by the front porch and turned over the dirt so it would be ready to plant. The danger of frost was probably past, so we could buy some impatiens and begonias from Dan's store any time now.

After a late lunch, I walked into town to the *Herald* like I did every Sunday afternoon. Someone had taped a note on the front door that read *JAP LOVER*. I tore it off and crumpled it up. Apparently my editorial had hit a nerve with at least one person. I was sure I'd get a few letters in the mail as well.

I wrote my article about yesterday's victory garden event. Frank's articles were already on my desk, as well as a couple from Rex on war news. Ken had talked to Mike from Thrift Drug and his friends yesterday, and he had a short piece about them. I proofed the articles and took them downstairs for Donny to lay out when he came in. The ads Peggy had worked on were already there.

After that I sat in my office, trying to figure out what to do next with the information Ben had given us last night. I kept going back and forth in my mind over whether the feds should have arrested Adler and Smith already. I hated the fact that they were still there, causing damage and putting people in danger.

Plus they were murderers. I had no doubt that they had killed Moe and now Wilfred Tabor.

Did the feds even know Tabor had been murdered? They surely had suspicions that was the case, though. If not, Katherine would tell them. I had another thought. Shouldn't the chief be aware that the FBI was conducting an investigation in his jurisdiction? He had to know about it; he was just under no obligation to tell me—as a matter of fact, he probably couldn't. It annoyed me anyway. What else did he know that he wasn't saying? There was a lot I wasn't telling him either, and I planned on keeping it that way for the time being. I wasn't about to be told not to worry my pretty little head again.

I contemplated what to do next. Katherine would still gather whatever information she could, but it wasn't enough to suit me. I thought about Ben reporting what he had seen to the foreman. I had no idea whether someone in charge of the shop floor had the power to fire someone. If not, the foreman would have reported the incident to someone higher up. Katherine might know who he'd report to.

Another thing that puzzled me was Wilfred Tabor's murder. Somehow he must have found out Nazis were working for him and threatened to go to the authorities. There was a worse option that troubled me. What if he had known about it all along? I thought back to my first meeting with Tabor in his office. It had gone well until I asked if Moe had met with him on Monday the eleventh. Tabor was certainly anxious to get rid of me after that. Moe had been there; I was sure of it. Tabor must have known what was going on, and it was possible he'd been the ringleader. But why kill him, then? Maybe he'd had a change of heart and argued with Adler or Smith. Maybe they didn't want to take orders from him anymore. Things got out of hand and he was shot.

None of this explained the message left at Sam's store or the swastika painted on his door or the notes sent to others. It was possible none of that was related to what was going on at the factory. Sam and others had been targeted because they were Jews. These incidents were terrible, but I needed to focus on the sabotage and the murders. Thanks to Ben, I knew what Moe's big story had been. Now I needed to find out what Wilfred Tabor had known that had gotten him killed. First thing in the morning I'd make another trip to the Ironworks.

*　*　*

Monday morning turned out to be busier than I'd planned. Telephone calls about my editorial speaking out against relocating people of Japanese descent kept Peggy glued to her desk. By ten o'clock the tally of calls from people wanting to run me out of town was slightly lower than that of those congratulating me on speaking out. Of course, no one on the running-me-out-of-town side would give Peggy their names. The calls tapered off after that, and Peggy took a break in my office.

"I'm sorry about all that," I said. I handed her one of the cups of coffee I'd just gotten from our kitchen. "I only expected a few calls and some nasty letters, not a deluge."

"Comes with the territory," Peggy said. "At least no one's mentioned tar and feathers yet."

"Good point."

"What's new on the investigation front?" she asked.

I couldn't tell her why Katherine was working at the factory or that Mr. Tabor had been murdered, but I could tell her a little bit about Moe's papers. She deserved to know that much at least. I got up and closed my door. "You know the papers I found at Moe's that I didn't think amounted to anything?"

Peggy nodded.

"I was wrong." I got the papers out of my pocketbook and passed them to Peggy. "Katherine helped me decipher some of it—"

"I thought you didn't trust Katherine."

"She told me something in confidence that changed my mind. I wish I could tell you, but I can't. I'm sorry."

It didn't seem to bother Peggy that I was keeping a secret from her as much as it bothered me. "I would expect you to do the same for me," she said. "So, she helped you figure this out."

"Yep. But not all of it." I told Peggy we'd figured out what the *L* meant. "I decided I needed to talk to Ben Cline. There was a reason he was targeted. He obviously knew something."

"And did he?"

"Mostly."

Peggy could tell I was holding back. She slid the papers to me. "I won't ask," she said. "I know there's a good reason you won't tell me."

"I want to, I really do. I hope you'll understand when this all comes out in the open. Moe was killed over what he knew, and I don't want that to happen to anyone else."

She reached across the desk and grabbed my hand. "Promise me that there's no chance of that happening to you. Moe was savvy and he was murdered anyway. I don't like this. Not one bit. If you know what Moe knew . . ."

I patted her hand with the one of mine she didn't have a vise grip on. "Moe met with his killer. I have no plans to do the same. As soon as I figure out who it is, I'll tell the authorities."

"You'd better." She let go of my hand and stood at the muffled sound of the phone on her desk ringing.

"Hey," I said. "Did you just tell me I'm not savvy?"

She smiled as she opened my door. "If the shoe fits . . ."

I leaned back in my chair after she left. I wanted this to be over. And soon. I stood and picked up my pocketbook. The best way to accomplish that was to do what I'd already planned—make another trip to Tabor Ironworks.

*　*　*

Arnold Moss wasn't in his office. I continued down the hall, where Miss Lewis was at her desk, typing. She finished the sentence and looked up at me.

"Where can I find Mr. Moss?" I asked.

"I'm not sure where he is at the moment. I can try to find him if you'd like."

"That's not necessary. I'll just wait. How are you doing?" I asked.

Instead of answering my question, she said, "Thank you for writing such a lovely piece about Mr. Tabor. It will never be the same without him."

"I know it won't."

"Everything will be different now," she said. "I'm not sure I'll be able to get used to it."

"You worked for Mr. Tabor for a long time, didn't you?"

Miss Lewis nodded. "I've never worked anywhere else."

Just then, Arnold Moss came down the hall carrying a sheet of paper. "Miss Ingram! I didn't know you were here. How nice to see you." He handed the paper he was carrying to Miss Lewis. "Would you mail this for me, please? The address is at the top."

"Of course," she said.

"Come on back to my office," Moss said to me.

I followed him back down the hall and into his office. There were boxes on top of his desk where it looked like he'd been packing various items.

"Excuse the mess," he said. "I'm getting things ready to move into Wilfred's old office. After the funeral, of course."

"Of course."

Moss moved around to the other side of his desk and sat. He pointed to the chair across from him. "Have a seat."

I did.

"I suppose you didn't come to see me just to chat," Moss said.

"So it's official that you're taking over for Mr. Tabor."

"I thought it would be after he retired someday, not for something like this."

"It must be difficult."

"Not exactly, but certainly different. So what can I do for you, Irene?"

"I realized, with Mr. Tabor gone, that I didn't know a whole lot about the largest employer in the area," I said. "I'm wondering about the hierarchy here."

"Hierarchy?"

"Yeah. The chain of command. Who's in charge from the bottom up."

"Why do you want to know?"

"Like I said, I don't know as much as I should about the company. As the editor of the *Herald*, I should learn everything I can about the businesses in Progress."

Moss nodded. "That's an impressive task." He leaned forward. "Have lunch with me, and I'll tell you anything you want to know."

I almost refused for the umpteenth time, then changed my mind. If having lunch with him was all it would take to find out what I wanted to know, then so be it. I'd keep my notepad and pencil visible so if anyone saw us they'd know it was business. Besides, if I were a man, it wouldn't even be an issue. We were almost halfway through the twentieth century, for heaven's sake. It was time for things to change. "Okay," I said.

If he was surprised, he covered it well. "Terrific," he said. "Where would you like to go?"

I was sure the Woolworth's lunch counter would be out of the question, and so would Dempsey's Diner. Ava would have a field day if she saw me with Moss. There was a nice restaurant inside the train station. Bill and I had gone there on special occasions, like the night before he left for basic training. We didn't dine there often because it was expensive. Arnold Moss wouldn't have a problem with that. "How about Morrison's?" I said.

Moss agreed.

I almost changed my mind on our way out the door. What if Moss took it the wrong way and thought I was interested in him? I shook off the thought. What he thought didn't matter. Getting to the truth did.

Chapter
Twenty-Six

Test Blackout in Detroit a Success
—The Progress Herald, May 25, 1942

Arnold Moss must have been a regular customer at Morrison's, as the hostess seemed to know him. She led us to a table near a window overlooking the train platform. As soon as we were seated, I retrieved my notebook and pencil and placed them on the table.

"You don't have to be all business, all the time," Moss said. "Enjoy yourself for a change."

"This is business. And I am enjoying myself."

I'd hardly began perusing the menu when our waitress came to the table. "Hello, Arnie," she said. "What can I get you? The usual?"

"That would be great, Gina."

"One Scotch and water coming right up." She pivoted to me. "And you?" Her tone of voice turned icy.

"Just water for me, thanks. I'm working." I gave her a smile. She didn't return the smile. "Got it."

When she was out of earshot, I said, "Another girlfriend of yours?"

Moss grinned. "Why? Are you jealous?"

I rolled my eyes. "Not on your life, but Gina sure is." I went back to checking the menu. I was tempted to pick the most expensive thing on it but decided on a club sandwich instead.

Gina brought our drinks. She set the Scotch down gently in front of Moss, almost brushing his hand with hers. When she put my water glass down, she tipped the glass enough for water to spill out, just missing splashing it all over me. It was definitely a practiced maneuver. I needed to do something about it before she ended up spitting on my lunch.

I stared at her. "For the record, I'm here to interview Mr. Moss. I'm the editor of the *Progress Herald*. I'm pretty sure you or your boss wouldn't want it mentioned that the waitstaff here is subpar. Am I right?"

She whipped a towel from her waistband and began mopping up water. "I am so sorry. I'm just clumsy today. I'll bring you a fresh glass of water." She scurried off.

Moss burst out laughing. "You keep surprising me, Irene. For a kid, you sure know how to handle yourself."

"If it had been an accident, I wouldn't have said anything, but she did it on purpose. It made me mad."

Gina returned, we ordered lunch, and I opened my notebook.

"You said if I had lunch with you, you'd answer any question," I said. "I believe I asked about the hierarchy at Tabor Ironworks."

"Well, I'm the big cheese, as they say in the movies. Everyone else is under me."

"You can do better than that. There has to be a chain of command."

Moss took a swig of his Scotch. "Why do you want to know this boring stuff?"

"I told you. I want to learn more about the largest employer in Progress."

He sighed. "Directly under me there is another vice president, Wilfred's son—"

"Mr. Tabor had a son?"

"Yes," Moss said. "He's over in England flying planes or something. He was never involved in the company. He's only a VP because of his name. I've never even met him."

I found that really odd. Even if he wasn't involved, wouldn't Mr. Tabor leave the company to his flesh and blood? "What's his name? Why haven't I ever heard of him before?"

Moss shrugged. "Wilfred Junior. Goes by Will. All I know is that Wilfred Senior was married once. His ex moved to California, taking young Wilfred with her. I don't think he's been to Progress since he was four years old."

That explained why I'd never seen him. "Will he be home for the funeral? I'd like to meet him."

"I have no idea if he'll be coming. Miss Lewis would know."

I was glad I had left the car parked at the Ironworks. I could ask her when I returned after lunch. Gina brought our meals, and while I spread mayonnaise on my sandwich, I asked him who was next in line.

"Every department has a head, and each shop has a foreman on each shift. I don't know all their names yet."

I didn't ask any more questions while we ate. I tried to sort things out in my brain, which was still back on Wilfred Junior. What would he think of his father handing the company over to a stranger? If they had been estranged, maybe he wouldn't care.

I'd get the scoop from Miss Lewis. I wondered if my mother knew anything about Tabor's ex-wife and son. A prominent man's divorce would have been the talk of the town back then.

"How's your sandwich?" Moss asked. He had already devoured his BLT.

"It's almost as good as the one from Dempsey's Diner. And Dempsey's is half the price."

"I'll have to try it sometime."

Sometime probably meant never. I couldn't picture him in a diner unless it was three o'clock in the morning, he was sauced, and nothing else was open. I wiped the mayonnaise off my fingers and pushed my plate aside.

Moss pulled a pack of Camels from his suit coat pocket. "Are we done with the questions?"

I was finally getting around to what I really wanted to know. "One more. A hypothetical one."

"I'm all ears." He lit his cigarette and blew out smoke.

"Suppose someone sees another worker doing something wrong—wrong enough to be fired. Who would make the decision to let the employee go?"

"Wilfred would have, but it would have to be pretty serious."

"So Mr. Tabor would have been the one doing the firing? Not one of the foremen or department heads?"

"They'd make the suggestion, of course. But Wilfred would have made the final decision." He took a pull on his cigarette. "He would have already known about the infraction, even if no one had reported it. The old man knew everything that went on."

On the way back to the factory, I couldn't get those words out of my head. Moss parked in his designated spot. After he went inside, I sat in Pop's car, wondering how I could talk to Miss Lewis without Moss being around. I didn't know if her loyalty to Tabor Ironworks included loyalty to Arnold Moss. She'd be more likely to talk freely when he wasn't around. I decided to telephone her when I got back to the *Herald* and see if she could meet me somewhere. I headed back to work thinking about Mr. Tabor, convinced he had either known about the sabotage or directed it. I wasn't sure which at this point, but I was going to find out.

* * *

Rex was waiting for me when I returned. "I'm going to write something up on the test blackout in Detroit last night."

I felt dumb for not knowing about it but couldn't let Rex know that. "Great. How did it go?"

"It went well, from what I learned. Apparently neighboring areas like Pontiac and Windsor participated too, making it the largest blackout in the Midwest."

"That's definitely newsworthy," I said. "Sounds like it went a lot better than the test in Pittsburgh last year." The lights on the bridges had been left on. It would have given bombers an easy target if it hadn't been a practice run.

"Yeah. But that was before Pearl. I heard they're planning another one next month."

"If you get any details about that, let me know. Progress is close enough that it might be a good idea to participate."

"Will do." Rex went back to his desk.

Peggy came into my office after that, and I told her about my lunch with Arnold Moss.

"Why in the world did you do that?"

"I wanted to find out what happens to the Ironworks now that Mr. Tabor is gone." I filled her in about Tabor's son.

"Wow. I never knew he had a son, not that I keep track of everyone's lives. I wonder if Ava knows."

"I didn't either. Mom might have known. Divorce would have been a bigger deal back then. I'll bet a nickel that Ava doesn't know. It was before she moved back here." I felt a little superior for knowing something Ava didn't. It would be tempting to rub it in.

"So Mr. Tabor left the company to Moss instead of his own son?"

"That's what Moss says. I guess we'll know soon enough. I'm going to call Tabor's secretary and see if she'll meet me somewhere and give me the scoop."

Peggy stared at me. "Why would you care? You're not running a gossip rag here."

I shrugged. I'd said too much already. "I know that. I just find it interesting."

"Uh-huh." She stood. "I'm not buying it.

"There's nothing to buy," I lied.

"Just don't get in over your head."

"I wouldn't think of it."

* * *

Miss Lewis agreed to meet me right after work at a coffee shop near the factory. I called home to let Mom know I'd be late for dinner, then read and edited articles that had been turned in. I wrote a draft of my clothing and fashion article, since it was the fourth week of the month. I managed to come up with some ideas for summer fashions thanks to Mom's movie magazines and her Sears & Roebuck catalog.

Dorothy, Mayor Young's secretary, telephoned to say he'd settled on dates for the scrap drive and that Lily's posters had been printed and would be hung around town in the next few days. The scrap drive would last a week, from June seventh to the thirteenth, and the collection bin would stay in place until the war ended. When I hung up, I marked the dates on my desk calendar and wrote a quick piece for tomorrow's paper.

I took the scrap drive article along with Lily's small version of the poster downstairs for Donny. "The mayor just gave me the dates for the scrap drive, so these will need to be added for tomorrow."

"It's awfully late to be adding things." He studied the drawing. "Who did this?"

"Lily drew it," I said. "She designed the posters the mayor's office will be hanging around town this week."

"But she's just a kid."

"She worked very hard for this."

"I don't like it," Donny said. "It's not fair. I don't get anything printed in the paper. You're only doing it because she's your sister."

I was out of patience. "You don't have to like it. You just have to put it in tomorrow's edition."

"But—"

"Mayor Young likes her work," I said. "Do you want me to tell him we're not putting the poster that he approved in the paper because you don't like it?"

He sighed loudly. "I guess not. I'll find room for it somewhere."

"It had better not be on the last page, or you can explain it to the mayor." I left him grumbling about life not being fair.

* * *

The coffee shop Miss Lewis had chosen was within walking distance of the factory and a bus stop. I recognized some Tabor employees from the few times I'd been inside the plant. I nodded to them as I walked past and took a seat in a booth. Miss Lewis came in a minute later and sat down across from me.

"Thank you for taking the time to talk to me, Miss Lewis," I said. "I know it's been a difficult few days for you."

"Please, call me Colleen. It's been very hard." She shuddered. "I can't get the image of him the way I found him out of my mind. I don't want to remember him like that. And now, with the changes . . ."

"I can only imagine. I spent a mere hour with Mr. Moss today, and it was more than enough."

That elicited a tiny smile from her. "Mr. Moss is certainly different than Mr. Tabor. It will take some getting used to."

We both ordered coffee, and she filled me in on the details of Tabor's funeral, which would take place tomorrow.

"The factory can't be shut down," she said, "but some employees will attend. It will be small."

"What about Mr. Tabor's son? Is he coming to the funeral?"

Colleen looked surprised. "How do you know about Will?"

"Mr. Moss mentioned it. He said he was a vice president but had never shown any interest in the Ironworks."

"He's wrong about that. Will is training pilots in England and can't get away right now, but Mr. Tabor told me he's very interested in the company. Will has a degree in business and wants to be involved. I spoke to Will myself, and he says that as soon as the war is over, he's coming back here to run things."

Now I was the one to be surprised. "Does Moss know that? According to him, Mr. Tabor made arrangements for him to lead the company."

Colleen set her coffee mug down. "As much as Mr. Moss would like to believe it's permanent, it's not. Mr. Tabor would never in a million years have done that. His father started the company, and it will stay in family hands. Mr. Tabor planned on leaving everything to his son. I have proof."

"What kind of proof?"

"I witnessed Mr. Tabor's last will and testament a week ago."

Chapter
Twenty-Seven

Germans Launch Offensive Against Soviet Partisans
—The Progress Herald, May 25, 1942

"Mr. Tabor made a new will a week ago?" I asked.

"Yes."

"Why?"

Colleen hesitated. "I don't know if I should be talking to you about this."

"It won't end up in the paper, if that's what you're worried about. I'm only trying to understand some things. Mr. Tabor's death doesn't make sense to me."

She looked around the coffee shop. It was beginning to empty out as people went home for dinner. "I don't want to be overheard," she said.

"We could go somewhere else." I tried to think of a place devoid of people.

"No, this is fine. I'll speak quietly." She leaned forward. "Even before Mr. Moss came to work for us, Mr. Tabor hadn't been himself. He was always very reserved but still personable, if that makes sense. But for the past few months he was withdrawn and edgy. The slightest thing made him angry."

"Do you think it was the pressure of the increase in production for the war? Hiring all those extra people and adding lines had to be stressful."

"I don't know. The extra production was why he hired Mr. Moss. He needed someone to take care of that end of things while he handled everything else." Colleen pushed her coffee mug aside. "I don't think Mr. Tabor liked Mr. Moss very much. Mr. Tabor didn't care for some of the changes Mr. Moss wanted to make. He didn't like Mr. Moss being so sociable with the employees."

"You mean the women?" I asked.

"Not just the women. Mr. Tabor thought he was too lenient and let some people get away with too much. Mr. Tabor ran a tight ship. I know some of the employees prefer Mr. Moss, but it's Tabor Ironworks, not Moss Ironworks."

"Why did Mr. Tabor hire him then? He could have waited until someone better came along."

"Mr. Moss has impeccable credentials—Harvard Business, and I don't remember what else. Someone Mr. Tabor knew recommended Mr. Moss. Mr. Tabor hired him sight unseen."

That might have been a mistake.

"Mr. Tabor made the best of the situation. At least until a few weeks ago. One of the employees was beaten up in the parking lot."

"Ben Cline."

Colleen nodded. "Mr. Moss said he would handle it. I'm not sure what happened after that, but when that poor man was hurt again, they had a big argument the next day. I couldn't hear what they said to each other, but Mr. Tabor was more angry than I'd ever seen him. He closed himself up in his office and made a telephone call. It was odd, though."

"What was odd?"

"I hadn't thought of it before, but usually Mr. Tabor had me place his calls and put him on the line when I reached his party. He dialed direct that time."

"Had he done that before?" I asked.

"Once that I recall," she said. "And that was a few months ago."

While the waitress poured more coffee, I thought about the conversation I'd overheard after Ben Cline was injured. Tabor had told Moss he was worried, and Moss had told him he worried too much and that he had everything under control. What was he worried about? The bad press that might follow? Or something entirely different? "What happened after that?"

"Nothing really, except Mr. Tabor asking me to witness his will. We went to his attorney's office, and the attorney's secretary and I signed it."

"Does Mr. Moss know about this?"

"No, I don't believe he does. Mr. Tabor didn't want anyone to know. He knew he could trust me not to say anything. Until now, anyway."

"Do you know the contents of the will?" I asked.

"Not entirely, but one thing I do know is his son inherits everything and will be named president of the company."

I had a lot to think about on the way home, and none of it made any sense to me. Moss was confident that Tabor had left him in charge of the company. It was possible Tabor had, then changed his mind after their argument. Before talking to Colleen Lewis,

I'd thought Tabor might have been the ringleader of the—for lack of a better word—spies, but now I wasn't sure. Why would Tabor sacrifice his company, the business he had built over so many years and wanted to pass on to his son?

He wouldn't. Unless he didn't have a choice.

The only ones to benefit if Tabor Ironworks had to close were our enemies. I thought of the direct telephone calls Colleen had mentioned. Moss had said Tabor knew everything that went on in the plant. Someone could have blackmailed Tabor to either support or overlook any sabotage. He'd been forced into it. That would explain his change in demeanor. When Ben Cline was injured, Tabor had had enough. He'd tolerated sabotage, but not one of his employees almost getting killed. Moss hadn't taken care of the situation like he'd promised, and he and Tabor had argued. After that, Tabor shut himself up in his office and telephoned whoever was blackmailing him. Did he just quit, or did he threaten to go to the authorities? Wilfred Tabor knew he was a dead man either way. I had to find out who the ringleader was and if anyone else was involved besides Adler and Smith.

*   *   *

Mom had one of her meetings—I'd lost track of which one—that evening, but she'd left a plate for me in the oven to keep it warm. She'd also left a note on the table saying Katherine had called and was working a double shift and I was to make sure Lily got her homework done. I helped her with some English homework, but she was on her own with science and math. They'd never been my strong subjects.

I settled down in the living room with the latest *Photoplay* but I couldn't concentrate on the lives of movie stars. I flipped through pages filled with advertisements that ran the gamut from leg makeup to feminine hygiene. I tossed it aside. I tried the radio, turning the dial from station to station, but my mind kept going over and over the latest revelations and I finally gave up. I decided a hot bath might help me put my thoughts in some kind of order.

I soaked in the tub until the water cooled. I still hadn't made much sense of what I'd learned. After I dried off and got ready for bed, I went back downstairs and stretched out on the sofa to wait up for Katherine, but the next thing I knew I was waking up to sun streaming in the front window.

* * *

Wilfred Tabor was being laid to rest in Calvary Cemetery on the grounds of the First Methodist Church of Progress. I'd never been to a Methodist service before, let alone a Methodist funeral service. I was more familiar with hour-long Catholic funerals with incense, holy water, and prayers in Latin, and definitely no laypeople giving eulogies. Tabor's service was short and sweet. I don't know why, but it surprised me when Arnold Moss strode up to the pulpit and gave the eulogy. I'd expected him to speak solely about himself, but he focused on how Tabor had taken him under his wing and what he'd learned from him. It was only toward the end that he talked about leading the company into the future.

After the service, everyone walked to the cemetery next to the church. Chief Turner and Rally Johnson were standing by the road, waiting to direct traffic when it was finished. It bothered me a bit to see Rally in uniform standing next to my future father-in-law. That was where Bill would have been. I didn't really begrudge Dad the help he needed; I just wanted Bill to be home. I pushed the thought of my fiancé out of my mind and focused on the task at hand—covering Tabor's funeral.

There were quite a few Tabor employees present, including Colleen Lewis. She burst into tears when the casket was lowered into the ground. I headed her way as soon as people began leaving and was halfway there when I saw Adler and Vivian Anderson walking back toward the church. I pivoted and followed.

Adler put an arm around Vivian while they walked. So they were definitely seeing each other. I kept following, keeping far enough back that they wouldn't see me. When they reached the other side of the church, Smith was waiting for them. Adler kissed Vivian and waited with Smith until she crossed the street. I inched closer, keeping near to the wall of the church. At first I couldn't hear the conversation, but when I was close enough, I realized they were speaking in German. I knew about a total of three German words, and even if they'd said them, I wouldn't have been able to pick them out because they were speaking too fast.

It didn't take me long to decide what to do. It might be my only chance to talk to them. I backed up to the corner of the church, then walked toward them, like I was out for a stroll. My heart pounded. "Hey, wasn't that Vivian Anderson I saw you with a few minutes ago?" I asked when I reached the two men.

"Yes, it was. How do you know Vivian?" Adler asked in perfect, unaccented English.

I introduced myself, hoping my nervousness didn't show. "I wrote the article about women in the workforce. Vivian was one of the women I interviewed."

Adler smiled. He was deceptively charming for a Nazi. "It was an excellent article. Vivian was thrilled to be featured."

"Do you two work at Tabor with her?"

"What's it to you?" Smith said. There was no sign of an accent in his speech either.

"I'm writing an article about the funeral and the tragic death of Mr. Tabor. What did you think of him?"

Smith scowled. "We ain't got time for this."

"Can I speak to you another time, then?" I asked.

"Nope," Smith said. "We're busy. We gotta go."

"What about Vivian? Do you think she'd be willing to answer a few questions?"

This time Adler spoke up. "You'll have to ask her."

"Thanks," I said. "I will."

They walked away with Smith grumbling about "pushy broads." In English, of course.

If nothing else, my eavesdropping and speaking to the two men had verified what Ben Cline had said. What was Vivian's involvement? I'd spent only an hour with her, but she didn't appear to be stupid. Or naïve like Betty. What if her story about being a widow was just that—a story? It would be easy enough for me to check the death notices in the *Butler Eagle*. I'd call over there when I got back to the *Herald*. Even if it checked out, I didn't like that she was keeping company with Adler. And I especially didn't like that she could be involved in betraying her country. Women had done all kinds of things they wouldn't ordinarily do in the name of love. Vivian didn't seem the type, but I really didn't know her. She might just be a good actress.

All the mourners had gone by the time I made it back to my car, and Dad's patrol car was pulling away from the curb. I considered telling him about Adler and Smith, but there wasn't any real evidence against them yet. It would be better to wait until I had something concrete to give him.

Instead of going straight back to the paper, I decided to check on Colleen Lewis. When I arrived at Tabor Ironworks, she wasn't at her desk. As I walked back down the hallway, I noticed Moss's door was open. I knocked on the doorframe, and Moss looked up.

"Can't get enough of me, can you, Irene?" he said with a smile.

I rolled my eyes. "Give it a rest."

"How did you like my eulogy?"

I sat in the chair opposite him. "Actually, I was impressed. You didn't talk about yourself until near the end."

"I didn't think it would be appropriate."

"Since when does that matter to you?" I asked.

He shrugged. "It doesn't really. But I'm not completely heartless. Wilfred's death was hard on everyone."

"Even you?"

"Even me."

"Where's Miss Lewis?" I asked.

"I gave her the rest of the day off. I couldn't take her blubbering any more. I swear she's gone through a dozen handkerchiefs in the last few days."

"She suffered a big loss. She worked for Mr. Tabor for a long time."

"I know, and I understand that. Every five minutes she tells me that's not how Mr. Tabor would do it. I'm trying to win her over, but so far it's not working. Moss leaned back in his chair. "So what can I do for you, Irene?"

"Nothing at the moment. I just wanted to make sure Miss Lewis was all right. I saw your door open, so I thought I'd better say hello."

"You make it sound like a chore," he said.

"I didn't mean it that way. I'd better be going." As I got up, my pocketbook caught on the arm of the chair. It dropped to the floor and the contents scattered. Embarrassed at being so clumsy, I knelt down and began gathering everything up.

Moss came over. "Let me help you with that." He picked up the papers I'd taken from Moe's and handed them to me. "Writing in secret code now?" he asked.

"Not exactly." I wasn't ready to tell him what it really was. "It's only a few notes for an article I'm working on." I scooped up the photographs I'd been carrying around. I missed a couple, and Moss picked them up and passed them to me. One was the picture of Ben Cline and Richard Adler I'd shown him before. I half expected Moss to comment on it, but he didn't.

When everything was back where it belonged, I stood up. "Thanks for the help," I said. "That will teach me to clean out my pocketbook more often."

"You're welcome. It always amazes me what women carry around with them." He walked me to the office door. "Thanks for brightening my day," he said. "Even if it was an afterthought."

I walked back to the car wondering if I should have asked him about Adler and Smith, especially after he'd seen the photograph. Even if I told him what I thought, he'd dismiss it out of hand. He'd never believe he had spies and saboteurs in his midst. No, it was better to keep it to myself. For now at least.

*   *   *

When I got home that day, I had a letter from Bill waiting for me, which improved my mood immensely. Katherine had worked the daylight shift again, so she and Lily helped Mom finish getting dinner ready while I took the letter to the front porch to read.

Hello Beautiful,

You last letter was swell. I miss you, too. Fortunately, they keep us so busy here I don't have time to think about that too much. The Sarge is a tough S.O.B. but that's what some of these guys need. There's no telling where we'll end up so we have to be ready for anything. This week I got to drive a tank. It's not as easy as it looks! I did better than one guy who almost took out the Sarge and one of the barracks. Sarge can really swear a blue streak!

Dad said he's been interviewing some guys for my old position. When he hires someone don't give the new guy a hard time. Ha ha. And don't like him too much either. I'll be back before you know it.

The rest of the letter was very personal and made me blush. He finished by writing that he would try to telephone soon. I held the letter to my chest. I hoped so. Letters were nice, but I missed hearing his voice. Lily called me for dinner, so I folded the letter and put it back in the envelope. I went inside and slipped it into my pocketbook for safekeeping.

After dinner, Lily's friend Cindy came over and they went up to her bedroom—supposedly to do homework together. I helped Mom clean up, then Katherine and I settled on the front porch while Mom listened to the radio in the living room. It had been a warm day—seventy-six degrees—and it was still in the sixties. A perfect evening to sit outside.

Katherine lit a cigarette. "What's new? I haven't talked to you for a couple of days."

"I planned on waiting up for you last night, but I fell asleep. I didn't even hear you come in."

"I saw you there but wasn't about to wake you," she said. "Besides, I was bushed."

"I have a lot to tell you." I told her about my lunch with Arnold Moss the day before.

She raised an eyebrow. "That's not something I expected you to do."

"Me neither," I said. "I had been thinking about Ben telling us about the first employee he saw mixing bad bolts or rivets—I don't remember which—in with the good ones. That guy was fired."

"I remember."

"I got to wondering who made the decision to fire him."

"Why would that matter? Adler and Smith are still there."

"I know Ben said it was his word against theirs," I said. "But even so, something that serious would have to go up the line. I wanted to know what the chain of command was, so I went to see Moss. The only way he'd tell me was if I went to lunch with him."

"What a sacrifice," she said.

"Believe me, it was." I told her Moss had said that Tabor was ultimately the one making those kinds of decision and that Tabor knew everything that went on in the plant.

"Does that mean he knew about the sabotage?" Katherine asked.

"I'm sure he did." I told her what Colleen Lewis had said about the telephone calls Tabor had made. "I think he was somehow forced into doing something against his nature. I can't see how he would sabotage his family company otherwise. I think he had a change of heart and it got him killed."

"That makes perfect sense," Katherine said.

"It doesn't get us any closer to knowing who's pulling the strings." I told her the rest—from Moss saying Tabor had left him in charge to Colleen Lewis's revelations about Tabor's son to seeing Vivian with Adler and hearing Adler and Smith speaking to each other in German. I asked Katherine what she thought of Vivian.

Katherine inhaled and blew out smoke before she answered. "She's hard to decipher. I don't think she's had an easy life. I do find it odd she's keeping company with Adler. They don't seem like a match to me."

I agreed. "There's something that doesn't add up with her. I called a colleague at the *Butler Eagle* this afternoon to get information on Vivian's husband's death. He couldn't find anything, which isn't completely unusual. Some people don't want anything in the paper."

"But you don't think that's the case," Katherine said.

"I don't know what to think. My colleague's going to dig a little further and get back to me."

Katherine crushed her cigarette out in the ashtray on the metal table beside her. "I'm off tomorrow, but I'll try to get her to talk when we work together again."

The fire department whistle blared just then, and I stood. "I wonder what's going on." Minutes later, two fire trucks sped past. Chief Turner's car screeched to a stop in front of the house, and I ran out to the street.

"You should know there's a fire out at Tabor. Don't have details, but it sounds like a big one."

Chapter Twenty-Eight

Fighting Still Heavy in Kharkov
—The Progress Herald, May 26, 1942

I ran inside to get my keys and pocketbook. "There's a fire out at Tabor," I said to Mom. "I'm going out there."

"I'll drive," Katherine said. "My car's out front."

Fifteen minutes later we pulled up beside a police car. I didn't see Dad anywhere, but Rally and Jimmy were blocking onlookers from getting too close. I asked them if they knew what had happened.

"We don't know yet. Someone said an explosion, and others said they smelled gasoline before the fire started," Jimmy said. "The chief went to see what he could do."

Katherine and I hustled toward the plant. One whole section of the building was aflame. "That's the box shop," she said. "That's bad. All that cardboard."

"What's beside it?"

"The paint shop."

A chill went through me. She didn't need to say any more for me to know that would be a disaster. Paint and turpentine would go off like a bomb. They had to get the fire under control.

Factory workers streamed out of the plant, and three more fire trucks from neighboring towns arrived. Rex and Frank pushed their way through the crowd and came toward us.

"I heard the sirens and saw the smoke," Frank said. "What do you want us to do?"

"Use your best judgment," I said. "I trust you."

Rex must have seen I was shook up. He squeezed my shoulder. "You'll be all right, kid."

Matt was already taking photographs. I wouldn't disturb him. It seemed everyone knew what to do except me. Katherine started directing factory workers to the parking lot on the other side of the road. I needed to focus instead of standing there gawking.

I took Katherine's lead and moved to another area where workers were exiting the building. I pointed them to a second parking lot a bit farther down the road. Betty broke off from one of the last groups to exit and came my way.

"I can't believe this. It's so horrible," she said. Tears streamed down her face.

"Do you know what happened?" I asked.

She shook her head. "Someone said there was an explosion. Do you know anything?"

"I heard the same as you. Someone else said they smelled gasoline. We'll know soon enough."

Betty wiped her face with her fingers. "Have you seen Sylvia or Vivian anywhere?"

"No, I haven't. Are they working tonight?"

"Yes. Sylvia was on her break in the cafeteria."

The cafeteria was on the side of the building opposite the fire. "She probably came out over there." I pointed to where Katherine was helping out.

"I'm not sure where Vivian was working," she said. "I only saw her for a minute earlier tonight."

"She's probably over with the others, then. Why don't you go that way?" Once Betty left, I headed closer to the area where the firemen were working to put out the flames. There was little I could do except watch. And think.

The fire had to have been deliberate. The reported odor of gasoline. Someone hearing an explosion. I had no doubt that Adler and Smith had started the fire. Would they be long gone by now? And what about Vivian? If she was truly missing, she was with Adler and Smith, which meant she was involved. I turned and headed toward the lot, where I found Katherine standing with Sylvia and Betty.

"Vivian isn't here," Betty said. "No one has seen her."

Katherine and I exchanged glances.

"I'm sure she's around somewhere," Sylvia said. "Let's go look for her."

When they were out of earshot, I said, "I think it's time we talked to the chief."

Katherine nodded.

We found Chief Turner getting statements from a group of employees. "Do you have a minute? It's important," I said.

He excused himself and walked our way.

I gave him the Reader's Digest version of the last couple of weeks. I expected him to berate me for keeping everything from him, but he didn't.

"I knew some of what was going on," he said, "but not all of it." He tilted his head toward Katherine. "Your government friends have kept me mostly in the loop."

"Have you seen Adler, Smith, or Vivian Anderson anywhere?" I asked.

The chief shook his head. "They're probably long gone by now. Or . . ."

He didn't need to finish the sentence.

"As soon as the fire is out, we'll do a thorough search," he said. "I'll send out a bulletin and notify the feds."

He'd barely finished speaking when a fireman exited the building carrying a limp figure. I couldn't tell from a distance if it was a man or a woman. The three of us rushed over as the fireman laid the person down on a stretcher near an ambulance.

It was Vivian Anderson. Her hair was singed, and she was covered in soot. Her face was red from the heat of the flames. One of her arms looked badly burned. She opened her eyes. "Richard. Still inside," she croaked. Then she lost consciousness.

The ambulance attendants pushed us aside to assist her. Dad gathered up a few men and had one of them get Rally to join them. He then went to talk to the fire chief.

Vivian was loaded into the ambulance, and I asked one of the attendants if she was going to be all right.

"I don't know. She's in pretty bad shape. We're taking her to Providence."

I watched them drive away, then stood there with Katherine. Neither of us spoke. I supposed I should have felt sorry for Vivian, but all I felt was anger. How could she have put so many lives in danger, especially people who were supposed to be her friends? Another horrible thought popped into my head. If she'd been involved with Adler and Smith all along, she was partly responsible for Moe's murder. My fingers curled into fists. "Why didn't I see it?"

I hadn't realized I'd asked the question aloud until Katherine said, "See what?"

"Vivian," I said. "I've been looking in all the wrong places and all along it's been Vivian."

"I'm not following."

"Vivian wasn't only seeing Adler, she was in cahoots with him," I said. "We knew someone else at Tabor had to be involved in the sabotage. Someone else calling the shots. It was right in front of us."

"Oh my God. I can't believe I actually befriended her. I felt sorry for her that she'd lost her husband."

"I wish I'd figured it out sooner. She was the one who blackmailed poor Mr. Tabor and had Adler or Smith kill him when he stopped cooperating."

"At least she didn't get away," Katherine said.

That was my only consolation. Vivian would have to pay for her crimes. It was something, at least.

Thirty minutes later the fire chief let Dad know they could enter the building.

Dad sent Rally and two men to go around the back of the building on the side opposite where the fire had been. Dad and several others, including a couple of firemen, entered the doors near the paint shop. It wasn't long before the firemen dragged a body out of the same doors. Dad followed a minute later. One of the men with him identified the dead man as Richard Adler.

Not long after, Rally and a volunteer came out one of the doors supporting John Smith, who was putting weight on only one leg. Another man followed, carrying a gas can. They took Smith to one of the police cars, and Rally pushed him into the back seat.

I turned to Katherine. "I'm going to talk to Rally and see what I can find out."

"Unless you need me, I'm going to check on Sylvia and Betty. I won't say anything about Vivian other than she's been taken to the hospital."

"Good. I'll catch up with you later."

Smith was lying in the back seat of the patrol car, moaning, when I reached it. His right leg was at an odd angle just above the ankle. It hurt just looking at it, and I didn't feel a bit sorry for him.

"What happened?" I asked Rally.

"We found him crawling on his belly, heading for an opening in a fence near the parking lot," Rally said. "I don't know where he thought he was going, but he sure wouldn't be able to drive like that."

"Did he say how he broke his leg?"

"He was trying to enter the building from a second-floor fire escape and fell. Serves him right, in my opinion."

"I won't argue with you about that," I said. "What about the gasoline?"

"He never made it inside to do anything with it, thank God."

Smith moaned louder, then mumbled something in German.

"Why's he talking like a Kraut?" Rally asked.

"It's a long story," I said. "A very long story."

He gave me a look, then nodded. "I guess I'll read all about it in your paper."

"I guess you will." I left Rally to deal with his prisoner and milled around, talking to some of the employees. Almost all had heard by now that the fire had been deliberately set and were shocked that someone would do such a thing. I had a feeling they'd be even more shocked when the whole story came out.

*   *   *

I found Katherine standing with Sylvia and Betty. I filled them in.

"I can't believe I worked side by side with murderers," Betty said. "And poor Vivian."

"Don't poor-Vivian me," Sylvia said. "She was with Adler. If it turns out she was in cahoots with them, she deserves what she got."

"How could you say such a thing?" Betty asked. "Vivian was our friend. She would never do anything like that."

"Why else would she just about get burned up if she wasn't there to help?" Sylvia said.

Betty opened her mouth to speak, but I put a hand up. "We'll find out soon enough, one way or the other," I said. "I'll telephone the hospital as soon as I get a chance."

Two of the foremen were rounding up those working the evening shift in the areas not affected by smoke and water. Betty and Sylvia said so long and went back inside. Just like when Ben Cline was injured, production for the war must go on. I spotted Rex talking to Arnold Moss. I'd leave him to it. Katherine and I headed back to her car. We were soon joined by Frank and Matt. Frank hadn't met Katherine yet, so I introduced them.

"Hell of a night," Frank said.

That was an understatement if I'd ever heard one. None of us felt much like talking, so we stood and watched the waning activity. When Rex finally joined us, I asked him what Moss had had to say.

"Oh, you know. The usual. A tragedy. Blah, blah, blah."

I gave him a little smile. "An exact quote, I see."

Rex grinned. "Of course."

I told my staff to go home for the night and report back bright and early. I was too wound up to go home, and there were a few things I wanted to do. I asked Katherine to drop me off at the *Herald*.

While she drove, I asked, "What happens now? Will you be off the hook?"

She sighed. "I wish I knew. I guess I'll find out soon enough. I'm hoping this is the end of it. I don't know what more I can do."

"I'll be happy to put in a good word for you."

"Thanks. I appreciate it." She pulled up to the curb and told me to call when I was ready to go home. "I'm not going to be able to sleep anyway."

I went inside and made a pot of coffee. While it brewed, I went back to my desk and collapsed into my chair. It was only eleven o'clock, but I felt like I'd been up for days. It seemed like the fire had burned for much longer than three hours. Thank goodness they'd kept it from spreading. I thought about Vivian, still angry about the part she had played in the sabotage. What had made her want to betray her country and, worse yet, attempt to kill the people she worked with every day?

I got up, went to the kitchen, and came back with a cup of coffee. I considered adding a bit of Pop's Scotch to it, but I needed a clear head to think. Besides, the brew tasted heavenly and the booze would probably ruin it. While I sipped it, I decided the first thing to do was check on Vivian. I picked up the receiver and dialed Providence Hospital. When the hospital operator answered, I asked what room Vivian Anderson was in. I heard papers rustling as she searched the registry.

"I'm sorry," the operator said. "There's no patient by that name."

That was odd. "Are you sure? She would have been brought in by ambulance with burns from the fire at Tabor Ironworks."

"I do remember that, but the woman's name wasn't Anderson."

"It wasn't?"

"Let me check the book again," the operator said. Pages rustled one more time. "Oh, here it is. There's a Vivian Adler in room one-oh-eight—that's the burn unit."

Adler. As in Mrs. Richard Adler. That explained a lot. I asked to be connected to the nurses' station. When the nurse picked up the telephone, I asked how Vivian was.

"She's been sedated, so she's sleeping comfortably at the moment."

"Will she be able to receive visitors?"

"I don't know," the nurse said. "A government agent just arrived and will be sitting outside her door. It will probably be up to him if she can have visitors. Do you know why he's guarding her? What did she do?"

If the agent hadn't told the nurse, I sure wasn't going to. "I can't say."

"May I tell her who called?"

"Just tell her a friend from work." I hung up before she could ask my name. I doubted the feds would let her have any visitors. I was out of luck getting any questions answered—unless Dad had spoken to her.

I dialed the police station, Jimmy picked up.

"Hi, Jimmy," I said.

"I don't have anything to tell you yet," he said. "The feds just showed up, and they're interrogating Smith right now."

"That's all right. I just have a question."

"Yes?"

"Has the chief spoken to the woman who was with Adler and Smith?"

"He checked on her when we stopped to get that Kraut's leg fixed. Back in my day we'd have given him another broken leg to go with it."

Ordinarily I'd be amused at Jimmy's story. Not now. "What did she say?"

"Nothing," Jimmy said. "They'd just given her a painkiller, and she was down for the count."

"Has Smith said anything yet?" I asked.

"Nothing in English," Jimmy said. "I have a feeling he knows a lot of German swear words, though."

"I'm sure. Thanks, Jimmy. I'll check in again tomorrow."

Now what? I thought as I hung up the phone. Something still bothered me, but I couldn't put my finger on what it was. The perpetrators had been stopped. Adler was dead. Vivian was in the hospital under guard, and Smith was under arrest. I doubted he would talk, even if the government agents tried to beat it out of him. It felt unfinished. That little voice inside that always told me I was onto a good story kept nagging me, saying I'd missed something, that there was a piece of the puzzle I hadn't put in place yet. For the life of me, I couldn't figure out what it could be. If there was more, the answer had to be in something I already had.

I gathered up all the notes and scraps of paper I'd accumulated since this whole mess began and spread them out on my desk, trying to put them in some kind of order. The first thing I'd found was the note Moe had left for me, stuck in one of the books in his desk—*Berlin Diary*. I wondered if his choice of book had been intentional. This was what had started it all—Moe telling me his death wasn't an accident. I could almost hear his voice when I read it again. No big revelation popped into my head, so I pushed it aside.

The next item was the list of names—the one where I had found Sylvia. I picked up the calendar scrap. *TAB 10 AM*. Regardless of who Moe had met with, when I'd asked Tabor if Moe had come in that Monday, he'd been upset enough to ask me to leave. At the very least, Tabor had known about Moe.

I looked through the other items—the photos, the three pages listing the production lines, and some notes I'd jotted down. I went to the kitchen and poured another cup of coffee, thinking about Tabor. Something struck me then. Colleen Lewis had told the police that his office door had been locked when she found him. I realized I'd never asked her about that. Who else had a key besides Colleen and Tabor? Vivian certainly wouldn't have had one. The same for Adler and Smith.

I picked up the scrap of paper again. *TAB 10 AM*. Of course. It made sense now. *TAB* stood for Tabor Ironworks, and the *10* was likely still the time, but *AM* didn't stand for morning.

It stood for Arnold Moss.

I could have kicked myself for not seeing it earlier. I should have known it hadn't been a coincidence that the sabotage had begun shortly after he began working there. Moe must have figured it out. I'd been taken in by Moss's smooth personality. It didn't make me feel any better that I hadn't been the only one. I wondered how much of his charm and attempted friendliness had been an act to find out what I knew.

I thought about our last meeting just that afternoon. He had seen the photographs and the papers with the production lines listed on them. He had to have recognized the significance, especially when he'd had Moe's place and Sylvia's apartment torn apart searching for Moe's evidence. He'd accelerated his plans and had Adler and Smith perform what was supposed to be their final act of sabotage. They were probably all scheduled to leave town after that, except Adler was dead, Smith had been captured, and Vivian was in the hospital. That left Moss to get away scot-free.

Not if I had any say in the matter.

I picked up the phone and dialed the police department again. Jimmy answered. "I need to talk to the chief."

"He's still with that piece of garbage."

"What about Rally?"

"He's in there with him."

"Can you tell the chief to stop and see me as soon as possible? I'm at the paper."

"I'll do my best, but it might be a while."

I hung up and dialed my house. Katherine picked up on the first ring.

"It's me," I said.

"Ready to come home? I'll be right there."

"Not yet. Have you talked to your contact in the FBI yet?"

"Yes. He's down at the police station right now. Why?"

"I know who's been calling the shots. It wasn't Vivian." I heard a noise out in the newsroom. "Hold on a second." I listened but didn't hear anything more. "Sorry. I thought I heard a noise, but I was wrong. I know who's behind all this."

"Who?"

"Arnold Moss." The words were barely out of my mouth when he appeared in my doorway. He was holding a gun.

Chapter
Twenty-Nine

Fire at Tabor Ironworks Started by
Disgruntled Employee

—The Progress Herald, May 27, 1942

"Hang up the phone, Irene."

I hesitated.

"I mean it, Irene. Hang it up."

"Irene?" Katherine said. "Who's there?"

"Now, Irene," Moss said.

"I have to go." I dropped the receiver into the cradle, praying Katherine had heard him.

Still pointing the gun at me, Moss sat on the corner of my desk. "You've made things very difficult for me, you know." He didn't wait for an answer. "My, my. What have we here?" He picked up Moe's letter to me and read it. "How touching." He looked at each paper one by one and shoved them into his jacket pocket. "You've surprised me once again. I never imagined you'd figure it out until I saw those papers and photographs you dropped. I thought I was just a handsome playboy to you."

"Did anyone ever tell you that you have a massive ego?" I tried to sound braver than I felt. Inside, I was a mass of gelatin. I didn't want him to see my fear.

He ignored the question, although I hadn't expected an answer. "Who were you talking to just now?"

"Chief Turner," I lied. "The police station is close. He'll be here any minute."

Moss laughed. "You're a terrible liar. He's still interrogating my inept colleague. Who was it really?"

"Does it matter?"

"No, I guess it doesn't. I'll be long gone before anyone gets here. I have what I need. I couldn't take the chance of leaving any of those papers here."

"Where are you going?" I asked.

"Not that you really care," he said, "but I'll be on a plane to New York before morning, then Buenos Aires."

"You're not going to Germany?" The longer I kept him talking, the better.

"Eventually I will. And maybe back here after we win the war. The Reich will need administrators. I'll be perfect, don't you think?"

"Germany will not win the war," I said.

Moss laughed. "Of course Germany will win. America entering the war will only prolong things. It's just a matter of time."

"You're wrong."

"Believe what you want." He motioned with his gun. "Stand up, Irene."

I couldn't. My legs had turned to rubber. "Why are you doing this?"

"I can't leave any witnesses. You know that."

Unfortunately, I did. "No, I mean why the sabotage? Why betray your country?"

Moss laughed again. "Ever the reporter, aren't you? I like you, Irene, so I'll answer your questions." He sat down, still pointing the gun at me. "You've realized by now my loyalty is to the Fatherland, not to this country."

"But you were born here, weren't you?"

"I was, but my parents weren't. They came here after the last war. They rejoiced when Hitler came to power, and I moved with them back to Germany about ten years ago. They hated it here. So many foreigners. So many Jews. I wanted to serve Mein Führer in the military, but when they found out I had been raised in America, they found a better use for me."

"What about Adler and Smith? Were they born here as well?"

"Yes. There are many like us, Irene. If your president was smart, he would have rounded up all the Germans instead of the Japanese. You stopped those two, but you'll never stop all of us. Americans are stupid. We will prevail."

"What about Vivian? You haven't mentioned her."

"Richard made the mistake of falling for her. He thought he'd eventually take her back to Germany with him."

"So she was part of it."

"She didn't know a thing."

"But what about tonight?" I said. "She was there with him."

"I don't know why she was with him. That wasn't part of the plan. I told Richard to give her some excuse to have her use her ration to buy gasoline. Stupid woman fell for it."

I'd been wrong about Vivian. What else had I been wrong about? "Another thing I don't understand is how you got Tabor to go along with your plan."

"That was easy. Blackmail. Wilfred had made some—let's say—unwise financial choices earlier in his career. He used company funds for some large private purchases. He'd since made up for it, but that wouldn't have stopped the fines and penalties, not to mention the bad press."

I found it hard to believe that would have been enough to get Tabor to betray his country. "That can't be all."

"We also threatened his ex-wife. For some reason, he still held a torch for her."

That made more sense. "You keep saying *we*. Someone had called Tabor to have him hire you, and Tabor called someone to back out of the scheme. Who else is involved in this?"

"Like I said before, there are many of us working for our homeland. You don't need to know any more than that. Time's up, Irene."

Over Moss's shoulder I saw a barefoot Katherine slip into the newsroom. "Wait. One more question. You owe me that much."

"Frankly, I don't owe you anything, but I'll answer one more."

"Which one of you killed Moe?"

"Does it matter?"

"Yes, it does. It matters to me."

Over Moss's shoulder I watched Katherine tiptoe across the newsroom and toward my office. Katherine picked up a heavy crystal vase from on top of Peggy's desk.

"I normally keep my hands clean—except for old Wilfred, that is—so I sent Richard and Johann to take care of things."

"Johann?"

Katherine raised the vase over her head with both hands.

"You didn't really think his name was John Smith, did you?"

Katherine swung the vase down on Moss's head with all her might. The vase shattered as it made contact, and Moss slid to the floor.

*   *   *

The next few hours were a whirlwind of activity. After Moss went down, I called the police station again and told Jimmy what had happened. He made it over in record time. He handcuffed the unconscious Moss. He'd have had quite a story to tell about capturing a notorious spy if we all hadn't been under strict orders to keep it quiet. By government order, we were to say the fire at Tabor had been started by a disgruntled employee who had perished in the blaze. It bugged me that no one would know the true story, but I took comfort in the fact that I'd had a little part in stopping the Nazis—at least in Progress.

The FBI took custody of Moss and Smith and transported them to Pittsburgh. Katherine was now off the hook, and the agent in charge said her record would be expunged. After the agents left, Katherine and I sat in the newsroom with the chief, Rally, and Jimmy. Rally couldn't stop staring at Katherine. I didn't want to burst his bubble by telling him Katherine's days in Progress were numbered.

"I still don't understand how the incidents with Sam are connected to the spy ring," I said.

"They weren't," the chief said. "I questioned Smith about that. It's been ingrained in him to hate Jews and just about anyone who isn't a full-blooded Aryan. He said they were only having a little fun."

"What's going to happen to Tabor Ironworks now?" Katherine asked.

I answered that question. "I'll talk to Colleen Lewis. I imagine she's already notified Mr. Tabor's son about the fire. I doubt he'll let it be closed. There are some good people there. Colleen knows more about that company than anyone. She could probably run it."

"What is the world coming to?" Jimmy said. "I can't imagine a woman running a company like that."

I grinned. "The world is changing, Jimmy. Someday it'll be a common thing."

Dad winked at me. "Yeah, Jimmy. Look who's running the *Herald* now."

* * *

I was all alone when my staff began arriving around eight. I had a fresh pot of coffee percolating in the kitchen, and I had removed any evidence that anything had happened overnight. I had just finished my fabricated articles on the fire. I understood that the feds were still searching for anyone else Moss was associated with, but in my opinion, they were long gone and off to their next target. Time would tell.

Peggy came in just as I pulled the sheet of paper out of my typewriter. "Have you been up all night?"

"Do I look that bad?" I asked.

"Truthfully? Yeah, you do."

"Thanks a lot. What a friend you are."

"How bad was it?" she asked.

I gave her the official disgruntled employee version.

"What a terrible thing for someone to do," she said. "And he died in the process. He could have destroyed the entire factory, and then what would have happened? All those people out of work. I just don't understand some people."

"Neither do I, Peggy. Neither do I."

Peggy's telephone rang, and she went to answer it. Seconds later she told me it was Chief Turner and transferred the call to my desk.

"How are you, Irene?" he asked.

"I'm all right. Tired."

"I'm at the hospital trying to talk to Vivian Anderson. She wants to see you. She won't talk to anyone else. If you can spare the time, would you mind coming out here?"

*   *   *

Ken let me borrow his car, so I didn't have to go home to get Pop's. I parked behind the police car in front of Providence Hospital. After I explained that Chief Turner was expecting me, the receptionist directed me to Vivian's room on the first floor. I walked down a long hallway and turned right. The chief was leaning against the wall outside room 108. He straightened when he saw me coming.

"Thank you for coming out," he said. "I know you're busy."

"Never for you. Where's the guard?"

"I sent him for coffee. Told him to take his time."

"Why won't Vivian talk to you?"

"I told her about Adler," he said. "I imagine she's afraid she's in trouble."

"*Is* she in trouble?" I asked.

"Most likely," he said. "Even if she wasn't involved in the plot, Moss told you she purchased the gasoline Adler used to start the fire. That can't be taken lightly." He opened the door and held it for me, then followed me in.

Vivian was lying in bed and opened her eyes when she heard us enter. She looked much better than she had when she was put into the ambulance last night. The skin on her face was still slightly pink, but all the soot had been washed away. Her entire right arm was covered with a gauze bandage. Only the tips of her fingers showed.

"Hello, Vivian," I said.

"Thank you for coming," she said, her voice still raspy from the smoke.

"How are you?" I pulled a chair over beside the bed.

"I've been better."

"Chief Turner said you wanted to talk to me."

Vivian looked over at him. "Can I talk to Irene alone, please?"

Dad nodded. "I'll be right outside."

As soon as the door closed, Vivian said, "I feel so stupid." A tear slipped down her cheek.

I reached for her good hand. "Tell me what happened."

"Will you make sure the police know that I had no idea what Richard had planned?"

"I'll tell the chief what you tell me, but it's not up to me what happens next."

She nodded. "I thought he loved me. I never would have married him otherwise."

So she really had been married to Adler. "How long ago?"

"On Saturday. How could I have been so stupid?"

I didn't have an answer for that.

"I'm sure that's not what you want to know," she said. "You want to know about the fire."

I nodded.

Vivian took a deep breath, which made her cough. She reached for the glass of water on the nightstand and took a drink before launching into her story. "Richard and I were scheduled for the evening shift yesterday. Just after lunch he got a telephone call. I don't know who it was. John, maybe. He went out for half an hour, and when he came back, he asked me to fill two cans with gasoline because he'd used up his ration. I wondered how he had managed that, but I didn't ask. I should have."

It must have been Moss who'd called him, not John Smith. He was the one giving the orders to Adler and Smith.

"I filled the cans and put them in his truck. We drove to work as usual and started our shift. I went looking for Richard when I had my break and saw him carrying one of the gas cans into the box shop. I couldn't figure out what he was doing, so I followed. There was no one in there except Richard, and he began pouring gas everywhere." Her voice broke.

"Do you need a break?" I asked.

She shook her head. "I tried to stop him. He kept pushing me away, telling me to get out, that he didn't want anything to happen to me. He pushed me out the door, and seconds later it was in flames and he was still inside. I tried to get to him, but I couldn't. There was too much smoke and it was so very hot. The next thing I knew, a fireman had picked me up." Tears filled her eyes. "I don't know why he would do such a thing. It was a good place to work. I don't understand why he would try to burn it down. Why did he do it? Why?"

I didn't have any answers she'd want to hear.

* * *

That Saturday, Lily and I helped Katherine load up her car.

"I wish you didn't have to go," Lily said. "I'm going to miss you so much."

Katherine put an arm around Lily. "I'll miss you too." She reached into one of her boxes and pulled out three records. "Maybe these will make you feel better."

Lily took them from Katherine and read the labels. "Oh! All three are Frank Sinatra! Thank you!" She ran into the house with her treasure.

"Are you sure you want to do that?" I asked.

"I am. I don't need them when I'm going to be singing with the real thing."

I grinned. "You're going to be a star someday."

"I doubt it, but I'm going to give it a shot. Anyway, singing backup for Frank at the Hotel Astor isn't too shabby."

"Certainly not."

Mom and Lily came outside to say good-bye.

"Thank you for opening your home to me," Katherine said to Mom.

"I wish you luck," Mom said.

Lily hugged Katherine, and I did the same. Katherine got into her car.

"Keep in touch," I said. "I want to know how you're doing."

"I will."

I was surprised I had tears in my eyes as she drove away.

* * *

Three weeks later Lily was waiting on the front porch when I got home from work. She waved a large envelope in the air. "It's from Katherine! Quick, open it!"

I laughed. "Can I put my pocketbook down and kick off my shoes first?"

"If you have to."

We went inside, and Mom came out of the kitchen. "You'd better open it quick. She's been jumping up and down ever since the mailman came."

"I wonder what it is." I studied the envelope and turned it over slowly, knowing it was torturing my baby sister.

"If you don't open it right now, I'm going to die!" Lily said.

"I sincerely doubt that." I picked up the letter opener we kept on the hall table and sliced open the envelope. There was a note attached to two eight-by-ten photographs. I read it aloud. *"Irene, here's one picture for you and a special one for Lily. I'll talk to you soon. Xoxo, Katherine."* I pulled out the two photographs. "Get a load of this," I said. The one on top was of Katherine and Frank Sinatra onstage. Katherine was gorgeous in a sequined gown with perfect hair and makeup. And Sinatra? Well, he was Sinatra.

"She is so beautiful," Lily said wistfully. "And so lucky. Singing with Frank."

I gave the picture to Lily so I could look at the next one. I grinned. "Oh, Lily," I said, handing her the new photo.

She let out an ear-piercing scream. "Oh! I can't believe it! Oh, I'm going to faint!"

"Let me see that," Mom said.

It was a head shot of Frank Sinatra. That wasn't the best part though. In the bottom right-hand corner he'd written, *To Lily. All my love, Frank.*

The telephone rang just then, and I picked up the receiver. "Hello?"

"Hello, beautiful."

"Bill!" My smile was wider than Lily's. I had thought the package from Katherine was a good way to end the day. This was even better. Much better.

This was perfect.

Acknowledgments

First of all, thank you to my marvelous agent, Melissa Jeglinski, who has patiently endured reading and making suggestions on the multiple proposals I've sent to her over the last few years. Thanks for everything!

Next is my fabulous editor, Faith Black Ross, who helped make this book so much better. I really enjoy working with you. I hope we get to work on lots of books together. And thanks to the entire team at Crooked Lane. You're awesome!

Thank you to the readers who have read my other books and kept asking when I'd have another one released. I hope you feel your patience was rewarded and you like this new book as much as I do.

Finally, thanks to the writing community, especially the mystery and historical fiction authors. All of you are so generous with your time whenever I have questions. I greatly appreciate it!